Ask Not...

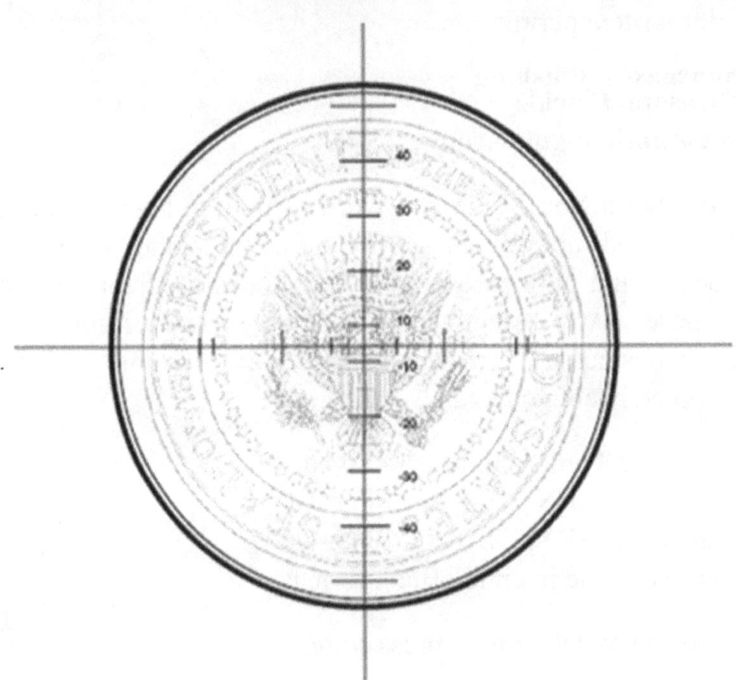

A JFK Thriller
by
Tom Avitabile

Suncoast Publishing
Sarasota, Florida
www.author-guide.com

Ask Not / Tom Avitabile. -- 1st ed.
Paperback ISBN 979-8-8677453-0-1
Hardcover ISBN 978-1-7351849-4-4
Also available in epub/eBook format

www.tomavitabile.wordpress.com/

Also by

Tom Avitabile

The Eight Day

The Eight Day – (author preferred)

The Hammer of God

The God Particle

The Devil's Quota

Give Us This Day

Forgive Us Our Trespasses

Coming soon:

Aquasapien

Wife and Death

Dedication

To Miss Troncone, my 4th-grade teacher
at P.S. 76 in the Bronx, who explained to me
what a loss the assassination of President Kennedy
was to our nation. And for the A+ she gave me
on my composition about him on 11/26/1963.
"Gee, she was swell."

Preamble

The content of the book was largely discovered in my research for the screenplay Ask Not. Prior to that, I had no idea how pervasive conspiracy theories were. It is safe to say only about half of the **looney tunes** and some of the **Hmmm, makes ya think** theories are presented here. I hope you, like to be wrapped up in a warm conspiracy, story as I do, and flutter between the possible and the improbable.

Have fun!

Cover Quote

On Friday, November 22, 1963, KBOX, Action Central News reporter, Sam Pate, was in Mobile News Unit #4 covering President Kennedy's motorcade, broadcasting live as it paraded through Dallas.

"It appears as though something has happened in the motorcade route..."

This utterance was the first inkling aired of something amiss. It now appears that 60 years later, this tragic event is still mired in uncertainty.

What is past is
PROLOGUE

"Bless his heart," Mary said to Jean after she smiled at the nice policeman who told them they had to walk all the way around the plaza.

"We have to hurry he'll be here any minute," Jean said.

The two women hustled and when another cop wasn't looking, they darted across the three-lane road to the middle of the grass. Mary looked around, "This is a good spot. Let's do it from here."

They had discussed exactly how they would do this. It required coordination and split-second timing. For if they were to get the shots off, Jean needed to be fast as Mary took the shots.

A roar and the sounds of sirens echoed coming down Main Street. "Mary, hurry he's almost here."

Mary was lining up the shot, she moved her position three feet to the right and four feet back. Jean didn't see this as she was looking up the street. She was biting her fist, stamping her feet, her nerves getting the best of her. She turned, "Mary..." She snapped her head all around and found Mary, now behind her. "Tell me when you are moving."

"Oh, shush. We can get a better shot from here. That man and his wife and kids were in the way."

Jean followed where Mary was now aiming and immediately understood. "Good."

Mary was removing her kerchief when the roar and the sirens were on top of them.

Mary's finger was poised to shoot. Jean stood where they had practiced; for when the shooting started. Jean looked across Elm Street, "Any second now, be ready."

Mary was glad Jean was giving her the heads up while she focused on the shot. Not taking her eye off the camera.

"Mr. President. Mr. President!" Jean yelled.

Mary pressed the shutter. Jean immediately pulled the Polaroid from the camera so Mary could take another shot.

"He turned and looked right at us. Did you get that? Did you get him?"

"Um hmm," Mary said as her finger pushed down again. With the click of the camera came a loud bang. It startled Mary.

Jean screamed. "Oh, my God. Oh my God!" She was hyperventilating.

Another bang.

She let out a bone-chilling scream. Mary joined in. The unimaginable horror was in front of them. Mary instinctively dove to the ground, pulling her friend Jean, who was standing there screaming, down with her. The camera and the film went flying. They don't notice the supersonic snap of a bullet that burrowed into the ground three feet to their right.

CYRUS SHAW STOOD ON THE CURB OF ELM STREET AS THE MOTORCADE PASSED. ACROSS THE ROADWAY FROM HIM WERE MARY AND JEAN

Sixty seconds earlier:

As he stood across the way in his straw cowboy-style Stetson, 43-year-old, long-haul trucker, Cyrus Shaw, was angry but resigned to the fact that he couldn't make his second delivery of the day, the cops had every street shut down. So, he lit up a Lucky and joined the crowds of people lining the roadway. His toes were right on the edge of the curb now. The crush of the crowd behind him almost had him in the street. He swiveled his head to his left as he heard the motorcade and motorcycles turn onto Main. He glanced over his shoulder at the yellow Hertz Rent-a-car sign with the clock on it that read 12:30. Maybe after he dropped his load of schoolbooks at the depository, he could still make his last stop in Fort Worth before 5. Although, the Friday afternoon traffic would be a bear, if this ended quickly, there was a chance.

As he took a long drag on a Lucky, he watched with great interest two women across the way in the plaza, fumbling with a camera and moving around. The one in the kerchief was cute. The other one was as jumpy as a long-tailed cat in a room full of rocking chairs.

Police motorcycles rumbled by with lights flashing and sirens blaring, then a couple of cars passed in front of him. Then a limousine, a stretch, no top. He could see the governor of Texas and the president of the United States sitting right there behind him. His pretty wife, who was all over TV, was in a pink getup that she must have been baking in, what with being under the scorching, Dallas midday sun.

Some young girls next to him were screaming like he was Elvis or something. A woman a few feet away was lifting her grandchild up to be able to see better. The little rug rat was waving a cheap American flag. Probably made in Japan by nips, the ex-marine, who was wounded at Guadalcanal, thought just as a loud bang rang out from over his shoulder, then two more, maybe from somewhere else. He didn't care or look. He hit the dirt and covered his head with his arms at the sound of the first gunshot.

There was a lot of yelling, and he could hear the powerful engine of the limo rev up as it took off. People were screaming. Some crying. He chanced to look up. It was pandemonium. Something brushed his cheek. Thinking it was a bug, he swatted it. It was a polaroid that landed on the curbside in front of his face. Something caught his eye. He brought it close. In the corner was a red spot... BLOOD. He touched the drop on the upper right-hand corner of the white photographic paper backing... it stuck to his finger.

He got up staring at the scene with his cigarette dangling from his opened mouth.

Looking around, he saw people running up to the wood fence behind him screaming. He was turned around by the sounds of a tussle next to him, a man in a suit was wrestling a camera away from an old man. The two girls taking Polaroids, who were standing not far from him across the street, were being questioned by another man in a suit. He saw him flashing some kind of identification. Cyrus watched as other people in the crowd were being relieved of their cameras and being led away. He unconsciously slipped the photo into his pocket as he watched a bus go by with reporters hanging out of the windows snapping pictures.

Suddenly, he was spun around by a policeman, "You got a camera there, sir?

Cyrus, still in shock just shook his head, no.

The officer gave him one more look. "What's in the pocket?"

Cyrus pulled out what was in his pocket. The cop looked down and seeing the Oklahoma traffic citation, grunted and threw it to the ground, and was off to the next person.

Cyrus was surprised it wasn't the Polaroid. He bent down and picked up the speeding ticket. He looked around; people were crying, pointing at the spot where the president was shot, and many were hugging one another. *They ain't gonna let me unload any damn books today.*

He stepped back through the crowd and walked to his truck five blocks away.

Pecox, Texas hardly deserved a dot on the map. It was mostly scrub-brush and dried-out arroyos. It was a landscape that could care less about the rusted old trailer, permanently parked up on blocks that marred the vista. Cyrus' unhitched, 52' Mack semi-tractor pulled up to this, three-room, no longer mobile, home. He climbed down and headed inside, flicking away a cigarette, and coughing as he did.

The 30-year-old house trailer started out small but was now even smaller with the inside crammed with cases of Marlboro, Winston, and Lucky Strike cigarettes. The boxes were in every conceivable space, leaving only two seats around the table, a worn high back chair, and half a mini sofa, in front of a 15-inch Sears black and white TV, propped up on a case of Tarrytons. Except for the brand logos, all the other writing on the boxes was in Spanish.

Cyrus' common-law wife, Maria Gonzalez, was very frail for her 52 years. She sat on her half of the couch alongside some Chesterfield cases, watching the television coverage of the assassination. The reception this far out was weak, the picture was snowy and often ghosted. Her madre, in her 80s, sat crossing herself as they showed pictures of Jackie Kennedy at Love Field.

Cyrus started opening drawers looking for something. "Where's my damn camera, Maria?"

Clutching her rosaries, she looked up with tearful eyes, "The President Kennedy has been shot!"

"I know that. I was there."

Her mother, who didn't speak English, sat mesmerized at the screen.

Maria crossed herself, "Dios Mio, that must have been horrible."

Cyrus ignored her and finally found the camera bag in the small cabinet over the smaller sink. He removed his Polaroid camera, then searched around the bottom of the bag and came up with a gray plastic tube. "You should have seen it. Maria, there was cops and G-men everywhere. They was takin' people's cameras and ripping film right out they hands."

He sat at the table, lit a Lucky, and took a long draw. He removed the photo from his pocket and started to peel back the developer-coated flap. His right eye was closed as the smoke from the Lucky billowed into it. But as the picture was revealed under the backing that eye also opened wide. For the second time today, his jaw dropped, and he was awestruck. He took the sponge "fixer" applicator out of the gray tube and wiped it across the picture.

The staticky sound of the TV cleared at that moment. "All we know at this time is that 3 shots were fired at the presidential motorcade from a lone assassin perched in the 6th-floor window."

Cyrus looked at the photo.

"...of the Texas School Book Depository building. I'm just getting word that police have found a rifle..."

Maria came over to him, looked at the photo then the TV, then the photo, and again at the TV. She was confused. She leaned in and whispered to Cyrus. "Madre Mia, maybe you should show them this picture."

"I can't do that. What if they start nosing around?" He picked up a pack of Luckies and waved it at the cigarette cases. "This is all contraband." He pointed to the bottom of the pack where there was no tax stamp. "Besides, they'd find out about Mom and send her back."

Maria's eyes widened.

"Comprende?" Cyrus said still unnerved by what they saw in the picture.

On Sunday morning, Cyrus was out in front of the trailer. He, Dan and Gus were loading cases of smokes into a white Ford Econovan. Maria and her mother were glued to the TV ever since Friday afternoon.

Dan brought out the last three cases in his arms and slid them into the truck. "TV says they're moving the shooter, and no matter what you say, Gus, this Lee Harvey guy was just some lone nut. He's a loser like they said on TV." He closed the rear doors and turned to Cyrus. "So, Wednesday for the Parliaments?"

"Should be, I am making a run to Nuevo Laredo on Tuesday. Come by Wednesday before 8, I got a early run to El Paso."

Cyrus took a tally.

Gus closed the side door, "No "nut" can shoot like that, Dan. Not at a moving target," he held his hands like he was aiming a rifle and shaking like a leaf. "The God damn President and the Governor no less."

Cyrus was just letting them talk all morning. At times just shrugging. He kept it all business, "Let's see, 20 cases of Winstons. 10 cases Luckies. Make it fifty even."

Gus peeled off five tens and continued making his point. "I'm telling you as sure as the sun is gonna rise tomorrow it had to be a crossfire. Two, three men."

"Bullshit! They only found one guy!" Dan said.

"If Oswald lives, then it was just him. But if he had some partners, I bet you they shut him up, good." Dan said as he held his hand to his head like a gun and pulled the trigger.

The sound of a gunshot rang out from inside the trailer, Maria screamed, and the three men rushed in.

Maria and her mother were sitting in shock, eyes glued to the TV screen.

The announcer was also in shock. "He's been shot! He's been shot! Oswald has been shot!"

"Son of a bitch, they did it," Cyrus said.

Gus started laughing, "I told you. They shut that old boy up real good."

"Hot damn." was all Dan could get out.

Cyrus snapped out of his momentary shock in time to grab the Polaroid off the table before the two men saw it.

A few minutes later, the men in the truck pulled away. Cyrus and Maria stood in the doorway. Cyrus took the photo out of his breast pocket.

Maria looked at it and then at her man, "Promise me you'll destroy that picture. They'll kill you too if you show anyone what you got."

Cyrus walked over to an open oil drum.

Maria stayed at the door. "Cyrus, burn it. Burn it! Please promise me!"

Cyrus lit it with his Zippo lighter.

Maria watched.

He took out a cigarette, lit it, and inhaled as he watched the speeding ticket burn.

1993

1 | HANK LARSON

"Flaps 20 percent." Pilot Hank Larson ordered as the giant 747 lined up on the approach to runway 22 right at New York's JFK airport.

The cockpit radio squawked, "Flying Tigers 107 you are at the outer marker."

His co-pilot, Bill was adjusting the radio beacon finder to JFK tower as he said, "I am looking forward to a hot bath and Lydia at the Hawaii Kai."

"I thought that was over?"

"Yeah, didn't she say Aloha, Bill?" Rob, the flight engineer, seated behind them said.

"I did too. But before we took off, I checked my messages, and there she was all sweet and sexy...so."

"Wheels down," Hank ordered.

The plane shuddered as the new turbulence caused by injecting a few tons of tires into the airstream changed its aerodynamics.

On the ground, the huge ship pulled up to its hash marks on the flight line and the engines wound down. Nonscheduled flights like cargo and charters parked outside the main gate areas and service stair trucks were the primary means of planing and deplaning.

The first out was the first officer, Bill, followed by Hank the Captain who dons his aviators. Rob the engineer was last to hit the service steps. To their right, a passenger 747 was deplaning its passengers to a shuttle bus. Its tail markings read, Heli Holland.

"Charter flight from Amsterdam," Bill said.

They reach the bottom of the steps; Hank and his crew notice the smiling faces already snapping photographs.

Hank put his go bag down on the tarmac, "Bill, check that right aileron. They felt sluggish. I'll check left."

"Okay, skipper," Bill said as he and Rob walked the 110 feet under the fuselage to the other wing tip.

As Hank was looking up at the left aileron, he didn't see a little girl playing with her doll while her parents were taking video of the newly arrived group.

A gust of wind blew the hat off the little girl's doll. She ran after it.

A rolling DC-10 was approaching.

The little girl was after the hat, every time she got close it flew further away. The plane loomed larger, coming at her.

Hank glanced over and saw the little girl running into harm's way. The little girl was running right into the path of the oncoming wheels.

Hank was running flat out. His hat flew from his head.

The little girl bent over unsuccessfully for the hat while holding her dolly.

Hank, with his arms whipping, puffing through his cheeks, was closing in on the girl. He tried to yell over the scream of the engines. "Hey! HEY! Come here! LITTLE GIRL!!!

But she didn't hear him and was on her knees now in front of the jet trying to catch the hat.

Bill turned in the direction of the yelling, "Holy shit!" he said, as he took off 100 yards behind.

The plane was starting its take-off roll and was right on top of her. Her dress and hair started to be pulled in the direction of the giant turbofan engine's intake. Caught up in the rush of air, she was screaming as she was starting to lift off from the intake vacuum.

Hank made a diving grab and got her by the ankles. It became a tug of war he had to win. He scrambled for a foothold. His foot skidded over the asphalt. Now he was being sucked into the vortex!

His hand caught one of the buried taxi lights that are countersunk into the pavement. He was stretched and pulled, with one hand on her ankle and the other in the slot in the pavement, he strained. His sunglasses got sucked off.

The blue light gave way as it was ripped out but stopped by the metal wire conduit which snapped taut and held. But the jolt caused the little girl to let go of her dolly. The engine sucked it right in, making a slight shred noise, heard over the rumble. A puff of grey smoke exited the rear of the engine. As if satisfied by the doll's sacrifice, the plane passed. Hank pulled the little girl into his arms. He was comforting the crying child as his co-pilot then her horrified parents rush up.

The father grabbed his little girl. The mother signed to her. The little girl, rubbing her eyes, signed back. The mother grabbed the little girl and held her tight. The woman's eyes met Hank's. She tried to speak but couldn't. Hank rubbed the girl's head and smiled at the mother. The mother signed to the father who, with tears in his eyes, took Hank's hand and clasped it inside his own. Hank's co-pilot handed him his hat.

As they walked into the Flying Tigers flight operations center, they were met by a round of applause from the eight people in the office.

One of the pilots patted him on the shoulder, "Nice going, Hank."

Judy, the scheduling coordinator, smiled at him. "That little girl's lucky you were in-bound today." She handed him some messages. "Your brother called, said..." she read from the note, "...something came up, he had to fly out of town. Said to tell you 'This could be it, the big one.' and that he's sorry. He'll be back late tonight. Will call you tomorrow."

"Great, he can't make the game tonight. Thanks, Judy. Oh, I almost forgot." He reached into his go bag and pulled out a box of cigars and handed it to her. "Your grandfather still smoking Cuban wrapped?"

She lit up. "You remembered. Oh, he's going to be so happy. Thanks, Hank. Here let me..." She reaches for her purse.

Hank held up his hand. "It's the least I could do for a World War Two ace."

"You're the ace."

Hank's friend and chief pilot, Brian Miller, walked up. "Hank, heard you saved a little girl. Meet me in my office in 5, I got to hit the head."

Hank hadn't been in Brian's office since the two Airforce pilots signed on to the freight hauler right after the Iraq war.

As the New York Center Operations manager and chief pilot for Flying Tigers, it was large and sprinkled with trophies from various softball leagues and memorabilia from Gulf War One. He looked at Brian's 'me wall'.

A crossed pair of M-16s served as the centerpiece of a collection of framed photographs. One, in particular, was a squadron shot of ten or so guys in front of a B-52 circa 1991. The banner read, The Hell Raising 43rd Bomber Wing.

Brian came in and sat at his desk.

Hank took the chair across from him. "My brother Ben can't make the game tonight. Want to go?"

"Yankee game?"

"Two seats over the dugout."

"You're on. How is that crazy brother of yours?" Brian said as he reached back into his credenza and brought out a bottle of McCallan 18 and two glasses.

"He's probably off on another wild goose chase. Hey, I'm impressed, why the good stuff."

"Not every day you save a little kid." He poured generously. "Yeah, your brother, I read one of his articles last week. He's a pretty good writer."

"He's wasting his talent, writing about UFOs, Loch Ness monsters, and other unsolved mysteries for that skin mag."

"Nice looking ladies in that particular publication."

"I was starting to worry that you actually just read the articles."

2 | THE NEGOTIATION

A ring of crust from an eaten-out sandwich hit the dust as Benjamin Larson, wiped his mouth on his sleeve. He was driving his rented Subaru jeep by an old, weather-beaten, sign reading - Entering Pecox, Texas, USA Pop. 1245

Hank's brother was on a freelance assignment reporting for Man's World Magazine. He was sweating like a pig. Sweat stains are blooming under the arms of the mismatched jacket to his pants. Food stains liberally decorate his shirt, most of which are hidden by his ugly tie which, as part of the motif, also displays a few gravy stains. On the seat next to his short, 230-pound frame, was a metal Haliburton Briefcase.

He approached the tattered remains of the gate with a weathered sign that reads, Pecox Quarry and Gravel.

Begin here "He must live in a quarry," he said to himself.

Dust kicked up as he drove through the remains of a gate.

He pulled up to the only place someone could live in, a rotting old, rusted trailer. He got out and stretched. He grabbed the Haliburton case and a smaller one and turned toward the door. A long, lean man in his early 30's, Howard Lance, swats at a fly. Benjamin walked up to him. "Hello, are you Cyrus?"

"I'm Howard Lance. I'm the one that called you. He's in here." He disappeared inside and Benjamin followed.

Benjamin sensed right away that this tiny trailer was a hermit's refuge. It felt even more claustrophobic by the layers of built-up nicotine discoloring the cheaply paneled walls. A picture of a Spanish-looking woman sat on the dresser with black bunting around the frame.

In front of him, still smoking, was a frail, emaciated man with protruding bones. Almost a breathing skeleton.

Ben put his cases down on the table, "Cyrus?"

He placed a device on his throat. It buzzed and the sound came out through his mouth. "Yes, that's me."

Ben was taken aback, he sounded like a robot from a sci-fi flick.

"Cyrus had to have his larynx surgically removed because they were cancerous. He needs that Sonovox thing to speak." Howard said.

"Nice to meet you. I'm Benjamin Larson from Men's World."

"Did you bring the money?" rattled out of Cyrus' throat.

"Excuse me?

"Hold it tighter," Howard said pressing his hand into his own throat.

Cyrus adjusted the position of the box. It was clearer. "Did you bring the money?"

Benjamin was a little thrown by his directness. "If I am satisfied as to the authenticity of the photo..."

"It's real, all right." Said Cyrus. With that, he got up and hobbled over to a space above the wheel well of the trailer. He removed a dusty old plastic plant and opened a hatch. He pulled out an old Premium Saltines tin. He opened the tin and removed the now yellowed photo. He handed it to Benjamin. "I was there when he was killed."

Benjamin handled it gingerly by the edges inspecting it. Even knowing what it was before he came there, still, he was startled by its content.

Howard filled in the blanks. "When Cyrus needed money to pay his wife's medical and funeral bills, he tried to sell me that at the library."

Benjamin was half listening as he was riveted to the photo. He opened the smaller case and pulled out a vial.

Howard continued, "I remembered you wrote that piece on Lincoln and Kennedy. I got your number through the writer's guild."

Benjamin placed a few drops of liquid on the back corner of the photo. The drop remained clear.

"What's that you're doing?" Howard asked.

'Alkaline trace. Any chemical treatment to accelerate aging or the appearance of it turns it blue."

"How long does it take?"

"A few seconds."

"Well, she's still clear so I guess that means something," Howard said smiling at Cyrus.

"Mr. Shaw, how did you come to have possession of this Polaroid?" Benjamin said.

"I took it from..."

Howard cut him off, "What he means is... on that day, Cyrus had a truckload of schoolbooks to deliver in Dallas, but because the President was in town, he couldn't get his truck near the building..."

"The Texas School Book Depository?

Howard didn't know, he turned to Cyrus who nodded. Then he continued, "So he waited right there."

"You witnessed the assassination?

"The whole top his head blowed' right off!" Cyrus said through the buzz.

"Why did you..." he turned to Howard, "Why did he wait till now?"

"His wife, she died last week, that's why he needs the money. She was always ascared that they'd be killed just for having that picture. So, she made him promise to burn it. But he didn't. He never even told anyone he was there that day, till last week, when he told me."

He turned to Cyrus, "How come you're not scared now?"

"Been 30 years. Nobody cares no more."

Benjamin considered the merchandise and the source. "Well, Mr. Shaw... We have a deal."

He pulled out of his breast pocket a standard release form and a pen. Unfolded it on the table. "This is a release granting me worldwide rights to this picture in perpetuity and the right to interview you when the book takes shape."

Howard interrupted, "Er... Something's come up."

Benjamin expected some kind of last-minute hardball. "Uh, uh, uh! We had an agreement!"

Howard held up his hands in a halting gesture, "Now, I know we did... it's just that this fella, another writer, called this morning and offered us twenty thousand. He'll be here at three."

"Look my plane <u>leaves</u> at three!... and I didn't come all this way to take part in an auction."

Howard crossed his arms and tried to act nonplussed. "Then I suppose he'll get the photo."

Benjamin sighed, "What's <u>his</u> name?"

"Just like you, he insisted on secrecy."

"Well, how did this other "writer" find out about this if it was our secret?"

"I guess I bragged a little after I made the arrangement with you, then it kinda' got into the newspaper here."

"The newspaper?! Some fucking secret! Do you have a copy of the paper?"

Howard looked around and then came up with the disheveled newspaper. He pointed out the article.

Benjamin scanned it. "Librarian Howard Lance... Brokered a deal... Cyrus Shaw... Artifact..." He looked up at Howard, "Artifact?"

Howard shrugs his shoulders. "I thought it made it sound more valuable."

Benjamin then played a little hardball himself. He opened the Haliburton and turned it toward Cyrus. In it was $10,000 in twenty-dollar bills. He thumbed a stack, like playing cards, right under Cyrus' nose. "Ten thousand cash, going back to New York in about 30 seconds. It'd be a shame, Mr. Shaw, if the other collector doesn't show or has a change of heart, then this will be as close as you'll ever get."

Cyrus was physically reacting to all that cash. He looked at the two men and tried to talk but only a rasp came out, then he put the SONOVOX to his throat. "Give him the photo."

Cyrus grabbed the case hugging it.

Benjamin placed the release on top and handed him the pen then slid the photo into a black plastic envelope.

Howard pleaded, "But Cyrus, the other fella ain't seen that photo yet!"

Benjamin retrieves the release. "Cyrus, enjoy the money." He took his case and left the trailer. He climbed into the jeep. Howard came to the door.

As the jeep pulled away, Howard vented his frustration. "That other fellow truly did call, you can wait and see for yourself. He'll be here at three... I wasn't lying... Damn!" He kicked the trailer door.

3 | THE FRIENDLY SKIES

The American Airlines 737 had just taken off. The plane was at a steep angle of ascent just after leaving the ground. Benjamin was squeezed into an economy-class seat. He reached up to open the air conditioning vent. He realized he was sitting next to a "white knuckle flyer."

"Never get used to it, taking off."

"Fly much?" Benjamin said as he reached down under his seat and brought up his leather briefcase onto his lap. He opened it and took out his Compaq laptop. He reached up to the overhead and turned on the reading light.

His row mate still talked as he watched him. "Fly too much! Hell, I'm on my way to Hong Kong. 8700 miles, 3 takeoffs, and landings."

"Cycles... It's called a cycle when a plane lands and takes off again."

"You a pilot?"

"No, my brother is. I'm a writer."

The plane bounced over a pocket of rough air. The businessman grimaced and talked to distract himself while putting a death grip on the armrest between them. "What kind of... things do you write?" he said in a voice he was trying hard to control.

"I specialize in feature magazine articles on the paranormal, the occult, and unsolved mysteries."

He jutted his chin towards the thing in the envelope on Benjamin's lap. "That what you're working on now?"

No. This is like finding the Rosetta Stone or the ending to an unfinished Shakespeare play."

"Which play is this the end of?"

Benjamin smiled as he held up the envelope, "Camelot."

Just then the pilot came over the intercom. Everyone instinctively looked up as if they could see the pilot speaking. Benjamin looked down out the window.

"Ladies and gentlemen, we've just reached our final cruising altitude. I'm going to shut off the seat belt sign. On the left-hand side of the airplane directly below is the old Pecox County quarry. From this altitude, the rings of dugout earth make the shape of a giant heart..."

Looking down, Benjamin could barely see Cyrus' trailer as it was a mere darker scratch on the tan landscape. "Son of a gun, it does look like a heart."

Then he saw a plume of dust. He made out that it was a vehicle approaching the trailer. He looked at his watch, it was 3:04, he smiled and dangled the photo in the window. "Sorry Charlie, I got there first." He pulled down the shade, put the photo in the case, reclined his seat, and closed his eyes.

18,000 feet below a rental car pulled up to the trailer. A tough-looking, no-nonsense type, with a strong physique visible under his suit, got out with a briefcase and walked up to the door.

Howard greeted him. "Mr. Dalton?"

"You Howard?"

"Yes. Sir."

30 seconds later, "You sold it?! For a measly ten thousand? I offered you 20! God damn it! We had a deal!

Howard had both his hands patting the air to bring down the anger. "Now, I know we did Mr. Dalton, but this here other fella, he was in a hurry, and Cyrus here, he didn't want to take a chance at losing the money."

Cyrus sat with the Haliburton under his arm. Mr. Dalton rubbed his hands over his face and blew air through his fingers. He studied the two for a second. "What was this guy's name?"

"Now, I couldn't tell you that, see, he wanted to be kept secret just like you."

Mr. Dalton took out a stack of one-hundred-dollar bills and started to peel off 20 of them and made a counteroffer. "Look, all I'm asking you to do is help me make my twenty-thousand-dollar offer to this other gentleman... and here's your two-thousand-dollar finder's fee in advance." He stuffed the money in Howard's hand. "You'll be doing him and yourself a favor, Howard."

It didn't take long for Howard to see the logic in this. "I never got his address or nothing just his name and phone number in New York."

Howard handed him the number and turned away to count his money. He didn't get to three when Dalton put him in a sleeper choke hold.

With Howard wriggling and dangling off his 200-pound frame, Dalton approached Cyrus' face with a ratty, Hula Girl pillow in his other hand. Cyrus started to tremble and without his sonovox all he could do was honk.

As the wheels of Benjamin's American Airlines 737 touched down at New York's LaGuardia Airport, he too had a pillow in his face, as he wiped his sweat on it.

The stewardess welcomed her passengers to New York City over the plane's speakers. Benjamin rose and slipped on his jacket.

His seatmate was bending over under the overhead. "Hey, nice meeting you." I look forward to reading the article."

"Thanks, Nice chatting with you too. Take it easy, okay."

In the terminal Benjamin found his name being held up by a town car driver.

Dalton was looking out through the window of an American MD-11 as it continued its climb up from the Austin Airport's runway. The Haliburton was sitting under his seat, with his right foot in front of it.

The pilot came on the intercom, "Ladies and gentlemen, we've reached our cruising altitude, and the weather all the way to New York this evening is clear and smooth so I'm going to shut off the seat belt sign. Those of you on the right side of the cabin might want to look down and see the Pecox County Quarry, or as the locals call it, the rock store. You'll notice the rings of hallowed out earth make a heart shape..."

Dalton looked down, a column of smoke rose from the burnt-out shell of the trailer, thousands of feet below.

He pulled down the window shade and closed his eyes.

4 | TOO HOT TO HANDLE

Ben had the cab he took from LaGuardia wait as he went up to his apartment for as long as it took to drop off his bags and open the safe. He spun the dial and replaced the picture on the wall that covered it. On the way out the door, he noticed a stain on his shirt. He stepped into the kitchen and ran the faucet for a second, long enough to get his finger wet. He dabbed it over the stain. Now he had a darker stain. He looked at his watch and just closed the button on his sport jacket with a hard tug. The buttonhole became a button oval and the jacket stretched to its theoretical limits. He headed out the door with half the stain visible above the first button.

"PJ Clarke's please."

The Checker cab pulled out into traffic. He checked his watch again.

The driver noticed him in the rearview mirror, "Running late?"

"Amazingly, the plane got in early, but there was no gate for them. So, we sat, and then all of a sudden, we were 20 minutes late to the gate."

The driver's hand motioned to the car's radio, "Yeah, they'd been talking about big storms in the Midwest, lots of planes all screwed up. Got a big date?"

"Business meeting."

"We should be there in 15."

"Thanks." Ben watched lower Third Avenue go by, he smiled, he had it. The elusive holy grail of the king of all conspiracy theories. Only with this missing piece, there would be no more theory. It would suddenly become history. A history that carried his by-line.

"What business ya in, if you don't mind me askin'"

"I'm a writer." Then he thought for a second, "…and a historian."

"Geez ya mean like a professor or sumptin'?"

"Nah, nothing like that. I freelance for a few magazines and one or two newspapers."

"There' a lot of money in that?"

"There is now!" He smiled to himself as he turned back to see 47th Street passing by.

"Okay, that'll be 25.50 with the wait time."

Ben handed him a twenty and a ten.

The driver noticed Ben's hand still sticking through the Plexiglas divider. So, he made change.

As Ben left the cab, he handed him three-dollar bills.

The driver grumbled to himself, "I guess, there ain't a lot of money in historical writing." Then he jumped as there was a knock on the window. He looked up, it was Ben.

"Can I get a receipt?"

"Really?" The cabbie said.

Inside PJ Clarkes, Ben went to the back room. His agent, Floyd Segal sat before an empty basket of bread. "I was about to give up."

"Sorry, the plane…"

Floyd held up his hand. "No problem. So, tell me…"

"I got it?"

"Yeah, great?"

"Was it worth the 11 grand?"

"Worth a million!"

"I like the sound of that. Let me see it?"

"Are you kidding me, it's home in my safe."

Floyd's demeanor shifted. "I see."

Ben picked up on it. "Floyd, I'm telling you this is it. The one thing the world's been looking for."

"Your world, the rest of us are looking for the fountain of youth, or a hot stock tip." He looked at Ben. "Assuming this has all the weight you say it does…"

"It does."

"Then we are going to need it verified."

"I verified it."

"Third-party Ben. Who's going to believe you or me."

"That can cost a pretty penny, plus we might have to let it out of our hands."

"Already covered that."

"One of my clients is all over this crazy-ass Kennedy stuff. He can verify it."

"Who's this?"

"Peter Salvo."

Ben whistled, "You rep him?"

"Yep, for almost 6 years now."

"And you trust him?"

"He's a big nerd. Worse than you."

"And he can lend provenance?"

"Him and maybe someone he trusts, but that will be better than some lab or third-party investigator. Cause with him you can walk the piece through the process."

"So, I never have to let it out of my site."

"Exactly. Okay, so what is this? When can I see it?"

"You can come back to the apartment with me after dinner."

"Can't gotta catch the silver snail to Huntington, wife's got me volunteering later tonight at some charity thing. But tomorrow, I'll come to you before work." He pointed to the table. "Are you gonna have anything?"

"Nah, I got to get back, I'm beat."

Floyd peeled off some bucks and parked them on the table on the little tray with the bill on it. He tried one more time. "Ben, what is it?"

"Proof that Oswald wasn't the only shooter!"

"No shit!" It sunk into Floyd's brain for a few seconds.

"Is this safe?"

"Safe? What do you mean?"

"Salvo is always saying how 166 witnesses to the assassination have disappeared. Are you monkeying around with something that'll make you disappear?"

"Nah, it's been over thirty years, no one cares about that stuff anymore. Besides this changes history! You can't stop that."

"Just the same, you know what?"

"What?"

"You deal with Salvo. I don't want to go anywhere near the friggin' thing."

"Suit yerself."

Super self-consciously, Floyd looked all around their table.

"New York City information, what number are you looking for?"

"Operator, maybe you can help me. I just flew into New York, but I lost my friend's number, and I..."

"What's his name sir?"

He looked down at the piece of paper Howard handed him. It read, ar2 611-1214. "Benny, er. Benjamin Larson"

On the wall in front of him was an ad for the Greenwich Village Jazz Club. He read that address to the operator. "In Greenwich Village... Bleeker Street, I think."

"I'm sorry sir, I show two Benjamin Larsons, but I don't see any listing on Bleeker Street."

"Are any of them close to Bleeker?"

"Well, I have one on 87th Street and one on 57th.

"Could be 87th.

"That number is 645 - 74..."

He looked at the number on the paper it started with 661. I'm sorry I remember now; he lives at 585 East 57th or something like that and I believe his number started with ... 611."

"I only show one other listing for a Larson, Benjamin but it's at 637 West 57th Street. That number is 611."

Getting what he wanted he hung up before she could finish.

West 10th Street was short but exceptional. Treelined, classic brownstones and a gentle vibe that lulls you into an all-is-right-with-the-world outlook. All of which made Dalton think, *there must be big bucks in writing*, as he walked down the picturesque street, silver Haliburton in one hand and the piece of paper in the other. He arrives at the apartment building on the block. He looked both ways, then proceeded up the steps.

At only 5 stories, NYC city did not require an elevator. As he reached the top, not out of breath, he peered up the steps. There was a red metal door with a bar across with yellow letters proclaiming; ROOF - KEEP THIS DOOR LOCKED AT ALL TIMES. He smiled, pleased with the layout.

Two hours later, from his perch at the top of the stairs going to the roof, he heard the scraping of the grit on each step as they laboriously climbed the last flight.

Benjamin reached the landing at his apartment door. While he was fumbling for his keys, Mr. Dalton padded down the steps, his automatic cocked and ready. As soon as Benjamin had the door open, Dalton came up quietly behind him and put the gun to Benjamin's back. "Make a noise, and I'll kill you."

Benjamin went instantly stiff.

"I want the photo you bought from Shaw today."

Nervously, Benjamin jerks his head up and down. "It's in the safe. Who are you?"

He smacks Benjamin across the side of his face with the side of his gun. "Shut up and get me that picture."

Benjamin was reeling from the blow, rubbing the side of his head.

With an unsteady hand, Benjamin opened the safe. He passed the photo in the black plastic sleeve behind him to Dalton.

"Shut the safe and spin the dial... Are there any copies?"

He shook his head, no. As he spun the dial, Dalton put him in a sleeper hold. As Benjamin slid to the floor, Dalton inspected the envelope. On it was a label that read," Property of Benjamin. H. Larson - Kennedy Polaroid Photo Original. Nov. 22nd, 1963." The envelope also had the warning, "Keep sealed and away from light." He nonchalantly broke the dot seal and slid out the photo. Casually checking to see if there was something inside, he slid it back in and scanned the messy apartment. He saw the electric heater in the living room under the window.

5 | THE NOT-SO-FRIENDLY SKIES

At 5'11, flight attendant, Christine Demarco, towered above the other flight attendants on this flight. Therefore, she was the first choice to deal with any unruly passengers. At the moment, she was all business, dealing with a Mr. Dalton in seat 33A, by the window, the only one in his row. The point of contention was the Silver Haliburton sitting on his lap.

She was mid-sentence, "...no, it's silver. But you still have to put it under your seat or in the overhead."

Dalton noticed the other passengers starting to look. He suppressed his dislike for this woman and compromised. He took the seat belt from the empty seat next to him and put it through the handle. "There, all secured. Happy now?"

"That's not..."

She was interrupted by the captain's P.A., "Folks we're number 1 for take-off. Flight attendants prepare for departure."

She looked back down and decided not to press it. She walked back to her station and pulled down the jump seat next to her co-worker Sally Hodges. As she buckled her 4-point restraint she gave it an extra hard tug, "Got a real winner in 33A."

An hour into the flight, the cabin service ended, Dalton looked around; everyone was strapped in, and the cabin lights were low. He popped on his overhead light and then opened the Haliburton. There, in the top's document pouch was the black plastic sheathed photo. He closed the case with the 10 straps of 10-dollar bills the fat man brought to the old coot in the trailer. He removes the photo from the black envelope and for the first time sees what it is. He did a double-take as soon as he realized what he was holding in his hand. "Holy shit!" he murmured under his breath.

Fire equipment and hoses are strewn all over the wet street. Flashing red lights bounce off every surface. Firemen with coats open and hats up are pulling the hoses in and disconnecting them from the hydrant, signaling the end of a fire. A Fire Chief in a white coat and hat came down the stairs of the 5-story building and spoke to two reporters, "It started in an electric heater in the top floor apartment. The drapes were too close, and they went up. The entire domicile was engaged. We have one fatality, who appears to have died in his sleep."

Looking up the reporter from the Daily News notes, "Lucky thing it was the top floor or the whole building would have gone up."

6 | A KINK IN THE PLANS

Dalton walked over to a bank of airport pay phones. He put down the case and dialed a number. When the call went through, he spoke in hushed tones. "This is Dreesan, I speak to the Admiral this second or me and the photo go right to the New York Times."

There was a momentary delay as the Admiral picked up the phone. "Dreesan, why this breach of operational security?"

"Sir, this picture has more to do with your own security, sir. It has to be worth much more than 200K to you, Admiral."

"So, you've examined it, against orders?"

"Yes, and now I can see why you, Admiral, were so interested in getting it back. I think the media would offer at least a million."

On the other end of the line, the stern face and scowling eyes betray the rage that Rear Admiral Brent R. Howser, USN Retired, was hiding in his otherwise calming voice. "Hold please."

He covered the receiver with his hand and turned to Sorrells, who handed him the phone.

He put the call on hold.

"Is he the only operative you've sent?"

"Burt Dreesan, his mission cover is Mark Dalton, we set him up as a go-between for a rich collector of JFK memorabilia."

"Have you used him before?"

"Yes, and for this he was the top candidate, lots of fieldwork. Very effective at containment. Never blew a mission and until right this minute, unquestionably loyal."

"I see." He brought the phone back up to his ear and nodded.

Sorrells took him off hold.

"A million is not an obstacle. Keep to the appointed drop tomorrow." He looked to his right, hitched his head, and Sorrells cut the call.

Burt Dreesan, former CIA agent and current assassin for hire, who outsmarted or outshot his way out of the most dangerous missions, without ever leaving a trace, hung up the phone with a shaking hand. He had just played hardball with one of the most ruthless and powerful men of this century. He took a moment to compose himself, then left the phone area.

He walked across the terminal and entered Airport Books. He perused the novels and picked one at random. He waited at the counter as the salesgirl finished up with a woman who he figured must have been going on a long flight as she had 5 hardcover books on the counter.

The salesgirl handed the woman a plastic bag with the books and a receipt.

Dreesan stepped up.

"Will that be all this evening?" She asked as she took an Airport Books bookmark and slid it between the pages, then bagged the book.

"Yes."

Dreesan came out of the store with the plastic bag. Directly in front of him were the long-term lockers. He reached into one pocket then the next. He looked around.

He approached the saleswoman from the bookshop locking up for the night.

As she was locking the pull-down gate, he spoke to her. "Er... Excuse me miss?"

7 | CHOOSING UP SIDES

When choosing up sides for softball, nobody ever picked "Lardo Larson," which always made him the last one left, the team that lost the toss for the first pick always wound up with him. It was the kiss of death, he couldn't run the bases, he threw like a girl, and he was an easy out at the plate. But Benny "Lardo" Larson had one thing going for him that ensured he at least got to play the game, namely, Henry "Hank" Larson.

Benny's older brother was always the first pick. He could smack the ball over the schoolyard fence, he could throw out a guy at home plate from center field, and he could usually beat out a routine infield hit. Very early on, Hank laid down the law, "If Benny doesn't play, I don't either."

Both sides agreed to this before the flip for who chose first. In many cases that coin toss determined who won the game.

It was the same at school, a year younger and 50 pounds heavier than Hank, Benny was a target for bullies and pranks. A few bloody noses later, nobody went after Benny, lest they suffer the wrath of his older brother. Even when Hank graduated a year before Benny from elementary or junior high and even high school, he would return, and usually, just a glare from him, insured safe passage in the halls and bathrooms of the school Benny still attended.

But it wasn't a one-way street between the Larson boys. Benny was a brain. He saved Hank from many a C or D in everything from

Algebra to English to Geography. Especially English. One side you always chose Benny for was the Spelling Bee. He could rattle off 'Autochthonous' like it was written on his hand. That was the word he won the State championship with. He was destined to be awarded a scholarship to Princeton for English Language and Literature.

Hank's dad loved them both, but he had a slight favoritism for his athletic son. Whereas Doris Larson was connected in a very maternal way to the boy she named after her brother, the physicist, Benjamin. So much so that in large part, Hank coming to the defense of his brother was really to protect his mom, who he knew felt responsible for coddling and keeping her younger son tied to her apron strings.

All of this made Hank, standing in a burnt-out apartment, thank God his mother didn't live to suffer the death of her little boy.

Hank wiped away the tears in his eyes as the locksmith was wrapping the hose around his acetylene tank after having cut the hinges off Benny's safe. The safe was the only thing that survived the fire that took his brother's life.

As much as he loved his brother, he was a slob. And having the drapes too close to the heater was definitely something in Benny's wheelhouse. He never made his bed. "Why? I'm only going to mess it up again tonight." He never washed dishes until there was no more room in the sink. He wore shirts until homeless people moved away from him on the subway, and he never ate anything that didn't become part of his wardrobe.

Hank peeled off ten twenty-dollar bills and handed them to the locksmith. "Thanks."

"Again, sorry for your loss." The locksmith rolled his tanks out of the charred apartment.

Hank took a deep breath and turned to the cut-open safe. There were a few hundred dollars in cash. A book, Flying Saucers Serious Business, signed by the author Frank Edwards. A notebook which seemed to be where he gathered his thoughts for writing a book on the restorative power of the Great Pyramid of Cheops. There was a piece of metal in a plastic sleeve. A typed label on it identified it as, 'Wreckage from Roswell Incident. Metallurgy identity undetermined by Hicken's Metallurgy Labs, Minot, Minnesota.'

He was leafing through some old, yellowed papers when two tall men in Stetson hats approached.

"Are you Benjamin Larson?

"No. I'm his brother, Hank Larson.

The two men reached inside their coat pockets and produced two ID wallets with star-type badges in them.

"Jack Connors and Willy Ritter, Texas Rangers. We need to ask your brother a few questions."

"Gentlemen, this was my brother's apartment. We buried him yesterday."

"Sorry, Mr. Larson. Did he die here in this fire?"

"Yes. Horrible."

Connors looked to Ritter with a raised eyebrow.

"What do you do?" Connors said.

"I'm a pilot for Flying Tigers, the airfreight haulers."

"Did you ever ship or haul anything for your brother?" Ritter said.

"No. What's this all about? Why the hell would the Texas Rangers be interested in my brother?"

"Mr. Larson, your brother met with a known smuggler named, Cyrus Shaw, allegedly to make a purchase of some kind. That same day, Shaw and one Howard Lance were burned to death in Shaw's trailer.

"Yeah, so what's that got to do with Ben?"

"Mr. Larson, we found your brother's name and the notation "Ten thousand dollars, plus my one-thousand-dollar finder's fee," among Howard Lance's effects." Ritter held up the note in an evidence bag with a star logo on it.

"We did not, at that time, find the money or the material which your brother was willing to pay ten thousand for. We believe he killed them and absconded with the money back to New York." Connors said.

Hank scoffed, "Killed someone!?... Benny? Look, my brother was a writer, a quiet guy... his idea of a score was finding..." He read from the old, yellowed papers in his hand. "Testimony of Amelia Earhart's flight mechanic. Murder? Not Ben."

Ritter was unmoved, "The fact remains that he's at least a material witness to a double homicide, if not the murderer himself."

"Look it's all academic now, Ben is dead, or doesn't dead count as a valid excuse in Texas? So, if you'll excuse me, I have to get back to work in a few days and there is a ton of stuff..."

"You'll have to stop that, sir." Connors held out his hand, and his other hand brushed by where he holstered his gun. The subtle threat was not lost on Hank.

Almost on cue, an NYPD uniformed cop appeared.

"Everything here is impounded as part of a joint interstate task force homicide investigation. You can't disturb or leave with anything."

Hank took in the two serious men and the cop in front of him.

As he was leaving Ben's building, he ran into the super. "Hi, I am Benjamin Larson's brother Hank."

"Ben was a nice guy, always a great tip at Christmas. So sorry he died."

"Thank you. I'm going to be around for a few days to settle up his affairs. How do we handle the lease?"

The super gave him the name and phone number of the landlord. And Hank thanked him, gave him his number, and left to go back to his place.

8 | NEXT MOVES

The McCallan 18 was out again on Brian's desk. Hank was in the chair in front of his desk.

Brian was shaking his head at the news Hank had just told him. "And there's no way around this injunction until your brother is cleared of all charges?"

"What I can't get over is how they can drag my brother's name through the shit like this?"

"I guess innocent till proven guilty only applies to the living. The dead haven't got the same rights."

Just then Judy came to the door with the daily report sheets in her hands.

"Come in, Judy. Wanna nip?"

"Thanks, Brian, but I still got a ton of manifests to audit. But I'll take a rain check."

He nodded. "Did you hear about Hank's brother?"

"Yes, just now, while he was waiting for you to get back from the hangar. It's so sad."

He turned back to Hank, "So, what are you going to do about your brother?"

He slaps his hand on his knees, "I'm going to take a little trip to Texas."

"What are you going to accomplish down there, Sherlock?" he said as he sipped the smooth, silky single malt.

"Ben can't defend himself, but I can. My brother may be a slob and a trashy writer, but he isn't...wasn't a killer..." He looked off in silence, then had a thought, "Would you do me a favor?"

"Don't even have to ask Hank, you're on leave till you get this mess straightened out."

Hank got up. At the door, he stopped and turned. "See ya, Judy. And Brian, thanks."

"De Nada, I still owe you big time."

Hank leaves.

Judy can't resist. "What do you still owe him?"

Brian reached over to the "wall of fame" grabbed an 8x10 and handed it to her. "My life!"

She looked down at the photo. It's a picture of a burnt-out hulk of a crashed B-52 bomber.

9 | FOUR YEARS EARLIER...

"Roger, Big Daddy. Thanks for the heads up." He threw the rocker switch on the yoke under his left finger from down to up, switching his comms to interplane. "AWAC says we got unfriendlies in the neighborhood. Stay sharp." Hank turned to his first officer, Brian. "I knew this run was going too easy."

The Electronic Weapons Officer calmly spoke over the headset. "Radar lock."

"Hit the chaff and flares. Hold on, boys." Hank executed an immediate jink to the left and down. The huge bomber shuddered under the stress.

"Got a bogey closing, continue evasives."

Hank reversed the jink and the B-52 engines screamed as he pointed the nose up in a hard right-banked turn. "Blow more chaff."

Shards of metal foil shot out from under the wings of the Stratofortress, its sole purpose to confuse the radar targeting mechanism of the missile streaking towards it at Mach 2. The flares presented heat signatures much hotter than his engine exhaust with which to zero in on.

"Going to be close, Skipper," EWO said over the interphone.

One last jink hard left and then he hit the flaps, slung down the gear and the plane slowed 200 mph. Everyone's chest slammed hard against the 4-point restraint belts.

The missile detonated in the plume of chaff 200 yards to the right of the airframe. The immediate concussion knocked the plane left, and Shrapnel peppered the fuselage and the wings. Brian groaned. Hank looked over, his leg and his arm were smoking and bleeding, and daylight came through the holes in the fuselage. The co-pilot's whole side of the cockpit was ripped up. The instrument panels were smoking. Circuits were sparking as the shrapnel shorted them out. The controls suddenly got sluggish; it was hard to keep level. "Navigator, radio our position to Big Daddy." He tried one more time, but the yoke was barely budging. He reached down and threw the toggle to "Abandon." A steady bright red light bathed the gunner's section and the Wizzo sections. "Abandon ship men, I can't hold her."

The Navigators pulled down their face shield and yanked twice on their ejection seat release in their armrests. The floor out from under them was blown away by explosive bolts and they dropped from the plane. At 12 thousand feet the parachutes built into their seats deployed. The gunner's position egress blew the top hatch above their heads and their seats launched up and away from the aircraft.

Hank reached into his armrest for his eject pull. He turned to Brian, who was in agony.

"Pop the champagne, Bri. Time to leave."

Brian struggled to reach for the mechanism. He barely managed to pull it once. "One more buddy, come on."

Just then another alarm sounded. Low fuel. Hank assumed the wing tanks were bleeding dry. "Running out of gas, brother, pull it." He did. Nothing. Hank knew that the safety mechanism against accidental ejection required the handle to be pulled twice in succession within three seconds. "Pull it again, you timed out." Groaning as he did, Brain managed to pull it once and then again, well inside the three seconds. Nothing. Hank leaned over; he tried twice nothing.

Brain spasmed, "Hank, get out. The mechanism is fucked. Get your ass out of here," his body went stiff.

"Hang in there. I got this." Hank grabbed the reindeer antler yoke. With all his might he pushed and pointed the nose down; the landscape came into view in the cockpit windshield. His instrument panel was dead. All the round-dial instruments were zeroed out. He estimated he was now descending through Angels 10. The jet started shuddering even more than before.

On the pedestal, he throttled back the eight engines of the giant war bird. He reset the flaps and strained to pull back on the stick until he had the right rotation for landing. The desert was coming up fast.

"Hank, you maniac, you can't dead stick a 52, get the hell out," Brian said through groans and spasms.

"Hey, I ain't going to leave this fine 55-million-dollar aeronautical machine, let's see if we can save Uncle Sam some chump change."

"Get out!"

"Shhhh." He wrestled with the yoke but there was no throw. The ground was coming up fast. *"Shit"* He remembered that the wheels were down. He grabbed at the glass-tipped wheel lever and pushed it up. With a dead panel, he had no up indicator telling him the wheels were up and locked and wheel well doors sealed. If the wheels were down, they could catch on the terrain, and they would cartwheel in a ball of flame leaving a dark charred mark in the sand. He was coming in fast, he set his flaps full and maxed the spoilers for air braking. He just had to go for it. He knew the glide ratio of the behemoth jet, he was about to ditch on the desert floor, was a narrow vortex. He decided to throw the engines into reverse at 100 feet. "Hold on Brother, this is going to be bumpy!"

The odds of rotating perfectly by eye, and flaring out onto the desert floor, then skidding unobstructed to some kind of stop was pretty low, but it was the only chance his co-pilot had of surviving.

He was hoping to hit at just the right angle with the tail first. Too steep and the tail would break off, sending him into a cartwheel, too shallow and he'd auger the nose into the dirt, the plane might, if it held together, flip head over tea kettle as the inertia drove the aircraft to pivot on its nose, a different kind of cartwheel, but just as deadly.

His luck, if you could call anything about this lucky, was that it was high noon. The sun was directly over the wings, as he approached, he watched the shadow. His head on a swivel, checking ahead and the size and shape of the shadow rapidly growing as he descended the last 100 feet. He popped the drag chute, designed to save brake meat during normal landings, right now he needed all the slow he could get. He had no yoke throw as the stick fought him every inch of the way. His arms were cramped, so he put his whole body into it.

The tail hit first; it was like a gut punch. He tried hard to push the yoke forward, but the plane was destined to do what it wanted now, any control he could have had was gone. Planes only maneuvered by introducing, lift and drag around the control surfaces. There was only ground beneath them, hence the only airfoil was pushing down. His jet was now just a hockey puck on a rough and unforgiving surface. All he could do was brace for impact.

In an explosive event, the wings sheared off. He felt the heat at his back. The cockpit tilted sideways as it gouged the desert floor. His chest was welted by the force of the restraint straps cutting through his flight suit. He couldn't believe how fast the fuselage was going, almost like the engines were still attached. He glanced behind him. There were flames in the tunnel just behind the cockpit.

The bomber was skidding across the sands like a Roman candle, its rear, a flame. The tail section separated and spun around to a stop breaking off one of the rear horizontal stabs. Now lighter, the plane slowed and eventually ground to a halt listing at an angle to the left.

Hank hit the center release on his belt and climbed against the tilt to Brian. "Got to go, bro."

There was no way out, B-52 crews entered the jet from the entry hatch in the belly. There was a chop ax back in the tunnel where there was an area where it was theorized that you could chop your way out. But no one had ever tied it. Besides, the tunnel was fully engulfed. He scootched over Brian and hit the ejection firing mechanism in his seat then turned away as the explosive bolts blew the hatch above the seat away and the empty seat catapulted out of the bird. Skylight poured in. He lifted Brian up. "Grab the edge."

In total agony, Brian reached up with his left arm as Hank pushed him out the top. A look to the rear confirmed the heat he was feeling on his face. The fire was being drawn towards the fresh oxygen in the cockpit. As soon as Brian cleared, Hank scrambled up, using the yoke as a step.

Once outside the jet, he swung Brian over the side. The tilted angle the jet rested in made the distance to the ground less and Brian made a reasonably soft landing in the sand. Still, he screamed when he hit. Hank slipped and landed hard. He got his wits about him and dragged Brian 100 feet from the flaming wreck when he collapsed. The fuselage was now totally engulfed in flames.

Hank held Brian sitting up. "We're good, Buddy." After a few seconds, Hank took a deep breath, he gently laid Brian down on his back. He stood up and scanned the terrain.

His last known position put him on the wrong side of the battle line. They were in Iraqi controlled area. He hoped his men survived the egress, and their homing beacons on each ejected seat were being picked up by rescue choppers. One of the three ball-shaped canisters of LOX, liquid oxygen, boiled off in the inferno that was his ship, belching out a ball of flame.

He decided to put more distance between them and dragged his first officer 300 feet until they were behind a berm. He looked up. Two columns of thick black smoke, one 1000 feet to his right from the burning wing tanks. The other in front of him was impossible for the Republican Guard to ignore. On the other hand, it was an aiming point for the Search and Rescue Helios.

There was a first aid kit in the ejected seat that was now lying on the sand. He made his way to it and also checked that the beacon wasn't damaged by the no-altitude ejection.

He treated as many of Brian's wounds as he could. He looked up. A plume of dust was heading toward them. This wasn't good. He pulled his 9 mm Baretta and searched the skies for any sign of S&R. "What are you going to do, fight the Iraqi army with that pop gun?"

"I don't know, you good with eating locusts?"

"Fried or chocolate covered?" he winced.

"Let's hope we never get the choice." He moved Brian behind a higher part of the berm. He kept low. There was a shot that they wouldn't be discovered.

An Iraqi BTR 80 troop carrier approached the first fire by the sheared-off wings. They didn't dismount and kept a safe distance away from the heat. After a few minutes, they turned and headed for the burning fuselage.

With his back against the berm keeping low Hank saw two dots in the sky. He hoped it was S&R and not unfriendlies.

At the burning wreck, they changed tactics. the back opened, and four Iraqi soldiers emptied out. They walked around the wreckage at a safe perimeter. Hank peeked over the berm and saw one of them notice the drag marks in the sand that led right to them. Hank turned and saw two choppers were inbound. The soldier unstrapped his AK-47 and cautiously followed the trail. The sound of the choppers caught his ear. Hank racked the Baretta and took a deep breath. Hank was about to spring up and shoot the soldier, as he hoped he was momentarily distracted by the helicopters. The soldier looked up at the choppers when he was twenty-five feet from them. He yelled and ran back to the troop carrier. A woosh over Hank's head resulted in the troop carrier exploding in a fireball. Mini gun bursts cut down the soldier. The Apache was sporadically firing and killing the scattered soldiers as the Huey landed. Two crew members scrambled out.

"Bring a litter," he yelled over the rotor noise.

One of the crew went back and brought the stretcher.

"You're on your way home." The crewman said to Brian as he and his partner lifted him onto the stretcher.

"You hurt?" The crewman asked.

"No, I'm good. Let's get out of here."

As the Huey lifted off and turned away, the Apache fired two missiles into the fuselage, just to be certain there was nothing for the enemy to recover.

Judy sat wide-eyed after Brian finished his telling of the time Hank saved his life, "Wow, boss, That's an amazing story. And that's why you don't wear short sleeve shirts?"

"Not pretty."

Judy was in the Army as a comms specialist E6. In fact, most of Brian's hires were vets. There were grunts, and sailors, and a few airmen. 4 or 5 of his employees still served in the National Guard.

Judy remembered at one point when Talon Air, a cargo start-up, was suspected of having sabotaged the jet-A fuel to one of Flying Tigers 74's. The entire fuel system and pumps had to be replaced at a cost of $240,000.

The men of the Flying Tigers wanted to go over there like a combat operation and raid their offices. 'Brian's Brigade,' they called themselves. Only Brian's levelheaded command style stopped these gung-ho guys from playing army again.

After that, Brian got everyone who wanted it, a membership at a gun range out on Long Island, and the fellas got to at least fire off some rounds and have a few beers. That bravado would have to suffice in the civilian world. Talon went belly up within 6 months, mostly because Brian dropped the cargo rates to such a low altitude that Talon crashed... financially.

Although she knew Brian and Hank were friends, she didn't know until just now that they had such a deep history.

10 | $5,000

Hanks's phone rang, "Hello."

"Mr. Larson?"

"Yes, this is Hank Larson."

"Mr. Larson before your brother died, we met and made a deal."

"Well, I don't know how I can help you."

"Can we meet?"

"Again, I don't really know anything about my brother's business."

"Please."

Hank was taken aback " *Please?* What kind of deal?"

"He was going to write about something I have."

"Well, I am not a writer, so I don't think I can help you."

"Then can I have my 5,000 back?"

"Your what?"

"I paid your brother to write a story and introduce me to Senator Browning."

"I don't know him, and I don't know anything about any 5,000 dollars. I'm sorry but he's dead and I am just trying to clean up his affairs. How did you get my number?"

"The super at your brother's building, I went there, and he told me about the fire."

"Well, I'm sorry but I really can't help you."

"Then take my number, in case anything comes up."

Hank doubted anything would "come up" but wrote down the number anyway and ended the call.

Hank took a shower, went into the kitchen, and scanned the fridge; cream cheese, onion dip, three beers and a past date quart of milk, and a hopeful second shot at a slice of pizza in aluminum foil from before his last trip. He tossed the slice, dumped the lumpy milk down the kitchen sink, and decided to go out to eat. He got dressed and headed downstairs.

Out on the street, a man approached him. "Mr. Larson?"

"Who wants to know?"

"Dennis Meeks, we spoke on the phone an hour ago?"

"Look, Mr. Meeks, as I told you, I don't have anything to do with my brother's business or what he did or did not do."

Then Hank had a disturbing thought. "Mr. Meeks, how did you find me?"

"The super of your brother's building."

"The super only has my number."

"I work at NY Tel. I used the reverse directory."

"Well, you shouldn't have bothered because we are done here." Hank turned and walked off.

Meeks called out. "Can I at least have my package back?"

Hank stopped and turned around. "Package?"

Twenty minutes later they got out of a cab at Ben's building. "If you sent it last week, then it wasn't in the fire. Let's check with the super." Hank said.

They went to the super's apt, 1E in the back of the first floor.

Manny Delgado was watching wrestling on Channel 9 when there was a knock at his door. He was in a wife beater and boxers. He went to the door. Looked through the peephole, seeing two guys he opened the door. He recognized both men. "Oh, I see you found Mr. Larson's brother."

"Has a package arrived for my brother since I left this afternoon?"

"A whole bunch came in, give me a minute to get dressed and we'll go to the package room."

There must have been 50 keys on the super's oversized ring as he somehow knew exactly which one fit the lock on the package room's security gate-like door. He started moving around the boxes. "Let's see. 5H, 3C."

"That's it, the FedEx box," Meeks said.

Manny grabbed it and confirmed, "You D. Meeks from Patchogue, Long Island?"

"Yep, that's me."

Manny handed over the box to Hank.

"Thanks," Hank said.

Outside the room, Manny locked the metal grate and went back to his apartment in the rear.

Meeks and Hank walked out into the street.

Hank looked at the box, "What's in here?"

"Nothing, can I have it?"

Hank shrugged, "Sure." And handed it over.

"Your brother still owes me my five thousand bucks."

"Take it up with him next time you see him."

"Very funny." Meeks turned and headed down the street.

Hank watched him leave. He thought about Ben and laughed about how his brother could really bring them out of the woodwork. He snapped his fingers and went back inside the lobby.

He took out his brother's keyring and opened his mailbox. There were a few envelopes and a True Flying Saucers & UFOs Quarterly. There was a trash bin next to the mailboxes and he tossed the mag in. He rifled through the envelopes and threw out 2 that were junk mail but the last was a handwritten envelope addressed to Ben. The return address in the corner was D. Meeks. 265 Oakdale Rd. Patchogue, NY. He held it up to the fluorescent light in the hall but couldn't see what it was. He slit it open with the box key and a personal check folded into a blank sheet of paper fell out and onto the floor.

Hank trotted out to the door and looked down the street, but Meeks was gone.

The next day Hank stopped at the post office and mailed the check back to Meeks' return address from the envelope.

11 | LARSON BEST LAID PLANS...

Dreesan located a perfect spot on the map. He rented a car and got to it 20 minutes before the others were scheduled to arrive. He purchased bolt cutters earlier in the day. The truck yard was empty this time of night and his scouting of the location told him they simply locked up at night with a padlock and chain. He pulled over to where the fuel truck was. At the rear of the truck, he removed the cap on the hose fitting, then he opened the valve and a torrent of gasoline flowed out of the truck.

A few minutes later, Dreesan had positioned himself behind a concrete building.

A car pulled up and stopped twenty feet away from his car. The two men inside got out, one was Lawrence Briggs, who at 30 was already an ex-prize fighter. He sniffed, looked down, and immediately realized what they were standing in. "Get back to the car now!" he said to Ned Croft.

Dreesan stepped out from behind the structure, lit his lighter, and called out to Briggs and the other man. "Don't move, you'll never get away fast enough." He was holding the lighter over the edge of the pool of gasoline."

"And if there are any snipers. If they hit me, same result. You fry. Is my money in the case?"

Croft lifted the case as he nodded.

"Now you, with the briefcase, get into my car and drive over to the gate. Leave the case on the seat and walk back or your friend here is toast."

"Where's the merchandise?" Briggs asks.

"In a lifesaving place. Once I'm out of here, I'll call with the location."

"That's a sucker play. No dice."

"You don't have a choice. I got the drop on you." He let go of the lighter and caught it at knee level, still lit. "Boom."

"Okay. Do what he says, Croft." Briggs orders.

Ned drove Dalton's car over to the gate and came back but didn't stand in the gas.

"Okay, if the money is in there, I'll call the Committee with the location of the photo. If not, we do this all over again, but for five million."

Dreesan reached into his back pocket and pulled out two sets of handcuffs. He threw them to the men.

"Now if you fellas would handcuff yourselves to that pipe there, I'll be on my way."

Just then a breath blew out the lighter, and Dreesan was blown back five feet by a stun gun thrust into his cheek.

"Fuck you." J.D. Belson pocketed the stun gun, "I hate this little prick."

"Jesus, what took you so long?" Croft said.

Dreesan was now hogtied to the pipe in the pool of gas. A solid punch rocked his face. Briggs rubbed his fists as Belson squatted down to look him in the eye to interrogate him. "Where is the original photo?"

"Go to hell."

Another punch landed. Blood flew.

Belson checked his jacket to see if any blood got on it. He looked up to Briggs. Briggs understood and moved around so that the blood would fly away from Belson.

"Listen, you are out of options here. Tell us where the photo is or you're going to die slow and painful."

"I am going to cut out your heart and then kill you," Dreesan said spitting blood.

Another punch, from the other direction, knocked out a couple of teeth.

Belson got up to leave. "Get this pig-headed, special forces grunt to the safe house where we can work him more scientifically... and leave his car somewhere public."

"I'm gonna try one more thing. You got a handkerchief?"

Belson handed him the one in his pocket.

"Go easy. He can't die until we find out where he hid the photo."

Belson walked off in the direction he came from. Briggs crouched and soaked the hankie in the gas, Dreesan was sitting in.

"Hey buddy, you got a cut here. Let me see that."

He dabbed the cut with the gas rag. Dreesan screamed. He then rung out the rag over his head as more stinging liquid flowed into his cuts.

"You were gonna fry us, huh, big man."

He waved the lighter in a threatening manner. Dreesan focused on the flame and then bellowed from deep within, "Fuuuck Yoooouu!" as he lifted his leg and brought it crashing down on Briggs' forearm. The lighter hit the fuel. Flame erupted everywhere. Briggs rolled out of the inferno and Man 2 threw his jacket over him, smothering the flames. Briggs was badly burned.

The flash from the flames turned Belson around, He saw Dreesan spasm as he was engulfed with fire. "Shit."

Colt ran over, "That guy's toast. Briggs is burned bad; he needs a hospital."

"Are you nuts? Take him to the safe house." Belson said.

12 | LOCAL NEWS

Hank rumbled down the road past the same "ENTERING PECOX' sign his brother did. The sun was getting low in the sky. He had been traveling all day.

As he drove up to where the trailer burned, he saw how intense the fire must have been. Only one corner of the metal skin of the trailer stood, the rest had melted creating slags of metal that dripped from the bottom edge of the frame.

He cautiously stepped onto the floor of the trailer. All this man's worldly belongings and furniture were mostly rubble and ash on the deck of the trailer. He kicked around some of the charred remains. He picked up a blackened tin that caught his eye. He could barely read 'SALTINES' on the side. He shook it, it was empty, so he threw it back down out of frustration.

Twenty minutes later, Hank was at the Pecox Telegraph Newspaper. Three people were working in the small-town paper's office. A woman got up from her desk to greet him. "Howdy there. Can I help you?"

"Yes. It's a long story, but I'm looking into the events surrounding the fire out at the quarry?"

"Are you a lawyer?"

"No, it's personal. My brother may have been involved." Just saying those words struck Hank as wrong. "I mean, I am trying to prove that he wasn't."

"Who was your brother? Does he live around here?"

"No, he lived in New York."

"Where's he live now?"

"Excuse me?"

"You said he lived in New York, where does he live now?"

"He died."

"In the fire?"

For the first time something registered in Hank's brain, "No, not this fire, one in New York." *Coincidence?* "I'm sorry let's start again; I am Hank Larson."

"Millie Hensley, nice to meet you, darlin'"

"I really don't know what I am looking for, but I need to know if my brother had anything to do with the two men who died out there."

"What makes you think he did?"

"The two Texas Rangers that came all the way up to New York to accuse him of it."

"Those boys can be dead serious."

"Can you help me?"

"Don't know if I can, darlin', but sit right down we'll start with the story on the fire."

She brings him a copy of the paper from 4 days ago. Under the headline, "TWO LOCAL MEN DIE IN FIRE" are the pictures of Howard and Cyrus

"Did you know Cyrus or Howard?"

"Knew Howard, he was an assistant at the library, used to come 'round here and pick up the papers for their periodical section. Cyrus was a shut-in up at the ol' quarry. Never met him."

"I heard he was a smuggler."

"He certainly was. He's been running illegal cigarettes up from Mexico for decades, till Sheriff Perkins made him stop around a year ago."

"Is this all there is about the murders?"

"Well, there was the little blurb I wrote about two days 'fore it happened." She handed Hank another newspaper and opened it to

Page 3. She pointed to a small article. "Shame, the way I understand it, Cyrus was due to cash in on something good, before he died."

"Thanks." Hank read the article:

Assistant librarian Howard Lance, reports that he has brokered a deal between Pecox resident Cyrus Shaw and a New York feature writer for the rights to a historical artifact from the day President Kennedy was shot. Mr. Lance declined to relate how Mr. Shaw came across the artifact.

Hank looked up, "How did you find out about this?"

"Down at the Rattlesteak..."

"The what, now?"

"It's a place out on the highway, most everybody in town goes there. Howard was there the other night celebratin' his deal and I asked him some questions then wrote the blurb for the paper the next day."

It was dark and Hank almost missed the turnoff to the county road where the place was. As he pulled up, a neon snake wriggled around the words RATTLESTEAK on the electric sign above the local watering hole. Hank pulled up to the outside and went in.

Everyone inside was blue jeans, Stetsons, and cowboy boots, even the women. He felt like a dude in an old western. Still, he stepped up to the bar. "Beer, please... and what'ya got to eat?"

"Specialty of the house. Barbecued rattler. The best in the west." The barmaid, in short shorts and a halter top, said.

"You like it?"

"Mister, I make it, using my grandpappy's secret recipe."

"Well in that case... serve 'em up." Hank now understood where the rattle 'Steak' came from, he kept thinking Millie Hensley had a speech impediment.

"Whatcha drinking, mister?"

"It's Hank, what cha got on tap?"

"Lone Star, Lone Star, and Lone Star."

"I'll take the last one."

"Good choice, Bubba!" she said with a smile.

As she turned and drew a beer for Hank. He looked over at the two men sitting on the stool next to Hank.

"Excuse me... I'm trying to find out about Howard Lance and Cyrus Shaw. Maybe you knew them?"

"You don't look like a Ranger?"

"No, I'm..."

"...a stranger. Got nuthin' to say to you, mister. Now, just let us finish our beers, okay Bubba?"

The rattler was tasty, but some parts were best left uneaten. He washed it down, ordered another, and asked the barmaid to break a single into quarters.

"Gonna try your luck at pool?"

"I ain't having any other kind."

She gave him a warm smile. "Cheer up. Some nurses get off at 9. Your luck might change."

She winked.

"No, that's not what..." but she was already down the other end of the bar.

Hank waited his turn and put the 4 quarters in the coin slide and the balls dropped into the end of the table. He racked them up.

A man who had been playing earlier came over. "You plan to play all by your lonesome?"

"More fun playing against someone else. You game?"

"You ain't from around here are you, mister?"

"No, down from New York. Hank Larson's the name." He held out his hand.

"Bufford Polk, and is pool your game?"

"I play occasionally."

"You ain't no traveling pool shark, hustler type are you, Hank?"

"Nah, I make my money the honest way. I work for a living."

"Whataya do, Hank?"

"Pilot, You?"

"Dispatcher for a trucking firm." He finally shook his hand.

"So, you're not a shark either, right?"

Bufford just smiled.

They were on their third game, a tiebreaker, each having won one. They were also on their third beer, which was an icebreaker.

Hank was lining up his shot as he tried to get some information out of Bufford. "So that's all he said?" he missed the corner pocket.

Bufford had a setup on the 2-ball in the side. "He was just all boiling over with himself. All fired up on having made a deal with some dude from New York. They say that's the guy who killed him and the old coot."

As Bufford took his shot, Hank noticed a big guy in overalls who watched from a table in the corner.

Bufford was good and won the tiebreaker but stayed and then teamed up with Hank against two fellas from the bar. Everyone was half in the bag, so it was a sloppy game. Keeping score was a challenge so they just hit the thing around and challenged each other when a difficult, or even an easy shot, lay before them. Lots of laughing and a few jokes.

Before he knew it, the bar was empty. Even the man in overalls had left. Hank thought, *"Just my luck, I should have talked to him. He's probably the only guy in town who watches everything that goes on around here."*

"Hey, wanna settle up? It's closing time." The barmaid said as she wiped down the bar.

Hank finished his beer and threw down a twenty and turned on the stool to leave but the barmaid poured him another drink.

"This one's on me."

"You haven't told me who 'me' is yet."

She smiled, "Carla."

"Well, thank you kindly, Carla. Is that how you say it down here?"

She corrected him, "Is that how y'all say it down here."

"Duly noted, thanks. To what do I owe the pleasure?" He asked as he lifted his beer to her. She had poured herself a shot and tink'd his glass. She downed it and slammed it on the bar.

"You look like a man where it ain't all going his way."

He looked down and made circles with the coaster on the bar. "Got a friend named Brian. He and his wife talked me into going to a murder mystery weekend once - I didn't want to go." He smiled at the thought and looked up at her, "Had a great time, though. Solved the crime and won 500 bucks and another weekend! From then on, I was hooked. Went 10, 15 times. I was good, but that was just a game. This is real, a real nightmare. I keep coming up empty."

"You let the nurses slip right through your fingers."

"Not why I was here."

"Well, I don't know about that, but Lucinda, the redhead," She held her hands out in front of her chest, "She was checking you out like you was a prized bull."

"Well, I would have only 'steered' her wrong."

"Hey, that's pretty darn funny for a New Yorker." She leaned in over the bar, "You know, I've been overhearing you all night, running around here like Perry Mason, asking all these questions. I take it that it's your brother that they say killed them two up at the quarry?"

"It's a long story, might take another beer."

"I gotta close, but I got some cold ones in my fridge?"

Hank was intrigued, he didn't expect that. His head was so tightly wrapped in proving his brother's innocence that he missed the big-boobed redhead and, apparently, this slim, trim woman with the great legs and a beguiling smile. One that he was sure increased her tips substantially. It worked on him, he shelled out a twenty. "Lone Star?"

"Bud. Can you handle that?"

"In your case, I'll sacrifice."

"See you are smart as well as funny. You wait outside, I got to lock the front and take the garbage out the back. You got a car?"

"Yes. You can follow me, I'm just 5 minutes down the road. I'll pull around front after I lock up. Won't be more than a few."

Hank winked and followed her to the front door.

"Don't you go running off now."

"And miss a Bud? Perish the thought."

She locked the door, smiled, shut the lights, and headed to the back.

Hank headed to his car. As he was about to start it up, a man appeared at the window, startling him. He stuck a jagged-edged knife through the open window. The blade pinched his neck. He looked up looking only with his eyes, lest he stab himself.

The hand it was in belonged to the big guy in overalls who he saw watching him in the bar. He said in a slow drawl, "Git out slow."

"You're the boss."

The guy in overalls held the knife through the window, then whipped it around the frame and right back at Hank's throat. "Where is it?"

"Where's what?"

Overalls punched him in the kidneys. Hank winced.

"Don't fool with me, now. Do you have it?"

"No, I don't have it."

Overalls pushed him up against the car and brought the knife up to his cheek.

"I'll carve you up like turkey, boy. I want it."

"It's in the trunk."

Overalls smiled. He grabbed Hank's shoulder and prodded him with the knife toward the back of the car. Hank opened the trunk. Overalls glanced in it while keeping the knife on Hank. With an inside move with his forearm, Hank blocked the knife arm while he delivered a full fist punch to the face. Overalls wheeled but started to steady himself. Hank, seeing that the hand with the knife in it was hanging over into the trunk, slammed the lid down. Overalls screamed and withdrew his hand grabbing his wrist. Hank slammed the trunk again locking the knife in. With his leg, Hank pushed Overalls over. His face was down in the dirt, with Hank's foot on his neck, out of reach of his arms.

"Now what the hell are you talking about? What do you think I have?"

Out of the night, blue lights flashed from a sedan that pulled up. Hank was surprised to see Connors and Ritter, the two Texas Rangers, get out. Ritter reached for his cuffs and knelt to secure Overalls' wrists.

"Didn't figure you to like fried rattler."

He chucked his thumb over his shoulder back at the bar, "It's her gran-pappy's recipe. You guys ought to try it.

"You want to tell us what happened here?"

"This nut came out of nowhere; he thinks I have something of his."

"Well, do you?"

"Now I do."

Connors looked to Ritter with a 'now we're getting somewhere' look.

Hank opened the trunk. Connors, disappointed, pulled out the hunting knife. Ritter had got Overalls up and was putting him in their car.

"You'll come with us to make a statement."

"I'm not pressing charges."

"Why not?"

"Cause, fellas, I got a more pressing engagement."

On cue, Carla's blue Ford pickup came around to the front. She leaned over and spoke through the passenger window. "I leave you alone for a minute and you get into trouble."

"They were just leaving." He turned to Ritter. "Totally her idea. See ya around, fellas."

"Look, we're on to you. We don't like you sticking your nose into this thing."

"Can I go?"

"Whatever it is you think you're doing, if you withhold anything, I'll slap you with obstruction of justice," Connors said.

He got in his car and started it up. She pulled around him and he followed her into the night.

Ritter turned to Connors, "Wait till he finds out she's a cop."

Connors walked over to their car. Crouched down to be at the same level as the window. He handed the knife to Overalls. He grabbed it with a hand that had the open cuffs dangling from it, and said, "He ain't got it. Don't even know what it is."

"Thanks, Bailey, how's the wrist?" He asked.

13 | BACON AND EGGS

Carla's house was a single-family ranch, with a front yard and a rocking chair porch. She got out of her pickup and Hank got out and met her by the porch steps.

"One question, Hank."

"Shoot."

"You ain't married or nothing, are you?"

"Nope, mostly nothing. You still want to invite me in?"

"What did you say you did again?"

"I didn't but I'm a pilot."

"Shit."

"What?"

"Bang a lot of stews do ya?"

"I fly boxes around."

"Huh?"

"I fly for a cargo airline."

"Sounds good." She turned to go up the steps.

He added, "But truth be told..."

She froze on the top step. Waiting for the shoe to drop.

"In turbulence, I do bang a lot of boxes."

"You tried too hard on that one...fly boy."

They went inside.

"Beers in the fridge, unless you'd like something a little stronger?"

"Nah. You had me with Bud."

"Suit yerself, I'm going get out of this outfit."

Hank controlled himself. It was a softball, but he had swung and missed a few times tonight at being witty. He went to the fridge. "You want a beer, too?"

"It's only right," she said from the bedroom.

Hank wondered what was going to return to him in the kitchen as he found the bottle opener and opened the long necks; sloppy oversized shirt and sweatpants, black pushup bra, and garters, or...

Carla came out in a tank top and slacks. Bare feet. Hair up in a ponytail. "Go sit in the living room, silly."

He grabbed her beer and sat on the couch. She joined him.

He held up his bottle, "To a wonderful case of southern hospitality."

"To solving your mystery."

"Thanks."

"What was going on with the cops before?"

"I truly don't know. This big guy, you might remember him, he was in the bar tonight wearing overalls?"

"Yeah?"

"Well, he comes after me with a knife and claims I have something of his."

"Did you?"

"No, I had no idea what he was talking about. He must have thought I was someone else. Anyway, the real strange part is, these two Rangers, who came up to New York to arrest my brother, must have been following me since I got here. They showed up, but after I got the upper hand."

"Wait a minute. Was that the guy in the back of their car? Was that the guy from the bar?"

"Yeah."

"Someone was playing you, Hank. That's Winston Bailey. He's a Ranger too."

"No shit! So, they set me up?"

"I'd say."

"Son of a bitch, they were really convincing."

"Well, I'm glad you're not a fugitive on the run."

"Hardly."

She slid over closer to him. "I mean, it wouldn't be proper for a woman like me to bring a criminal into my house."

"You never know what could happen," Hank said playing along and getting a little closer himself.

"I mean you could have just grabbed me and had your way with me," she said, her breast touching his arm.

"And that would be a bad thing?"

"Not if you're gentle."

"I can do that."

She kisses him on the lips. "Promise me one thing?"

"You realize that at this point you could get any promise you want, don't you." He kissed her.

"You'll leave in the morning?"

That caused him pause, "Wait. Are you married? ...or something?"

"No, I just like to keep things simple. A little fun, some cum, then run."

"I never heard that before, I got a lot to learn about Texas women."

"New Jersey, buckeroo, but a Texan since I was 10 years old."

He looked down at her tank top. "And look how you've grown since then."

She reached down and grabbed his crotch... "My, my you too."

The smell of bacon frying was truly nature's alarm clock. Hank awoke in her bed. He went to the bathroom. When he came out, he passed her closet. Hanging there were three police uniforms.

He entered the kitchen. "You are going to spoil me."

"It's part of the service. You serviced me, I service you."

"The pleasure was all mine,"

"That's the way it usually goes, but you are extra specially generous."

"I'll take that as a compliment."

"Honey, you can take that to the bank if you ever decide to become a gigolo."

"So, who's the cop? An ex-boyfriend, husband?"

"Me."

"Whoa."

"Relax. I'm just a dispatcher with the county. I don't arrest nobody, just talk all day to the boys on patrol."

"With that voice, what a distraction."

She affected her radio voice. "1 Baker 6, answer to the 210 hundred block of Wisconsin Avenue. Man with a gun. Be advised, plain-clothed units responding."

"Wow. I'm looking right at you, and I can't believe that's you. You are all business aren't you."

"Been doing it for 10 years now. Kinda' gets to where you have to be."

"Can I ask a question?"

"Anything, baby."

"Last night, when you asked me if I was a rooster in the stewardess hen house, if I had said yes, would that have been a deal breaker?"

"No, baby, more of a resumé enhancement."

"Carla, you are just full of surprises."

"Over easy or scrambled?"

Hank helped with the dishes while Carla got ready for work. She came into the kitchen in her uniform.

"Wow. That's... I mean... Gee. Do you have another 10 minutes?"

"Down boy. Wasn't last night enough?"

"Can't get enough of a good thing."

"That's sweet," she kissed him on the cheek. "What are you going to do today, Perry Mason?"

"Do what I came here to do. Probably go back to the paper, see if I can dig up anything else."

"Millie Hensley, her little brother was in my homeroom in high school. She was a big deal up in New York, she was working at the New York Times. Then her daddy got sick she came back here to take care of him. Lord knows her brother, Phillip, wasn't worth dirt after he got mixed up in drugs. After her daddy died, she never went back to New York. When old man Parker died, he ran the paper, she stepped in and never left."

"I'm hoping she knows something about the Kennedy assassination. Somehow that has to do with my brother. But I'm just fishing without any bait."

"You know, now that you mention it, and I don't know if this will help, but Jack Crowley left the afternoon of the fire."

"He knows about the assassination?"

"No, he went fishing like he does every year. He'd of passed the quarry on the way to the interstate. Should be back today. It's a long shot, but you could talk to him. Maybe he saw something."

"Jack Crowley, huh? Where would I find him."

"He's been away for two weeks. He'll probably hit the General Store on Main Street at some point to stock up."

There was a moment of silence. They look at one another.

Hank started to talk, "You know..."

She stopped him. "I know, baby."

He took a deep breath. "Carla, have a great day at work."

"Good luck today, Hank."

One last lingering kiss.

"You can let yourself out-, the door locks behind you."

Hank watched her leave. Flying all over the world, many folks would assume he was knee-deep in sexy, willing women. Not so much. Few and far between was more the pattern. But for the life of him, he never met anyone as... as... playful... as Carla. He remembered a line someone once said about how to be a success, 'always leave them wanting more.'

He wondered who was last with her and who would be next. He knew that was going to happen, after all, she had a 24-count box of condoms in the drawer in her nightstand. Half empty.

14 | THE BIG CATCH

The poles and the mud told Hank that this was Jack Crowley's Wagoneer. He had returned, two weeks from the day that Hank's brother, Cyrus, and Howard had died. The smell indicated that Jack had a run of good luck and plenty of fish to dry for the winter. Hank caught him coming out of his grocery store.

"Excuse me, Mr. Crowley, Mr. Jack Crowley?"

"Who wants to know?"

"My name is Hank Larson; heard you went fishing. Smells like you charmed 'em right onto the hook."

"Been fishing since I was five. What are you fishing for, mister?"

Hank smiles, "Did you know Howard Lance or Cyrus Shaw?"

Jack threw his thumb over his shoulder. "Just heard inside they was killed!"

"The day you left."

"What are you saying?" Crowley asked as he loaded a box of groceries into the back of the Wagoneer.

"Please don't get me wrong, I'm not saying anything, I'm asking. Asking for anything you might know about it that can help me clear my brother's name."

"Who's your brother? What's he got to do with this?"

"Well, my brother died that same night, up in New York. Somehow, the Texas Rangers think he was involved with the two deaths down here."

Crowley took in Hank for a moment. Then he spat on the ground. "Listen, this may not help you, I mean if you're looking to clear your brother, but as I was heading out, I see this fella stopped by the side of the road, had a map out. So, I slow down, ask, you know, "Could I help you?" He was definitely not from around here. He asked the way to the quarry."

"What time was that?"

"Oh, must have been about 2:45 'cause I made the interstate by 3:30."

"And where was this?"

"On the only road outta town. About 10 minutes from the quarry. He missed the turn-off, the old sign's worn clear through to the wood."

"That fits the time of death in the paper, at 3 to 4 that afternoon.

"I'm no cop but I'd say that puts your brother there when it happened." Crowley got into the Wagoneer and started the engine.

Hank was deflated, but something was still nagging him. "Yeah... I'm no cop either, but... Jesus, what's bugging me is that the Rangers haven't found any fingerprints or anything."

"Maybe he wiped everything down, like in the movies."

"Ben?" He scoffs, "Ben never cleaned up after himself in his whole life, the fat, little slob. Look thanks for the info..."

"Fat Slob? We talking about the same guy? You could cut yourself on the creases of this guy's suit. Military neat, you know the type. And he weren't little neither."

Hank brightened. He reached into his back pocket and pulled out his wallet. He opened it to a picture of Ben and him at a ball game. "Was this the man?"

Jack squints, "No. No, that ain't him. This fella was a tall drink a water, built like a Sherman tank."

Hank let out a deep breath, "You remember what this Sherman tank was driving."

"A rental. An Oldsmobile."

"How do you know it's a rental?"

"Fred Myers, he got stuck with a whole bunch of Cutlass Salons, you know the Aerobacks. He rents them over by the airport real cheap. The way I figure it, in 20 years he might make his money back."

"Mr. Crowley. I don't know how to thank you. You've set my mind at ease."

"Glad to have helped. You have a good day now."

"You, too."

He drove off.

Hank decided to go back to the paper.

"...like a Sherman tank. Didn't ask for Cyrus though, just the quarry. That's what I told him." Crowley said to the two Texas Rangers who were waiting for him when he got home.

"And he said, you eased his mind?" Connors asked.

"Word for word?"

Connor turned to Ritter, "This is starting to get interesting."

Millie Hensley closed the file drawer and turned back to Hank, "It's real thin Mr. Larson. This new 'military' guy might not have even gone near the place."

"That's why I was hoping you could tell me if Cyrus was ever in the army?"

"Grabbing for straws there too. As far as we know from his obituary he was never in the army. I don't think there is any connection."

"Well, doesn't it seem more than a coincidence that both Howard's and Cyrus' deaths and my brother's ended in fire?" At that moment, a thought he had been harboring surfaced again. This time like a kick in the head.

Hensley sees the change in his face. "What?"

"I am starting to think that Ben didn't die in any fire caused by an electric heater. He was murdered! Just like Cyrus and Howard. And...

She jumped in. "But the County Sheriff and the Rangers ruled the deaths accidental."

"Can I see that article again?"

She still had that issue paper over on the composing table and handed it to him.

He skims it. "Not exactly." He read out loud. "There was no evidence of foul play, so the cause of the fire was still undetermined as of our deadline. However, the Fire Chief says the domicile was heated by an illegal use of a pool heater put into service to heat the trailer. He offered that the victims could have succumbed to carbon monoxide poisoning before the mobile home was engulfed in flames, most likely from the same faulty heater. Adding, that was his personal, probable cause but not an official position. Carbon monoxide poisoning has recently been cited in the death of tennis star, Vitas Gerulaitis in New York last month. A badly installed pool heater..." He stops reading. "A heater again."

So, you think this military man, whoever he was, may have killed Cyrus and Howard, flown to New York, and then killed your brother and stole whatever it was?

"Maybe my brother had already left before this guy showed up."

"So, you're saying this goon was after the artifact..."

"Only he didn't count on Benjamin showing up before he got there, maybe."

"Well, that's one possible explanation, but it's all fancy guesswork."

Hank grabbed the phone locked on one thought. "He didn't count on Ben! He didn't count on..." He spoke into the phone, "Yes, the number of Austin Airport, flight operations, please.

"Mind?"

Hank flashes the hook and dials again.

"No. Not at all, darlin' I'm going to go get a coffee, you want one?"

"No, thank you." The man on the other end answers using his last name.

"Flight operations, Phillips..."

"Good afternoon, Mr. Phillips, my name is Captain Henry Larson..."

Hensley came back into the room with her New York Times coffee mug as Hank was finishing the call. "Thank you for looking it up. High ceiling, no mechanical delays. Thanks, you've really helped me. Thanks, I will." Hank hung up.

She took a sip, "Good news?"

"American had a 4:30 flight arriving 6:45 at LaGuardia. That fits into the time frame of the trailer burning, a flight to New York, and my brother's death sometime before midnight."

"Sounds good, but how are you going to prove that this soldier type Crowley met was even on that plane?"

"Being an airline captain, even with a cargo airline, has its perks."

Hank was able to wrangle an economy class seat as a courtesy from the AA flight operations center in DFW, on the same flight he suspected his brother's killer took, out of Austin. He had a few hours beforehand. He walked over to the diner, ordered a coffee and made his way to the payphone, and thought he'd give it a shot. He dialed '411'. "Yes, I'd like the number of the county Sherriff's office, please?"

"The non-emergency number?"

"Yes, please."

"I can connect you, for an additional 25 cents."

Hank fished in his pocket and dropped a quarter into the phone.

"Thank you. Connecting your call now. Have a good day."

They picked up in two rings, "County."

"Yes, I am trying to reach a dispatcher, Carla?"

"I can take a message."

"Can I speak to her?"

"We don't transfer calls. I can get the message to her, and if she chooses to call you back, she will. What number can she reach you at?"

"I'm leaving town, so I am at a payphone, and I just wanted to say goodbye."

"How long will you be at this number?"

"My plane leaves in three hours."

"Okay."

"Thank you." He hung up.

As a pilot, Hank had been in the South many times and always had grits with his eggs. However, yesterday morning this diner served up the best grits he ever had. So, he came back and ordered two over easy, grits and toast.

He was mopping up the eggs with a piece of toast when Carla entered.

"I was expecting you to call me back, how did you know where I..., Right! You're a dispatcher."

"Reverse directory. We use it when somebody is cut off or can't speak."

"I'm so glad I got to see you again."

"Note said you were leaving today?"

"I think I may be on to something. Flying back to tap a favor."

"Sounds promising..." She looked him right in the eyes. It was a soft look. Almost vulnerable.

It registered with Hank, "I couldn't leave without saying goodbye. I never met anyone like you."

"I am sure you meant that only in the nicest way."

"Of course. There's something about you..."

"Because we jumped into bed from jump street?"

"Well, that's part of it. But look, what do I know? Usually that only happens when someone is using you as a hammer, to bang out the dents in their life. As a guy, sure you go with it, but somewhere deep down, it's kinda like you took advantage of someone who was hurting or angry or looking to distract themselves from a shitty life. Guilty in a way. But, you've got none of that, not that I can see anyway. You, you are just purely in it for the, as you say, fun. And I have to tell you, that goes a long way to make me feel really good about last night."

"No guilt?"

"Yeah, I guess that's what I am trying to say. Just like being in love, you know, when there's no guilt over sex."

"Okay, so you had to see me one more time, to explain to me how you are walking away with nothing more than a good time."

"Did I do the wrong thing?"

"No, baby. You know, no one has ever talked to me the way you just did. You're a sweet guy, you know that? Although I ain't too sure some of those skeletons aren't hanging around my closet, I do feel good about doing what comes naturally. But, and I guess you earned this, I felt different with you too."

"Care to share?"

She turned to the counter, "Doris, can I get a cup?"

"Black, two sugars coming up." The waitress confirmed as she went to the urn.

"Guys at work hit on ya all the time, but I never play, because then they are there every day, whether it works out or not. The bar? Well, that is almost a guarantee of a drunken grope and romp in the hay. So, I am very selective."

"Oh, so you selected me? I am honored. Why?"

You didn't go for the low-hanging fruits." Once again, she made two cups with her hands but lowers them below her own chest.

"Grapefruits. I seen that girl turn a guy in 60 seconds flat. But you, you gave her no never mind. Right away you were one in a hundred."

"What if I just didn't like redheads?"

"Didn't think of that. Anyway, I guess what I am saying is, when I am ready to lock up into a relationship, it's going be with someone like you."

"Or me? You know what they say on TV, never settle for substitute brands."

"I ain't done with sowing my wild oats yet, cowboy. And I figure some lucky girl's going scoop you up long before my nesting gene kicks in."

"Now I feel bad."

She reached across the table and grabbed his hand, "Why, baby?"

"Because I am only one in a hundred, and you are one in a million!"

Doris brought the coffee.

15 | TICKET TO RIDE

Back in New York, Hank came through his apartment door with a grocery bag and the mail from the box downstairs. After he put the milk away, he sat at the kitchen table and went through the mail. "Address Unknown" was officially stamped on the envelope of the check he attempted to return to Meeks. He immediately wished he hadn't thrown away the original envelope with the return address at the post office after he addressed this one.

He shrugged and was about to tear up the envelope with the check in- it when he had a second thought. He opened the envelope and saw that there was no address printed under the name on the check, however, there was the account number. He debated over what to do. *Do I try to track down this guy? Does he know anything that could help me with Ben's death? Should I just let the check go, if it never gets deposited, then Meek's account is never going to be charged.*

He decided to turn in. He had to be in Queens early tomorrow.

"Thanks for doing this Dix."

"No problem, Cap."

Roy Dixon still called his old skipper of the B-52 they flew during the war, Cap. Right out of the service, Dix got a job with the IATA.

All the airline tickets went through their main computer located outside JFK in Queens.

They walked into the computer center, and Dix introduced him to a man in short shirt sleeves with different colored pens in his pocket protector. His eyes magnified through 'coke bottle' glasses. His name tag read, Michael Wells System Operator.

Wells shares his doubts as they navigated through the terminals and mainframes, "I don't know, Dix. Pulling a complete passenger manifest from an airline's system requires a court order and FAA release."

"Mike, just do it, okay? We're not looking for evidence. Just info."

"If we find the guy I'm looking for, you guys will fly free for a year. I mean it."

"Great. Me and a thousand packages. No thanks." Dix said.

They arrived at a free terminal. Wells took his seat. Dixon stood by and Hank was looking over Wells' shoulder. He placed a slip of paper down by the keyboard with the date he was interested in on it. "I'm looking for a man on American's 4:30 to New York, who bought a ticket or changed destination to New York at the last minute." He turned to Dixon who he had filled in on the story, "This guy couldn't have planned for Benjamin to get in his way. Wells, can your machine tell me that."

Wells blew air as if to say, "Humpf, I thought this was going to be hard.

Dixon brags a little. "Stand back Hank, you're about to find out why we call this guy the Wells of information."

The screen scrolled as Wells hit the keys like a stenographer taking fast dictation. The screen rippled then an old-style printer ripped out two quick bursts. The paper folds out and Dixon rips it from the machine.

"Wells, you've gotta make this stuff look harder," Dix said.

"Harder than using this legacy old dinosaur of a machine?" He hands the printout over his shoulder back to Dix.

Dix scans the paper, "Bingo. Two last-minute bookings to New York that evening. One's a woman. The other's a man. Changed destinations at the Austin gate from Phoenix, Arizona, to New York... Oh, you are going to love this.

"What?" Hank said.

"Because of the stupid rate schedules, it cost him an extra $129." He smiled and looked up at Hank. "He paid for the upgrade with an American Express card in the name of Harvey Dalton of Silver Springs, Maryland. He was assigned window, 33A.

"Wells, what was the equipment on that flight?"

"Seven three - stretch, why?"

"Cause unless I'm mistaken, seat 33A that our Mr. Dalton occupied is the one next to the wing emergency door on a 737.

"That's a stroke of luck!" Dix said.

"Why's that?" Wells didn't follow.

Dix fills him in. "Flight attendants have to make note of who gets these seats and be sure that these passengers are big enough and able enough to help, or at least not be in the way in case of an emergency."

"Yeah, and that gives us a shot that maybe a stew will remember this guy."

Wells hit more keys. "The American computer system shows it was a Dallas-based crew."

"Wells?... Could..."

"Already on it. Cross-checking the cabin service list out of D/FW with JFK."

"Hank, you know, not to piss all over this streak of good luck you're having, but we're into a sticky area here. The flight attendant's union doesn't like people browsing through their files. Too many cockpit men looking for a stew's number created a hornet's nest of trouble a few years back..."

The printer staccatos again. Wells interrupts them. "Cool, two of the five-cabin attendants from that flight are deadheading to D/FW from LaGuardia tonight." Wells ripped the printout and handed it to

Hank who jotted down the info on a piece of paper. "Roy, Wells, thanks. Even if they torture me, I'll never tell them that I got the stew's names from you guys."

Connors and Ritter are having a rough time trying to convince their superior officer, Colson, to continue their investigation into the quarry deaths.

"Forget it. You've already come to a dead end once in New York."

"But I know the brother's involved otherwise why would he be in Pecox digging for information?"

"Look, I said drop it! He's left our jurisdiction and I am not going over budget again just so you two geniuses can follow him back to New York... again! And would you mind telling me what happened to Bailey's wrist?"

16 | THE SECOND SALVO

Hank took a cab back from Queens to his apartment house on West 42nd by the river. Hank got out and walked into his building. As he was entering, he held the glass door open for an older lady walking a little dog, who reminded him. "Tenants meeting, Thursday night, Mr. Larson."

Hank nodded and noticed that down the street by the building's side gate, a man in glasses and Bermuda shorts with white socks and black shoes was talking with the superintendent of Hank's building as he was carting out two garbage cans on a wagon. The super pointed to Hank who was holding the door while the dog sniffed his pants leg.

The guy in the shorts followed Hank into the building as he entered the lobby, he just missed the elevator door as it closed.

Hank was watching from behind the staircase. When he saw the man react to missing the elevator by punching his leg, Hank smiled and snuck up behind him.

"You looking for me?"

He jumped. "Are you Henry Larson? I'm Peter Salvo, I was supposed to work with your brother. Can we go somewhere outside to talk?"

"Why can't we talk here?"

Peter leaned in, "Laser listening devices bouncing off the glass surfaces."

He's got a live one here, "Riiight."

People walking dogs and kids were rollerblading past as Hank and Pete sat on a bench and talked. Hank was bugged that Peter kept looking around. It was making him paranoid.

"...till his agent called, and then there was the fire, so I called the agent back and he said Ben had a brother who was a pilot. Then it was easy to track you down."

"But you don't know what Ben bought from Shaw either, do you?

"No, but if it is anything close to what he told Floyd…"

"Floyd."

"Floyd Segal, your brother's agent."

"Didn't know he had an agent."

"I had just agreed with his agent that I would help with provenance and assist him if there was a conspiracy side to the story. I've spent my whole life investigating the Kennedy Coup d' Etat, and I've written three books."

"Coup d' Etat, huh? So, who killed Kennedy?"

"He was going to start pulling advisors out of Viet Nam, which became the most profitable war in American military-industrial history."

"So, what did killing him accomplish?"

"The coup put people in power who wanted the war and had the clout to cover up the fact... And those people killed your brother."

"I don't know if this is good or bad, but you are the only other person who believes Ben was killed."

"In the past 50 years, over 166 assassination witnesses and investigators have met with suspicious or untimely deaths. Whatever your brother found got him killed, too."

"So, what do you want from me?"

"I want to go through your brother's things. Maybe something will lead to what he had."

"Who do you work for?"

"Myself. I'm a lone conspiracy nut," He smiled at his own witticism. "I get paid by writing and speaking and, as in your brother's case, consulting.".

"You actually make enough money to live doing that?"

"Yeah. Most of the time. If you help me and a book comes out of it, I'll give you 30% of the income.

"And what if we come up with whatever it is?"

"Floyd said that your brother said that what he had could prove that Oswald didn't act alone…"

"And if he didn't act alone then it was a conspiracy."

"Bingo. The reason for 30 plus years of speculation, research, and circumstantial evidence."

"So, then you must have an idea of what he had then."

"Sure, but which one? A second rifle, a mangled bullet, a picture of Oswald within the window without a gun, a CIA or FBI top secret report, a confession by another shooter, the proof the motorcade route was detoured in front of the sniper's nest, an associate of Oswald who helped him escape, or a hundred more things."

"So, again, what happens if we come up with whatever it is?"

"Depending on whether it is a class one artifact or not, then I could get my publisher to advance us a couple of hundred thousand or so."

Hank's eyebrows go up. "Who determines that?"

"That's why his agent called me. I can verify or bring in experts who can authenticate any item. Your bother insisted on the chain of custody throughout, and I can deliver that."

"Is that how you make your money? Writing books about this stuff?"

Partially, but I also get paid to speak, my talks are very popular, in fact, that's why I am here in New York."

"About this?"

"No, Jacob Leon Rubenstein," he said.

"Who's that?" Hank said.

"You know him as Jack Ruby."

17 | HOMEWORK

With Salvo and his brother deep into the Kennedy thing, Hank decided he needed to find out more. There were large Hawaiian leis around the necks of the two lions who stand guard over the steps of the 42nd Street Library on Fifth Avenue. Lots of lunchtime office and construction workers were eating lunch on the steps. Above the entrance was a large banner, 'South Sea Island Festival of Books.'

Hank made his way to the information desk, "Excuse me, where would I find anything on the JFK Assassination?"

The man at the desk gave him a momentary look that told Hank he was now considered a nut.

With a sigh, the man said, "Historical or Conspiracy theories?"

"Uh, I guess both."

The man jotted down two section numbers and handed the paper to Hank.

As he walked through the halls, the smell of scores of thousands of books reminded him of a school trip they once took here. Their guide for the field trip told them that the library had an enormous archive below Bryant Park, that stretched to 6th Ave from the back of the library and held incredible artifacts from history. That was the first and last time he ever heard the term, artifact. Now his whole life was turned upside down because of an artifact that could or could not be historical. If it wasn't so sad, and about his brother's death, he felt you could classify it as hysterical not historical.

On the library shelf were 26 volumes of the Warren Report. The 27th book in the series was the 888-page summary.

After about an hour, Hank realized two things. The thick book was like an index to the 16,000 pages in the other 26 volumes. And that the gist of it was everything the crazies denied with extreme intellectual chauvinism. The report was pretty much what he had heard over the years and reached the conclusion that he never bothered to question: One lone gunman, three shots, and no conspiracy.

He put the books back on the shelf and headed out of the library. He went to the Sabrette stand on the street. Under the blue and yellow umbrella, he ordered 'two dirty water dogs' as he and his friends called them growing up with mustard kraut and a Pepsi. He preferred that term over the other neighborhood handle, 'guts and nuts.' Then he, like scores of others, picked a step and ate his lunch.

He tossed his trash and entered the library again. This time to the 'whacko' section as he thought of it.

Oh God, he thought as he read the ninth, or was it the tenth, 'Who Killed JFK?' This one had it as the driver of the limousine, who for some reason was able to shoot the president without any other person on the planet seeing him do it.

One more and then I am out of here. This time he chose the book by the color, he was always partial to blue. This one was called, Kill Zone. He remembered that his row mate, Kyle, mentioned 'kill zone' on the plane. He read the blurb, *'There were 11 seconds of turkey shoot presented to LHO,'*

Lee Harvey Oswald, he decoded.

'11 seconds of full body, center mass opportunity, twice as large as the human head. 11 seconds of a slow-moving, primary target, closing to within 50 feet of him. And yet, LHO waited until the target passed him and was driving away, which presented a target the size of a honeydew melon that was 200 feet away on a downward angle and

moving away and to the left of his position...through a tree! Why wait? Because LHO didn't wait, in fact, he never shot anyone. He was eating lunch on the second floor, but by then the target was in the Kill Zone!'

Hank had to admit, that was a compelling question. He thumbed through the book. In the center leaf was a map of Dealey Plaza. It showed the limousine in the position of where the X was when he stood on Elm the other day. Three dashed lines converged into the drawn head of the president in the back seat of the rectangle that represented the limo. One dashed line went from the Dal-Tex building, right across the street from the Texas School Book Depository, but directly behind the limo. Another line emanated from the triple underpass directly ahead of the limousine. The last, traced a direct line from the Grassy Knoll, which jutted out slightly into the soft curve of Elm Street, making that shooting position just off the right front fender of the limo.

The firing sequence was denoted in numbered circles. The first shot that was fired was shown from the overpass in front of the limo and was marked with the numeral one. The numbers two and four emanated from the Dal-Tex building directly behind the limo, the third shot was indicated by a number three from the grassy knoll.

A note below read: '3 and 4 were nearly simultaneous, within one-tenth of a second apart. Acoustically, due to the echo in the plaza, sounding like one shot.'

He read down into the text, 'The fatal head wound came from the grassy knoll. Governor Connelly's wounds came from the fourth shot from the Dal-Tex, from behind.'

Hank's head was swimming. All of this was at once ridiculous and at the same time strangely compelling. He could see how you could get caught up in all this crap.

He thought about Ben. Was this the way Ben's mind worked? He always believed Ben's propensity for alternate conspiracies, occults,

UFOs, and ESP, was just a cash cow for him, and that he reported on it objectively as an observer and observer of the absurd.

He placed the book back on the shelf and realized there must have been fifty or one hundred more. He was sure at least a few had his wife, Jackie, being replaced by a duplicate who was an extraterrestrial spy from the moon, who was ordered to kill him for planning to invade the moon by the end of the decade. For a split second, he thought he might cash in like these authors and write a book about it. 'Jackie from the Darkside' sprang to mind as a title. She would have had to be from the dark side of the moon, so no one could see the civilization she was dispatched from. He laughed to himself; *it would be so easy.*

A man sitting next to him asked, "What's so funny?"

"Nothing, it's just..."

"Just what? You think there is something funny here?"

"C'mon, a secret service agent shot the President? Absurd."

"Got to agree with you there, but lone gunman, three shots, is just as absurd."

Hank's radar started beeping, he was about to say, 'I think I hear my mother calling me. Have a nice day.' Instead, he decided to engage, *why not, this is almost entertaining.* "So, what do you think happened?

"Not me. Senator Browning."

That was the name that Meeks fellow said Benny was going to introduce him to. Hank decided to hold onto that nugget lest he becomes a target of this guy's mania. "Who's he?"

"Ranking member of the Senate Select Committee on Assassination Records."

"When was this?"

"Four years ago."

"And..."

"Browning was the only one who said that there was a conspiracy to kill the president and that an earlier attempt had failed that month."

"In Miami? I heard about that one...somewhere."

"Miami? No. That's just from that TV documentary, and it was October and it was proven false."

Hank was about to ask, 'By who? Which conspiracy nut said another conspiracy nut was a nut?' This whole area of controversy was insane and self-perpetuating by conspiracy freaks. Again, he moderated his tone. "So, what's your theory?"

The man turned the book he was reading around and pointed to a sentence as he read it out loud. "The Chicago Oswald was also an ex-marine, sharpshooter, and known advocate of treating Cuba more fairly. He flew from Long Island to Chicago a November 1st, 1963. His presence caused the Secret Service to cancel the Kennedy's Chicago trip."

"Wow. Did they arrest him?"

"No, he got away. CPD and the local Secret Service office blew the investigation."

Hank rolled his eyes, *another unproven conspiracy theory.*

"But if this guy was a senator, then they knew."

"Except a week later he recanted. Somebody got to him."

A voice in Hank's head said, *A conspiracy, wrapped in a conspiracy, about a conspiracy!* He'd had enough. "Well, that's extremely interesting. Thanks for the info. Gotta go."

"Have a good day," the man said and returned to his book.

18 | BULL AND BEAR

Hank walked up Fifth Avenue, all the way his mind running over the facts, then he caught himself; *supposed facts*. His little muse of the ET Jackie as an assassin from the moon brought his mind to Kyle saying Jackie's uncle Georgie and Onassis were protecting her. He decided to walk over to the Waldorf.

He entered the ornate and historic lobby. He remembered that as a kid growing up, his entire family gathered around the TV on New Year's Eve to watch Guy Lombardo and his Royal Canadians play in the New Year right from the ballroom of this hotel.

He approached the front desk. "Is Mr. Kyle Mann still checked in?"

The frontman checked his flip file, "I'll call his room. Whom shall I say is inquiring?"

"Tell him Hank Larson...er. from the plane."

He waited for the seventh ring and then hung up. "Well, he hasn't checked out, and he doesn't answer his phone, you might try the Bull and Bear."

"Thanks."

The Bull and Bear was the hotel bar for the Waldorf Astoria hotel. Steeped in New York tradition, it was the very definition of 'classic.' As soon as Hank entered, he saw Kyle at the bar with a few other fellows.

As he approached, Kyle saw him. "Hey guys, here's my friend from the other night. Hank say hello to two guys who think the New York Yankees are gods and not just the luckiest collection of untalented players ever assembled. One of the men turned and shook Hank's hand, "...says the Red Sox sycophant! I'm Dave."

"Nice to meet you."

"Harry." The other one introduced himself as he also shook Hank's hand.

"So, Hank what brings you here?" Kyle said.

"To be honest, I wanted to continue our conversation from the other night."

Harry nudged Hank with his beer bottle, "Don't tell me you're an, let me clean this up, an assassination fanatic?"

"No, but my brother was, and I am trying to understand him better."

Harry weighed this and nodded.

"The guys have a seminar in a few minutes. I got an hour before I have to be on a panel. Wanna grab a table?" Kyle said.

They settled in the corner and ordered. When the waitress left, Hank got right to it. "You mentioned kill zone on the flight."

"Yeah, the best way to plan an ambush."

"What makes you so sure it wasn't just Oswald alone, or LHO, as you guys say."

"Been reading, huh?"

"Guilty."

"You hunt?" Kyle asked.

"No."

"Ever fire a rifle?"

"In the Airforce, basic training."

"Ever use a scope?"

"Nope."

"Okay, so eyewitness testimony and even the Warren Commission states that Oswald brought the gun to the depository broken down and wrapped up in a paper bag. He told anyone who asked that they were curtain rods. So, if you follow that logic, he had to build the rifle once he was in the building. Well, as soon as you remove a scope from a rifle like that Italian job he had, you have to realign the scope. That you do at a rifle range, live fire, and then adjust for center, fire again, and adjust until it is zeroed in. So that scope wasn't worth shit soon as he removed it. And to use the iron sights, when the scope is attached, on moving target playing peek-a-boo through a live oak tree and then get anywhere near the target is either a lucky shot, not to mention three lucky shots, or a lie."

"So, you are saying that Oswald wasn't the shooter?"

His words, "I'm a Patsy."

"So, who?"

"Three hitmen from the Corsican mob."

"The three hobos?"

"Tramps, the three tramps." Kyle corrected him like he was teaching him a new language.

"And they got him in this kill zone."

"A salvo of 4 to 6 shots."

Hank perks up, "Salvo?"

"Fusillade, crossfire, salvo."

"No, it's funny you used that word because Peter Salvo..."

"Wait, Peter, *Who Killed Kilgallen*, Salvo?"

Hank didn't catch that, "Who did what to who, Kilgallen?"

"Peter Salvo, the author. He wrote the definitive book on Dorothy Kilgallen."

"I thought he was a conspiracy nut..., no offense."

"None taken. Did you know who she was?"

"Yes, wasn't she on that old tv show, What's My Line?"

"Exactly. She was a newspaperwoman."

"So, he did a biography of her?"

"...and she covered the Jack Ruby trial, and it didn't add up to her. She wrote columns for the papers saying how Jack Ruby was a key mob figure and knew of the assassination beforehand. And that he knew Oswald. You can see that look of familiarity on Oswald's face when he came out of the crowd, just before he shot him. And she wrote how Ruby was well known to the Dallas cops and the cops would hoot and holler all night long at his Carousel Strip club. Sometimes the cops were up there dancing with the girls."

"So that's how he was able to waltz into the basement and kill Oswald?"

"Exactly."

"Wow. And they killed her?"

"Four different barbiturates were found in her system and trace residue on her glass. It was all covered up."

"Wait, how do you cover up a murder of a TV star?"

"Well, first you got to get someone in the city to send the body, found dead in Manhattan, to the Brooklyn morgue."

"Why?"

"You got to remember; the mob gave the Brooklyn morgue a lot of business. They had their hands in there to make sure certain causes of death were ruled in their favor."

"And no one noticed?"

"It was immediately ruled a suicide. One form was filled out, the body sent to Brooklyn, and it all disappears. Including I might add, a book she was two months away from publishing. She is quoted as saying, *If the wrong people knew what I know about the JFK assassination, it would cost me my life.* Ever write a book?"

"No, can't say that I have."

"Well, it could take 6 months to a year or longer. At two months away from publishing, you either have it finished or nearly. That's reams of paper. Yet not a sheet was found. She had a contract with Random House. And it all disappeared. No questions asked."

"Till Peter."

"Till Peter." Kyle agreed.

"Well, I am glad you are telling me he's the real deal, in the phony conspiracy world at least."

"Why? How do you know him?"

"He came to me after my brother's death. They were supposed to work on whatever it was..."

"The artifact?"

"Yes, whatever it was. He said he could get me a hundred grand advance on a book that he would write. That's when I was happy and content just believing it was Oswald with the curtain rods in the library."

"Look, Hank, I know all this stuff is a little out there. But at some level, it is just as valid, or just as preposterous, as the official version forced fed to the media and us."

Hank had heard that same sentiment from the guy in the library too. It reminded him. "Kyle, in all your travels, ever hear of the Chicago Oswald?"

"No, but I gotta run. Next time we get together you got to tell me all about it! Good talking to you, Hank."

"Have a good rest of your convention."

Hank was mildly surprised that Kyle didn't know what the guy in the library knew. Then he caught himself. A short time ago he didn't know or care about any of this. That made him consider that all he or anyone, who wasn't there or involved, only knew what was being broadcast. And he who controls the media controls the message. Or something like that. Something Rod McKuen once said. He watched Kyle walking down the corridor, in all respects a sensible levelheaded guy, *passion or hobby*," he remembered him saying. It was easy to see how you could get wrapped up in all this mind-bending stuff, but Hank had to stay true to his original purpose; to clear his brother's name.

19 | 7:29 TO PATCHOGUE

Hank decided to walk from the Waldorf and catch the crosstown bus at 42nd and Lex to go home. As he was waiting for the light to change, a man rushed in front of him and flagged down a cab. As he got in, he said to the driver, "Can you get to Penn in 10 minutes, I got to catch the 7:29 to Patchogue."

Hank watched the cabbie stick out his hand as he crawled his taxi across the street to get directly to the westbound street without going around the block. He was rewarded with honks. and a few choice comments about his lineage as he navigated across the midtown traffic.

As he walked, 'Patchogue,' rang in his head. *Meeks. He lived in Patchogue.* As he turned onto his block, he remembered that Meeks was looking for Browning and the guy in the library, and said Browning was the name of the ex-senator his brother was supposed to introduce him to.

20 | BILLABLE HOURS

"Harris, Browning, and Gould. How may I help you?" the receptionist answered the phone the next morning as Hank closed the white pages, which he never used before that. "May I speak with Mr. Browning?"

"Are you a client of Mr. Browning?"

"No, but I..." Hank hadn't thought this through, *what am I asking?* "Er, I may have some information from when he was a senator."

"Well, leave me your name and number and someone will get back to you."

"Someone, not Mr. Browning?"

"Sir, he is a managing partner at this firm and as such is very busy, and unsolicited inquiries just can't interfere with his schedule."

"I understand, thank you. I'll write him a letter. What's your address?"

425 Lexington Avenue was a building from the 1950s. It had a directory that was white letters on thin black slats that fit behind the glass. Harris Browning and Gould, LLC, was the only listing on the 15th floor.

Hank sat in the reception area and waited. He perused a brochure about the law firm. Their big area of expertise was governmental affairs. It caused him to wonder if he'd ever heard of a Senator or

Congressman Harris or Gould. Lobbying law firms were where most ex-politicos went to cash in on their prior membership the most exclusive club in the world. The professional photograph of Browning had him in front of the requisite law books on shelves and an American flag on the edge of the picture. He was right out of central casting for a Senator. Jowls, bushy eyebrows, and piercing eyes. The salt and pepper hair spoke of experience and survival in the blood sport known as politics. Eventually, the receptionist noticed and asked, "Are you being helped, sir?"

"I am waiting for Mr. Browning."

"Do you have an appointment?"

"No, but I am sure he'll want to speak with me."

"Sir, if you don't have an appointment, I am afraid I'll have to ask you to leave."

Hank looked around the empty area, "Am I taking someone's seat?"

"Sir, please. Without an appointment, you can't just sit here."

Realizing he'd given her enough grief, he raised his hands in a no-contest manner, "Okay. I'll just let myself out." He rose and headed out the double glass doors to the elevators.

The receptionist kept her eyes on him as she called down to security.

In the lobby, Hank went to the small cigarette and candy stand, off from the entrance. He bought a pack of gum. As he stood there, he noticed the security guard eyeballing him.

He decided a good offense was the best defense. He approached the desk. "You a vet?"

"170 Assault group Nam."

"43rd Bomber wing, 68-71. Pilot?"

"Crew chief. You?"

"Drove a Buff."

"Luxury!"

"No cup holders, but better than an eggbeater I guess."

"Roger that."

"Look, I figured you got a call about me. I need to have a word with Browning from the 15th floor."

"Yeah, they kind of hate that. What's your beef?"

"My brother died under less than normal circumstances, and I think what got him killed was the same thing that Browning worked on as a senator."

"So, you are warning him?"

"No, I just need to find out what it was. He might know something that could help me understand why my brother was murdered."

"Do you think he was involved?"

That threw Hank, "Um, no. No, I never even thought of that." His mind raced, he weighed the idea, but decided this now lawyer, couldn't have been involved...unless..., "Do you know this, Browning?"

"Just to say, hello, have a nice day, and the like. No real conversation."

"What state was he the senator of?"

"Texas, I think. His family made guns. You heard of Browning?"

"No, shit! Like the B.A.R.?"

"Browning Automatic Rifle and the Browning 1911."

"That .45 was my sidearm," Hank said with a grin.

"Hell of a gun. First pistol I ever fired..."

"So, is he an approachable kinda guy?"

"He's a politician, can look right through you while smiling right at you?"

"Gotcha. You mind if I wait for him here?"

"No can do, chief. After the call, it would be my job."

"Understand, I'll just wait outside."

"That would be best."

"Good talking to you."

"You, too."

Ten minutes later, the lunch crowd started pouring out of the buildings of midtown. Five minutes later, Browning came through the doors of 425, as a tall man in a dark suit held the door.

Hank approached, "Senator Browning?"

Instinctively the lawyer stopped in response to Hank's firm voice and looked at him.

"Sir, I was wondering if you can help me. My brother was murdered, and I think..."

"I'm sorry, Mr. Browning is late for an appointment. Excuse us." The man in the dark suit used courtesy words but put his body rudely between Hank and Browning. He then opened the door of a Lincoln Town Car for Browning to enter.

Browning stopped, "Who was your brother and why do you think I can help?"

"He was a reporter, and he was investigating what you said sounded fishy."

"What's your name?"

"Hank Larson."

"Benjamin was your brother?"

Hank nodded.

"Well, Hank, call my office. Tell Maria, I told you to set up a meeting. We'll talk then."

Hank was mildly surprised. "Thank you, Senator. Have a good day."

"You as well." He got into the car and the dark suit got in the passenger seat.

Hank went to the corner pulled out a quarter and dropped it into the payphone.

At 2 p.m. Hank came through the doors of Harris, Browning and Gould. The receptionist recognized him immediately. "I'm sorry but..."

"Ah, ah, ah. I have an appointment this time."

"You do?"

"Set it up with Maria, she had an opening today, so I came back."

Cautiously and with her eyes glued to Hank she dialed, "Maria, does Matthew have a 2 o'clock? There's nothing on my sheet."

"Oh, okay. Any other appointments? Okay." She hung up. "Just have a seat."

A few minutes later, Browning and the suit came through the doors. Browning did a double take when he saw Hank sitting there, "Mr... Larson."

"Yes, I called, and Maria said you had an opening at 3."

"Well, give me a minute to hit the head, and I'll have her come out to get you."

"Sure thing."

Hank figured since the firm had the whole floor, Harris, Browning and Gould, could only bring on one more managing partner, as Browning's corner office was grand and had an incredible view of the Empire state building and the city. *There can only be four corner offices.*

"Would you like anything? Water, tea coffee, something stronger?"

"No thank you. I don't want to take too much of your time."

"You have till 3:30, then I'll have to kick you out. Non-billable time and all"

"Fair enough. My brother, Ben, was killed after he bought some kind of artifact from the Kennedy assassination."

Browning's expression was somewhere between, 'Not this again,' and, 'Tell me more.'

Hank opted for the latter, "He purchased it in Texas. I don't know what it was. Because whoever killed him stole it."

"First, I am sorry for your loss. Ben was a unique man. I met him during the Select Committee on Assassinations. He was almost an expert witness, but the majority blocked all our witnesses."

"Wow. Benny never mentioned anything like that."

"And you're here because I am quoted as calling out the Warren Report saying, 'I just don't buy it. The whole single shooter just makes no sense.'"

"This is a very long shot for me and a big jump in logic, but before he died, my brother made a deal with a man who had something that he wanted Benny to write about and since Benny was also going to introduce him to you, I am guessing it was about the assassination.

"First I am hearing of it. Do you know what that was?"

"No, I handed it back to him, but his check came in the mail after that, and I noticed he lived on Long Island."

"So...?"

"Your name came up again when a guy at the library yesterday was telling me about the Chicago Oswald."

Browning's demeanor changed, "I see. And now you think since this man is from Long Island, and so was the Chicago Oswald, that maybe he knows about the other plot? Don't you think that's a pretty thin connection?"

"I don't know what I think, except this may be why my brother was killed, so I am here to ask you if there is any truth to this Chicago Oswald thing."

"Are you recording or memorializing this conversation in any way?"

Hank was thrown, "Why, no. No."

"I don't want to get into it now, and here, but someone approached me while I was on the committee about a shooter and something worse in Chicago. At the time, I wasn't in the majority, so I didn't have any sway with the chairman. Anything I brought up was immediately shit canned. Mostly because I didn't back his oil bill."

"Politics."

"Washington would be so much better if it weren't for politics."

"That's quotable."

"But you are not quoting or memorializing this in any way, or by any technological means?"

Hank nodded.

"Please answer verbally!"

"Er... okay. No, I am not recording this or anything. Does the name Meeks mean anything to you?"

It was a subtle tell, but Hank would have gone all in if they were sitting across the flop in Texas Hold'em.

"Okay. Let's table this for now."

Hank looked at his watch it was only 2:11. "But..."

"You are asking me about something that may be covered under three national security statutes and governmental regulations. I need to make a call, let's meet tonight at my home in Westchester. Maria will give you the address."

"Wow."

"Yeah, wow. I don't know why I want to help you, Mr. Larson. But perhaps, there's been too much killing and too much lying."

Hank had a sudden chill. "See you tonight, and thank you."

"Don't thank me yet. I may not be allowed to share anything."

On his way out the door, Hank nodded to the guard who was the crew chief from Nam.

21 | PBX

Hank sensed that Browning knew Meeks, and it nagged at him. It would be great to talk to Meeks before he meets with Browning tonight. But how could he reach him? Then he remembered how Meeks found him.

Hank headed over to 36th Street between 7th and 8th Avenues. There was a New York Tel building there. As a kid one summer, he rolled racks through the sweltering streets of the Garment District for $2.80 an hour. The phone building was air-conditioned to keep all the telephone equipment cool and if you stood out by the grate, it cooled you down, too. He met a lot of phone repairmen standing there. He learned a lot about PBX. It was the dial 9 system of outside calling an office would use. The phones, with the 5 glass buttons and a red hold button across the bottom, were called 1A2 K sets. He learned a lot from those guys. It got so, 'He knew enough to be dangerous,' as his dad would say about anyone who knew half a story or a half-truth.

Once again, he stood outside the large red brick building. Guys in blue shirts, with tool belts with test set phones hanging off them, went in and out. A rather large fellow was off by the side smoking a cigarette. Hank approached. "Hey, is Ronnie Buscul still a tester?"

"Ronnie? The foreman? Hasn't been at a test desk in 10 years."

"Is he in today?"

"Nah, he's on vacation."

"Are the blue's still running?"

That connected. "You know Ronnie."

"Yeah. From here," Hank said

"You worked PBX?"

"A little. Then I went into the air force."

"What's your name? I'll tell Ronnie you was lookin' for him."

"Sure, Hank. Hank Larson."

"Bill, Bill McVickar.'

"Well, Bill maybe you can help me."

"What?"

"Once and a while, Ronnie would look up a number for me, reverse directory kinda thing."

"Really?"

"Yeah, I used to give him a 5 spot, and he'd run it."

"5 spot, huh? How long ago was that?"

"Long enough that I guess it's up to 20 now?"

"That must a been 5 years back." He looked right then left, "It would be around 50 today, what with the cost a livin' and all."

Hank reached and pulled two twenties and a ten out of his wallet. Handed him only the twenty and said, "The rest when you get me the address."

"Next station stop, Patchogue. Patchogue next stop." The conductor said over the public address system.

Hank stood up as the train, packed with commuters, was pulling into the suburban station. His car was in the shop today for a brake job, and the train was probably faster than midday Expressway traffic.

At the station, scores of cars, most of them driven by women, waited in the crowded parking lot. All of them then jamming through the narrow two lanes of driveway back onto Division Street in a rush to get home to a martini or tuna casserole.

An Island Taxi was waiting. He walked over and handed the driver a piece of paper, "Can you take me to this address on Rose Avenue?" "Sure, that'll be my second stop. $5.50 to you."

Hank looked in the back seat, a woman was already in there. He assumed she was the driver's first fare. The cab waited as the train left, and sure enough one more person walked up. "Emanuel Church, Montauk Highway?"

"Sure thing, Pastor. That'll be the second stop. No charge."

"Thank you," the man in the collar said.

"That makes Rose Avenue the last stop, buddy." The cabbie said to Hank in the rearview mirror.

Hank just waved his hand ending in a thumbs-up gesture.

The detached house on Rose Avenue with the cracked concrete driveway could have used a little love and paint. D. Meeks on the flat black mailbox alongside the front door confirmed that his fifty was well spent.

He knocked on the door. He looked at his watch. He had three hours to get to Browning's house in Westchester by 9 p.m., as Maria had indicated. By now his car should be out of the shop and waiting for him outside the garage, with his spare key locked inside.

Meeks came to the door and was stunned to see Hank. "How did you find me?" He started scanning the street, a touch of fear in his eyes.

"Reverse directory. You taught me all about it."

"You still needed a Ma Bell person..."

"Let's say I went down memory lane and made a slight detour."

"Come inside," he said his head still on a swivel. "Why are you here?"

Hank pulled the bank check out of his shirt pocket. "It came as soon as you left."

Meeks stared at him for a few seconds. Then grabbed the check. "Were you followed here?"

Hank was thrown a little. "No, I..."

"Are you wearing a wire?"

"Of course not."

"Are you armed?"

"What?"

"Can I frisk you?"

"You better buy me dinner first!"

"Get out!" He headed to the door and swung it open.

"Just tell me that whatever you were paying my brother for, wasn't the thing that got him killed?"

That froze Meeks. He slowly closed the door. "Are you sure you want to know?"

"The more I find out, the less I want to know. Was it a JFK thing?"

"Did you find anything in your brother's possession about a Thomas Vallee?"

Hank rummaged through the recent history in his head. "No... nope, never heard of him."

"Want something to drink?"

"Water?"

They were sitting in the living room now, Meeks in a well-worn Lazy Boy recliner and Hank on the couch.

"I was Secret Service in 1963. Long Island Office. But in late October I got temporarily transferred to the PPD..."

"Philadelphia Police Department?"

Meeks smiled, "No, Presidential Protection Detail."

"You were in Dallas?"

"No, but I was on the advance team in Chicago."

"On Nov 2nd?"

"Very good, yes."

"So, you are the one who canceled Kennedy's Chicago trip."

"Well, I rang the bell, the bosses made that call based on what I found."

"So, you found the Chicago Oswald?"

"That's a cute name. Never heard that before."

"That's because you don't hang with the conspiracy nuts."

"And you do?"

"Reluctantly, in the last few days, trying to find out what got my brother killed."

"His name was Vallee, Thomas Vallee. I had a run-in or two with him out here on the island."

"He was from Long Island," Hank remembered.

"Yes, and we had him in our files here. But when our Protective Intelligence Squad pegged him as a threat to the president, I took a special interest, but we lost him or his whereabouts in mid-October. That is until he turned up in Chicago the day before the president's visit."

"And he was like Oswald?"

"In profile and background, it was almost like Vallee and Oswald were groomed, and their backgrounds, or cover stories, were crafted by the same agency."

"Agency?"

"CIA, NSA, FBI, or a few initials that are classified."

"So that's how you knew?"

"Eventually. But I was on the trail of a Cuban hit squad, two expatriates who barely escaped the Bay of Pigs. They, like the CIA, blamed Kennedy for the disaster."

"So, you were tracking them, not Vallee?"

"They lead me to Vallee. Turns out he was their patsy the way Oswald was set up in Texas."

"Wait, you are saying Oswald was a patsy too?"

"Only he and Vallee both didn't know it."

"But what did they think?"

"Hard to say. Vallee didn't know the Cubans, but they knew him. He was placed in a Chicago hotel that overlooked the motorcade route. There was another room a floor up that, as near as I could suss out, was also procured for one of the Cubans. The other was believed to be in a park across the street."

"Was there a grassy knoll in that park?"

"Very funny. But a crossfire nonetheless."

"Kill Zone!"

"Definitely. Just like Dallas."

"So, you arrested all of them?" Hank asked even though he knew the guy in the library said the SS and cops blew it.

"The Chicago field office and the local LEOs bumbled the takedown. They were all in the wind within 8 hours."

"Where were you?"

"I was called back to Washington on the second of November to report."

"So why didn't they stop Dallas?"

"When we lost the shooters, the bosses buried me and my report."

"Then the Dallas office never heard about Chicago?"

"I was railroaded. They put me up on some bullshit charges and I went to prison for 6 years."

"They shut you up."

"The alternative was a bullet, but I guess I had some friends at Treasury."

"Wow, that's a heck of a story, but if they quashed this, how does anyone outside the government know anything about this at all?"

"I approached the Senate Committee on Assassinations with the same package I sent to your brother."

"Senator Browning?"

"Among others, but they wouldn't hear me out."

"Hold on, when I spoke to Browning..."

"Shit! You spoke to Browning? When?"

"Earlier today, I am going to meet him tonight. That's why I came to see you before..."

"You fucking idiot. Browning is in on it!"

"In on what?

"The cover-up. He's an arms manufacturer. The people who killed Kennedy were shills for the military-industrial establishment, and still are. They are the only ones who had the juice to set me up, control the Warren Commission, and kill off many of the witnesses to the assassination. Hell man, they even put the head of the fucking CIA on the commission. He was there to make sure no other witnesses or conclusions saw the light of day."

"The fox in the henhouse." Hank said, "Why were you paying my brother to meet Browning then?"

"To put a bullet in his brain. He was an attorney back during the Warren Commission. He and Arlen Specter were thick as thieves. It was Browning who took my statement to the Warren Commission and then buried it. A day later, I was framed on a counterfeit money case from the year before I was assigned to the PPD. Said I shook down the counterfeiter. They probably offered the guy a better cell in order to get him to swear to their lie. It was Browning who ratted me out when I went to him."

"But he's the only guy who said the Warren Commission was bullshit."

"Words. Just words. Words that made me and a few others, I guess, who had evidence like I did, come out of the shadows, wrongly believing they had a fellow traveler, A champion for the truth. Meanwhile, he made us disappear, or be imprisoned as in my case. He played the same role again with the Senate Select Committee when he, strike that, they, elevated him to Senator."

"They?"

"Committee for a Strategic Superiority."

"Another Committee?"

"Here's another one for you, I am sure they rigged the election, put him on the Armed Services Committee," he said as an aside, "...where he always voted for the boys with the dangerous toys."

"This is so fucked up."

Meeks opened a drawer and pulled out a gun.

Hank stiffened. Sat back in the chair hands gripping the armrests.

"Are you sure you weren't followed?" He went to the window and cautiously pulled back the curtain.

He relaxed a bit. "Yeah, pretty sure."

"Great. Did you drive, where's your car?"

"It's in the shop. I took the train and cabbed it here."

"Were you alone in the cab?"

"A woman and a, a Pastor."

"A Pastor? Where did he go."

"A church, er. The Manuel, Emmanuel on Montauk Road."

"Highway... and that church is closed. Had a fire."

"Really?"

"When and where are you meeting Browning?"

Hank hesitated. He didn't know if this guy was a dangerous nut with a gun, out to settle a score, or a victim of the evil doers that all the conspiracy nuts point to. Hank did know one thing. He had to get out of there. The gun changed the equation. Especially if Meeks felt Hank compromised his safety. "Your name isn't Meeks, is it?"

Still looking out the window, gun up and ready, he confessed, "Meechum, Donald Meechum. I changed it when I got out of prison. Kind of my own, personal, witness protection program."

"Is your connecting with my brother the reason he was killed?"

"Possibly, if he talked to the wrong person."

"A person like Browning?"

"Like I said, the Senator was a wolf in sheep's clothing."

"What do we do now?"

"We?"

"You think there's a killer pastor out there, about to rain fire and brimstone down on us?"

"Inconclusive. You go out the back. Keep your head down. You are 2 miles from the train. Go to your right out the back door."

"You are letting me go?"

"Of course, what do you think I am."

"A guy with a gun?"

He pointed it at Hank. "Which reminds me, when and where are you meeting Browning?"

Hank skulked out the backdoor of Meechum's house. He kept looking over his shoulder as he made his way to the light of Montauk Highway. It was dark, and he was two hours away from meeting Browning. But Meechum strongly suggested, at gunpoint, that Hank just forget all about it. He was inclined to agree. He didn't know if any of this was real, or all compounded conspiracies. Or whether Browning was the bad guy or Meechum was. He was glad he was out of there.

On the train back to the city, he kept running over everything in his head. As the train pulled into Pennsylvania Station, he decided he couldn't be distracted from his commitment to clear his brother's name. All the conspiracies, senators, and Chicago Oswalds could go to hell. He swore he was off the conspiracy drug. They were all crazy.

22 | IN THE STILL OF THE NIGHT

If you needed some peace and quiet and sought a respite from the rat race of New York City, 20 miles or so to the south, Purchase in Westchester County supplied the quiescent calm and bucolic perfection that made it acre for acre the most desirable land for the escapees from the cacophony of humanity piled high in the Big Apple.

Meechum parked his car a quarter mile down the single-lane road that led to the 6-acre compound that ex-senator Browning purchased in Purchase.

Scaling the wall was a bit of a challenge to the ex-secret service agent who last was on the Chicago Oswald takedown 33 years earlier. Now at 66, complaining muscles and uncertain balance slowed his forward movement. But soon he would settle a score that went back to the Warren Commission and his subsequent incarceration in the fall of '63.

His preliminary reconnaissance, as fast and brief as it was, showed no outer perimeter infrared or sonic sensors, maybe. But more importantly, there were no security personnel. He was satisfied everything was safe for Hank Larson's arrival.

Five minutes later a car pulled up to the gate. The intercom box standing beside the driver's window was automatically triggered by the presence of the car.

"Good evening." The speaker squawked.

"Hank Larson for Mr. Browning,"

The gate separated with a humming noise. He drove the long driveway that culminated in a circular drive surrounding a fountain that wouldn't be out of place in any piazza in Rome.

He used the pineapple knocker on the door.

He was expecting an immediate confrontation with Browning, but still allowing for a butler or servant to answer the door. He had his gun in his waistband and an untucked shirt over it.

It wasn't the butler.

Brian Hosty, a specialist in "wet work," who served with Admiral Howser making problems disappear, opened the door. He had a military bearing and raised a gun with a silencer to his face.

"Larson, you have 10 seconds to tell me where Meechum is," Hosty said.

"Who's Meechum?"

"8 Seconds."

"I'm telling you I don't know any Meechum."

"Meeks. Meechum also went by Meeks. You met with Meeks."

"Look, I'm just trying to find out who killed my brother. I don't know any..."

The silencer's normal "pffft" was even more muffled as Hosty had pressed it right into the man's shoulder as he pulled the trigger, spinning him to the floor, with a bleeding shoulder.

Squatting down, Hosty held the gun above his nose and said, "Next one is in your forehead. Where's Meeks, now!"

When he hit the floor, his gun slipped out of his waistband but was still under his shirt as he lay there. The pain in his left shoulder was searing. His right hand was lying on top of the gun, under his shirt.

"Wait!" He groaned, "Don't shoot. I'll tell you."

Two loud shots rang out from under his shirt. One caught his tormentor under his chin and exploded out the top of his head. He fell back dead.

His shirt had caught fire around the hole the bullets made. He patted out the flames. Then he flattened out on the floor and drew short breaths. He heard someone come toward the foyer from an adjacent room.

"I told you I didn't want any shooting in my house. You goons from the committee..." Browning froze when he saw two men on the floor and Hosty's brains all over.

With great effort, he raised his head up from the floor, "Browning, you son of a bitch." He lifted the gun with a shaky hand and fired twice.

Browning went down with two in the belly. He rolled around the floor for a while panting like a dog after a summer run, then went still with a final death rattle.

With his left shoulder bleeding and throbbing he tried to right himself, he sat up as pain shot down his arm. His right arm! He grabbed for his chest. He fumbled to reach the nitroglycerin pills in his pants pocket but stiffened from the crushing pain now radiating all over his body. In agony, his last words were, "Oh, shit."

23 | WHAT WON'T THEY PUT ON TV NOWADAYS?

There was just a barely perceptible sound of flowing air in the sealed room. The faces of the serious men in the room reflected off the highly polished wood conference table where they were seated. Like most corporate conference rooms, but not nearly so benign, at one end of the room, were video screens. One large one was in the center and on it are displayed a green, night scope image. It was of a commando being met at the door by a scantily clad woman. She nodded and left. The commando waved in the person wearing the night vision camera in. As the camera passed the commando, it showed him talking into his helmet-mounted boom mike. A split second later, his voice came over the room's sound system. It was a little like a dubbed foreign film where the lips don't match the sound.

Admiral Houser was finishing up some paperwork and looked up at the screen as the voice was heard.

"Team one is in the nest." The sound was thin and crackled.

The Admiral went back to his papers as the flickering green TV image showed the point of view of the man wearing the night scope as he cautiously moved through the apartment. The image came to rest at the doorway into a bedroom. Two bodies were visibly entangled in lovemaking. The overly ornate braided epilates adorned the Generalissimo's uniform as it was slung over one of the bed posts.

The image whip panned to the first commando as he spoke, "Oh shit! What do we do? There's a woman in bed with him."

The Admiral smiled at hearing the nervous operative and spoke without looking up, still focusing on his paperwork. "Not our concern, stay with the target."

That order caused a change of tone, "Sir, we have target acquired, sir."

At the table, the men directed their attention to the Admiral. He finally looked up. "Proceed."

A spray of white-hot bullets traced across the image and crashed into the jolting bodies of the m8an and the woman. The Admiral nonchalantly pushed a button on the terminal next to him and the image on the screen changed to color bars, over which was the benign message, "END TRANSMISSION - THANK YOU FOR USING COM SAT 6."

"Send a communique to the Chancellor, tell him the opposition has been eliminated. He is in our debt."

"Yes, Admiral" came from someone at the table. He closed his pen, pushed the papers to the side, and, addressing the room, moved on to the next order of business. "What progress is there in the Texas situation?"

Nelson got up and walked to the center of the table. As he talked, he placed two overlapped photos face up on a palette scanned by a camera above the table. This created a rough split screen on the big video monitor. A kind of high-tech, school overhead projector. On one side was a black and white image cropped to show Cyrus in his straw cowboy hat in Dallas in 1963. The other, more recent one, was him from the newspaper article on his and Howard's death.

"We have tentatively identified the target in Pecox as previously designated Unidentified Cowboy 3. That brings the number of unidentified assassination witnesses, from the photo analysis, down to 14."

"Did he indeed have the missing Polaroid picture?"

"Inconclusive."

Nelson put a picture of Dreesan down on the palette.

The Admiral immediately spoke, "That's the greedy son of a bitch who held me up for a million?"

"We set him up with the identity of one Harvey Dalton, a recently deceased copier salesman from Maryland for this op. Unfortunately, the man terminated himself before he could apprise us of the location in which he hid the photo in question." The legal background of Nelson poked through his vernacular.

The Admiral banged the table. "God dam it! Who bungled his interrogation, I want his scalp?"

"Sir, that would be Briggs who was the operative assigned to retrieve the photo from Dalton, er, Dreesan. Briggs eventually succumbed to his first-degree burns in a safe house."

"Damn."

The intercom buzzed, "Admiral, it's your daughter on line two."

"I'll take it in the den." The Admiral got up to take the call and said to the room, "I won't be long."

Everyone waited. Nobody dared to even hit the head. Brent Howser was the worst combination of extreme power, ruthless morals, and a sixth sense of danger. Many, and certainly everyone in the room, thought him the single most powerful human being on the planet. Everyone stood when he reentered the room.

He waved his hand, "As you were." He sat and started right in. "Sorrel, what have you got regarding Polaroid 7?"

"We have an inter-agency silent search going for any traffic relative to Kennedy or the Warren Commission or the House Committee on Assassinations," Sorrels said as he put a UPI photo from the Plaza that was at an angle that showed Cyrus Shaw about twenty-five feet across the roadway from Mary Moorman and Jean Hill snapping their Polaroid pictures.

He continued, "Meanwhile, it is entirely plausible that given where Cowboy 3, er. Shaw was standing, he could have come across the missing Polaroid Land Camera photo number 7." Then he directed his comment to the new member of the committee. "Johns since you have never attended an 11/22 Executive Action proceeding, and with everyone else's indulgence, let me answer the question that we all asked when we were first read into this op. Johns, our people found the first 6 in Jean Hill's purse when we interrogated her that afternoon. They were innocuous, too far away, or had images blocked. A few were motion smeared. According to her testimony, Moorman snapped the 7th picture in sync with the rifle shot. The last picture, number 8, was still unexposed in the camera."

"We released those to the Warren Commission."

"Number 6 is in the report, but it's right after the neck shot, and before the headshot, so it was deemed releasable with no evidentiary value, but it could place 7 in the time frame to reveal what we are all here to keep classified. Any questions?"

"But no one has ever seen number 7, so we have no confidence that it is at all compromising. Is that right?"

"That was our hope until it emerged as an artifact in that business down in Texas. Now we must assume it has some evidentiary or incriminating content."

Johns nodded.

Nelson then turned to the Admiral giving him the floor.

"Can we contain this?" The Admiral asked.

Nelson held up a copy of the Pecox Telegraph, "The circulation of this small-town paper that carried the original notice is under a thousand. It never got out of that town. We were lucky that Jenkins came across it."

Jenkins, 40-ish seated at one end of the table, nodded. "I was visiting my in-laws who just happen to live in Pecox."

The Admiral cut in, "We can't operate on luck. We need solid intel and a course of action to eliminate or contain this matter. Any lead on where this blasted picture is?"

"Belson is backtracking the trail in Pecox now, sir. We should hear something shortly." Nelson said as he handed a copy of the newspaper to the Admiral.

"You tell them, no loose ends this time."

"Of course, Admiral."

24 | END OF STORY

To Millie Hensley, it was like Deja Vu all over again. For the second time this week she was answering a question from an out-of-towner in her office about the Quarry deaths. "The librarian himself came over and told me. I wasn't even going to run it 'cept I had a last-minute ad cancelation and had to fill 3 column inches." This fellow named Belson was imposing and very grim. Which in part accounted for her cautious replies.

"Did you see this artifact?"

"No." She glanced down. Under her side of the desk, on her lap was her reporter's mini-tape recorder. The record light was flashing.

"Has anyone else inquired into this?" Belson said.

"No."

"Is there anything else that you printed on either Mr. Shaw or Mr. Lance?"

"No. Where do you work, again?"

"The National Archives."

"Oh. How is Brendan Farley these days?"

"Who?"

"The director of the National Archives."

With that Belson got up, and walked over to the door. His body blocking her line of sight all the way, he turned the OPEN sign to

CLOSED. He then snapped his fingers, like he had just remembered one more thing. As he turned, he reached into his jacket pocket and took out his handkerchief. As he neared her, he pulled a little glass tube out of the same pocket.

"I must dig deeper into my cover stories." In one smooth move, he held the handkerchief over his mouth and nose while he shoved the glass tube under Ms. Hensley's nose. Before she could react, he broke the glass open with the pressure of his thumb and forefinger. A small puff of green mist was released. She shuttered and went stiff in an instant. The lightweight recorder hit the carpet silently. Her lips turned blue, as she gasped her last breath and slumped in her chair.

Belson took out his handkerchief, wiped the sign and the front doorknob as he left.

25 | IN A STEW-PER

Hank picked up his car from the mechanic and headed out to the airport. He parked in employee parking and shuttled into the terminal at LaGuardia. Hank made it just as the flight, that the two flight attendants were dead-heading back to D/FW on, was about to call for boarding. The departure area was crowded. He saw a flight attendant who appeared somewhat disheveled from her long day, her jacket flung over her luggage wheelie. She was sitting in the only seat that had an empty seat next to hers. As he approached, he read her ID tag. "Sally Hodges? I'm Hank Larson, Captain with Flying Tigers. Can I talk to you for a minute?"

"Sure, but they just announced boarding and I got a short turnaround for an early out of Dallas tomorrow."

"This won't take long." He sat.

"What's this about?"

"I'm trying to find out about a passenger of yours from a flight the Friday before last."

"Are you kidding? Look I'm beat. I've been working 6-on, 1-off for two weeks, and you're asking me about one passenger on a flight from almost three weeks ago?

"This is very important." Hank pressed.

"What could I possibly tell you about him?"

"Well, did he stand out in any way? I know he was in 33A. It's a bugout row, so I thought you might have noticed anything unusual.

Speech, demeanor, mustache, beard, limp, bad hairpiece. Did he order anything special? Did he sleep? Was he too nervous to sleep? Did he look like a soldier?"

Hank was trying hard to draw out any little detail. All Sally was drawing were blanks.

"I'm sorry I'd like to help but I don't even remember what city I was in last night."

"I know... Thanks for trying. Has..." He looked down, referring to his Blackberry, "Christine DeMarco shown up yet."

"Chris? Why are you asking about her?"

"She was on the same flight with you that night."

"She was? Are you sure you're just a pilot? How did you know where to find me and Chris?"

He sat straight up and mocked a serious tone, "I am actually sworn to secrecy?"

"Was it that horn-dog, Captain Weston?"

"Who?"

Just then they called for boarding.

"Look that's me. Hope you find whoever you're looking for."

Sally put her handbag atop her roll-along luggage wheelie and started for the gate. At that moment, Chris DeMarco came rushing into the gate area. Hank followed them both over to the boarding door. Hank overheard the ground agent giving the two stewardesses some bad news.

"Sorry ladies, only one company seat left. Seems a check-ride captain is needed in Dallas in the morning, and he's taken one of your seats," he said.

"Sally, you're beat, and you're going home. You take this flight. I don't have check-in for my flight 'til 7 tonight. I'll take the next one."

"You're a sweetheart. Thanks, Chris."

As Sally boarded. Chris turned to leave, and Hank approached her.
"Chris... Chris DeMarco?"

"Yes?"

"Hi, I'm Hank Larson, Sally suggested I speak to you about someone I'm trying to track down."

"Sure, but mind if we sit? I just ran all the way from the other side of the airport. My legs are killing me." She turned and led the way. Hank noticed her perfectly shaped calves.

"Me, too," he said under his breath.

They settled in the airport lounge.

Hank caught the waitress' eye. "Two Michelobs."

Chris added, "Got anything like pretzels or nuts?" She turned to Hank. "I'm starving."

Hank went through his whole spiel again and was surprised when she said...

"Oh! Yeah, him!"

"You remember this guy?"

"Like you said he was in the emergency row." She filled in the blank look on Hank's face, "My dad was a staff sergeant. I grew up with those guys."

Hank lost his place. "I'm sorry, what's that got to do with this guy?"

"He had it... you know that military look. That, I'm on a mission from God attitude. Mondo commando all the way."

Hank relaxed; he'd found his man. Then a chirping sound caused Hank to look around.

Chris opened her bag. "Excuse me." And took out an IBM Simon phone.

Hank was impressed. He for some reason hadn't gone mobile phone yet, though he understood it was better than his beeper.

She spoke into the phone, "August 10th? Hold on let me check." She pulled the phone away from her ear and started touching the keys. Then she looked at the screen. On it was a calendar. She returned to the call. "I'm good for the 10th. Okay, I will. Thanks." She hung up.

"Wow. Does it do windows too?"

"Not yet. We were given these as a part of a new program. It's okay, but the battery doesn't last long. And I can't always get a signal."

"Yeah, I am going to wait and see if they get better."

"You know what they call this thing?" She waved it before she put it back in her bag, "A PDA."

Hank thought for a second, "A Public Display of Affection?"

"Yeah, can you believe that?" She plucked a few peanuts out of the dish.

"What can you tell me about him?"

"The guy? He was a real winner, boy. He carries on a briefcase. A metal one, silver."

"So anyway, we're taxing and I'm on cross-check, and this guy's case on his lap."

"Go on, this sounds like it could be my guy."

"He wouldn't let me put it in the overhead. I joked with him about, you know, the crown jewels being in the case or something and he says..." She looked down and away as she remembered, "Oh yeah, he said," she feigned a deep male voice, 'The case stays with me, is that clear!'" She laughed, "It was like something my father would say. 'Is that clear?' So, I say, 'No, it's silver', meaning the case, but he didn't get it."

"Not a fun guy?"

"No, he wasn't."

"Who did you say you worked for again?"

"I didn't."

"So why do you want to know about some guy from a flight almost 3 weeks ago?" She popped a few more nuts into her mouth.

"I'm working with the IATA, ticket fraud division. This guy keeps bilking us for thousands in unpaid fares."

"Do you carry a gun?"

"Huh? Why, no... Why would you ask me that?"

"For a moment, it sounded like exciting work. I took this job to meet exciting people. Instead, all I get are invitations to the mile-high club from cockpit Johnnies."

"You mean pilots?"

"Only the assholes..."

"Horn-dogs?"

Chris was thrown a little, "How do you know that term?"

"Uh..."

"Don't tell me. You're sworn to secrecy. Anyway, I attract them like moths to a flame." She made circles in the air with the peanut between her fingers and popped it into her mouth. She tilted the bowl, but it was empty. She held it up to a passing server and waggled it.

"But you still like your job?"

"For me it's great. Lots of time off, and free airfare to spend it anywhere I want. Take my pictures and make notes."

"Pictures and notes? For what?"

"I love photography and I'm working on a book about... It's a little esoteric."

"Try me."

"Well, you see, I've got this pair of ruby red slippers, and I take them everywhere I go and photograph them."

"A photographer?"

"Well not professionally, obviously, but I had my brother, and I had our first darkroom when I was ten."

"Well, you certainly developed..."

She held up her hand as if to say, "Stop".

"Yeah, I've heard that one before. I've got some great shots of them in front of the Eiffel Tower, on top of the Empire State Building, on the steps of a temple in Tibet, an Iowa cornfield, the red against the dusty green. Then I take notes on the place and the people who come over and ask what the hell I'm doing."

"Sounds like a wild idea, what are you going to call the book."

"Just click your heels."

Hank took a beat then it registers. "Nice title, Dorothy. Now can I ask you one?

"Okay, shoot!" she said.

No gun!

They both touché.

"How can I put this; I mean..."

The waitress placed a fresh bowl of mixed nuts this time between them.

"...I'm curious. What's wrong with pilots?"

"Oh, they're, dashing, commanding, and more interested in flight time than quality time. I've sworn off them. After you get over the thrill of flying, most of them are boring. No excitement."

"No guns."

"Something like that." She cracked a large Brazil nut with her teeth.

26 | RED FLASHING LIGHT

Tommy Barnes got off the school bus and went right to the garage. He left his backpack on the old washing machine that his dad was going to fix someday, and grabbed his bike. He had three baskets on it, two on each side of the rear wheel and one big one in front of the handlebars. With those, he could carry 30 rolled-up newspapers. He could make his rounds and be home by 5 to start his homework before dinner. He was saving up for a 10-speed Racer, the blue one in the Sears and Roebuck catalog. He was halfway to the 86 dollars it cost. But he also used the money he made for other things, movies on a Saturday night, hamburgers and malts, and a big kit model of an M46 Patton Tank at 1/12th scale, which really slowed his savings.

He biked into town, threw down the kickstand, and entered the newspaper office. When he saw the closed sign, he was confused, but he tried the door anyway. It opened, and he went in. Five seconds later he came busting out of the door, screaming, "Help! Help! Someone Help!"

"One Charlie Baker, 10-15 at 345 Main Street, Pecox. Report of a deceased body. K" Carla called out over the dispatcher's microphone.
"One Charlie Baker, 2 minutes out, K" Was the radio response.

She went to the other screen and looked up the address to confirm her suspicion. "Damn," was all she said under her breath.

By the time Carla's shift ended at four and she got over to the paper's office, the county detectives were on the scene.

"Carla. What brings you out of the radio shack?"

"Was it Millie?"

"Yes. Looks like natural causes. Probable heart attack. We were just about to move her and notify the next of kin."

"Her brother, Phillip. He's either down by the freight yard or in lock-up or rehab."

"Juicer?"

"Ever since he found his mother in the kitchen, just like this."

The detective turned and looked down at the body now on a stretcher under a sheet. "Runs in the family, I guess."

At that point, a uniformed cop handed the mini recorder to the detective with his latex-gloved hand. "It's still recording."

The detective put on his gloves and held it by the edges. He looked at it for a second and hit the stop switch on the edge where he was less likely to smudge a fingerprint. Then the rewind button in the same manner. The tape made a Micky Mouse sound but in reverse. He stopped it and hit play.

"Did you see this artifact?" A male voice on the tape asked.

"No."

"That was Millie," Carla said.

"Shh," the detective said as he listened.

The male voice continued, "Has anyone else inquired into this?"

"No."

"Is there anything else that you printed on either Mr. Shaw or Mr. Lance?"

"No. Where do you work, again?"

"The National Archives."

He hit stop. "Well, well, maybe it doesn't run in the family."

"Jerry," Carla said to the detective, "This is weird. That man was asking about the Quarry murders."

"How can you be sure?"

"I met this guy..." She went on to tell him about Hank and his interest in the deaths.

An hour later, Jerry had the two rangers and Carla in the squad room of the county sheriff's office.

They were listening to the tape and were near the end.

The male was heard saying, "I must dig deeper into my cover stories."

Then a small snapping sound was heard. Then a thud.

Jerry stopped the tape.

"That's all there is?" Conners said.

"There's the sound of the door closing, then 12 minutes later the door opens, and the delivery boy says, 'Miss Hensley, Miss Hensley, you okay.' Then he ran out screaming for help. After that the sounds and conversations of the responding officers until I shut it off."

"Obviously, he isn't from the National Archives," Carla said.

"Why are you here again?" Ritter asked.

"She's the one who connected you guys and your person of interest, Larson."

"But you're not saying that's him on the tape?"

"No, that ain't his voice," she said.

Jerry held up the micro recorder, "We were ready to call this a natural, till we found this."

"This guy doesn't have a southern accent. Any strangers in town?"

"Mrs. Yates said she saw a man of average build, five-eighth, five-ten walking on that side of the street. But she didn't see him leave the paper. Just on down a little from it." Jerry said.

"Did he get into a car?" Ritter asked.

"If he did, she didn't see it."

"Based on the description, could be Larson," Ritter said.

"He's at least six, six foot one, and besides that ain't his voice," Carla said.

"Could sound different on tape?" Connors said.

"Maybe, but Hank's sweeter, nicer, this guy was digging and a drillin'."

Ritter rolled his eyes, "He's sweeter," he said to Connors.

Carla stuck out her tongue at him.

"What was the snap?" Connors asked.

"My guys were trying to figure that out. They are going to send the tape to the FBI lab. Maybe they can figure it out."

"Maybe it was the cap on a hypodermic?" Ritter said.

"Since this turned into a homicide, the coroner will check her with a fine-tooth comb. If there's a puncture wound hell find it."

"Could it have been her neck snapping?" Connors said.

"Wasn't broken, and again, blue lips and other indications of a cardiac event," Jerry said.

"So that's it, all we know is she was murdered but not by who," Ritter said.

Carla didn't look convinced.

Jerry caught on. "What?"

"When this guy asked her if anyone else came around asking? Well, she said no. But Hank was there at least twice, asking about this very thing. Why would she have said that?"

"She was protecting, Larson?" Jerry said.

"That's news? Larson could have led this guy to her." Connors said.

"They were working together?" Ritter said.

"Who Larson and Millie Hensley?" Connors said.

"No, but that's interesting, I meant this archives guy and Larson," Ritter said.

"Could be, or maybe he followed him, and that led him to Hensley. Either way you cut it, puts Larson back under the spotlight." Connors turned to Jerry, "Let us know what the coroner finds. Thanks for bringing us in. Good work."

"What about me?" Carla said.

"True," Jerry said, "Carla connected the dots on this, otherwise Hensley's in the ground as an open case."

Reluctantly Connors tipped his Stetson, "Much obliged, Carla."

"You're welcome."

That night at the RattleSteak, up against one of the columns on the bar, Carla placed a votive candle beneath a picture of Millie Hensley. Cowboys tipped their hats as they passed.

27 | MONDAYS SUCK

It was a good gig. After retiring from the NYPD with a work-related injury, Frank Lozano getting a cushy job as personal protection for an ex-senator was right up there with being on the mayor's detail. But better because it was pretty much a day shift. Browning wasn't a night person, he only went into the law firm three days a week, the rest of the time he was either at the Purchase House or the cottage, in Martha's Vineyard. Yet, Lozano drew a weekly salary. Even in the summer when sometimes Browning was up in the Vineyard for a month, and he was able to go fishing on his 32-footer, out of Camron's Bay.

It was a pussy detail. No one was gunning for the 80-year-old lawyer who served in the Senate for 4 terms. Mostly all Lozano ever confronted were a few oddballs and a couple of wing nuts who either had a beef, or new information on something he was involved with as senator. Most of these people folded like a cheap suitcase under his command police voice and body blocks. He was strapped but never had to touch the gun, except to clean it, and qualify once a year. It was a really sweet pad on his forced retirement with half-pay.

The ex-senator was in one of his writing modes. Working on another book about politics and the law. He loved all that professor stuff. He told Frank once that a book keeps you relevant and on TV. It also got you many lucrative speaking gigs. For an old man, now out of the political scene, staying relevant was better than three houses, a yacht, and the pied-á-terre apartment in Paris.

Last week Browning left for the cottage. When he got like that, in the book-writing mode, he gave all the staff the week off. Didn't shave or go out. He crammed and knocked out whole sections of his manuscript in big chunks.

Lozano pulled up to the gate and punched in the code.

That early in the morning he was surprised to see a car in the circular drive. It wasn't Judy's or any of the house staff's. Lozano pulled up behind it. He went up to the door and used his key. He opened the door, but it stopped ¾ of the way. Then the rank smell assaulted him. He gagged and pulled out a handkerchief to cover his face. He put his shoulder into the door and muscled it open. Bloated and discolored, the three bodies lay in pools of blood. Browning was furthest away. Two men were close to one another, one blocking the front door.

Lozano went into Browning's den. He opened his wallet and took out a piece of paper with some numbers on it. He picked up a pencil and subtracted 9 from each number and dialed the decoded string. It was picked up in one ring. "This is Halfback, tell the Admiral we have a situation red."

28 | CONNECTING THE DOTS

Three days later, back at the IATA data center, Hank met Wells and Dixon in his office.

Dixon started right in with the good news. "Since Dalton's original destination was Phoenix, we checked all the flights that were leaving New York Center for Phoenix the night of your brother's death and for the day after."

"We didn't even have to make an inter-line search. Harvey Dalton used the same carrier, American, to complete his trip."

Dixon handed a printout to Hank as Wells fills him in.

"Dalton took a 10:15 p.m. flight out of LaGuardia, direct service to Phoenix.

"Did you come up with anything, Hank?"

"On a hunch, I called information for Silver Springs, Maryland. Harvey was listed. Spoke with the widow, and it seems her husband died a month ago. Natural causes. Heart. Smoked two packs a day and carried an extra side of beef for good measure."

"So, he couldn't have bought that ticket a week after he croaked."

"I didn't have the heart to tell his widow that some guy masquerading as her dead husband is running up their American Express bill."

"Well, it most certainly looks like something's up here. You going to tell the police?"

"I... no. There's nothing to tie him to Ben's murder. Right now, I can't prove that this guy isn't anything more than a credit card swindler.

"So, then what are you going to do?"

"I'm deadheading out tomorrow in a company jump seat, to Phoenix. That's where this guy went and it's all I got.

29 | JUST THE FACTS

Hank was down in the laundry room. He was folding his laundry on the grey Formica table. "Hmmm," he walked over to the dryer, spun the drum, and found the other sock sticking to it. "Tried to get away, eh," he said to the sock. He needed to catch up on his laundry since he was heading out to Phoenix in the morning.

As he approached his apartment, a man and a woman were standing there ringing the bell.

"Can I help you?"

"Henry Larson?" the man held up a gold and blue badge. "Detective Moss, NYPD, and this is my partner, Detective Cammi. Can we ask you a few questions?"

"What's this about officers?"

"Detectives. May we come in, please?"

"Sure...detectives, but don't mind the place." He put down the laundry basket and took out his key." As he opened the door, he said, "I haven't been home much."

"What can I do for you offic... detectives."

"Do you know a Harold Browning?"

"I've met him."

"When was that?"

"Last week."

"When was the last time you saw him?"

"Then."

"Mr. Larson, his assistant said she made an appointment with you on the night of the same day you met with him."

"Yes. But someone I spoke with later recommended that I not take that meeting."

"Did you call either Mr. Browning or his assistant to cancel?"

"No."

Detective Cammi spoke up, "The assistant said you were pretty anxious to meet with him. Why the change of heart?"

"Total misunderstanding."

"About what?" she pressed.

"He was on a committee when he was a senator, and I wanted to clarify something he said on the record."

Moss jumped in. "What do you do for a living, Mr. Larson?"

"I'm an airline pilot." Moss looked beyond Hank to the model planes on the shelf by the TV. One knocked over on its side.

"Mr. Larson, can you account for your whereabouts on the night you were supposed to meet with Mr. Browning?"

"I was here. Hey, what's this all about?"

"Just a few more questions, Mr. Larson. Have you had any contact with Mr. Browning since that day?"

"I told you. That was the one and only time I ever spoke with him."

Cammi looked to Moss then to Hank, "The guard in the lobby said you were stalking Browning."

"Stalking? No, I was waiting to speak to him without his black belt secretary throwing blocks."

"Did you, in fact, get to speak to him in the lobby?"

"No, it was outside, by his car."

"What did you talk to him about?"

"Why are you so interested in me and what I said?"

The detectives had an eyeball conversation and Moss spoke for both of them. "We could do this down at the station."

"Hold on. What's going on here? You are asking me all these questions. Are you accusing me of something other than a lapse of business etiquette?"

"Just trying to clear up the inconsistencies in your statement."

"Wha...what inconsistency?"

"You said you only met with him one time. But his assistant said you had come back for a meeting in his office."

"Well yeah, I mean one time, meaning that day, that's all."

"Was it once or twice?"

"I, I guess it was technically twice."

"Was there technically any other time when you spoke with, met with, or communicated with Browning in any way?" Moss said.

"Wow. Give me a break. Just that day. Period!"

"You seem agitated Mr. Larson, why?"

"Because you are giving me the third degree and I still don't know what the hell this is all about."

"What was the name of the person who advised you not to speak to Browning?"

Hank threw up his hands, "Really?" He looked at both of them. They stood like statues. He capitulated, "Ah, what the hell, Meeks. Er, Meechum actually."

"And why did this Meechum advise you to cancel?"

"He knew more about what I was interested in and told me Mr. Browning would not be helpful."

"Helpful in what?" Cammi asked.

"In who murdered my brother."

That got them looking at each other. Raised eyebrows all around. "Let's start at the beginning," Moss said.

"You know, let's not. You haven't told me what this is about, and you are getting really personal, and personally, it's my business and none of yours."

"We can get a warrant. Compel you to talk, tie up your banking records, interview everyone you ever talked to from first grade on, and impound your car. Or you can just answer a few more questions. Your choice."

"Well, since you put it so nicely."

Twenty minutes later, they were sitting in the disheveled living room. Cammi had righted a chair and Moss was on one end of the couch Hank sat on. Their notepads were out, and the air was less chilled.

"We'll pull the DB-5s on your brother's death. Have you had any further contact with the Texas Rangers?"

"No, but they are like gnats. I can't believe I won't hear from them again."

Cammi chimed in. "You know, my brother was all into the 'who killed Kennedy' thing. Do you think this threat Meechum made was real?"

"He was an ex-agent. Or so he said. He had a gun and was as paranoid as can be. I don't know if what he was telling me was true or not. But at the time, I had had it up to here with conspiracy crap, so I just walked away."

"Well, thank you for your time. We may need to speak to you again are you planning on leaving town?"

"I'm still hopping jump seats around the country trying to find out what my brother had that got him killed. I'm flying out tomorrow to track down, to track, well I truly don't know what I am tracking down, but it's the only thing I have left. I am hoping I'll learn something. But in general, I never know the next place I am flying to or when."

Moss handed him his card, "Could you let us know when you are going out of town, just so we are aware."

"Sure thing."

They got up to leave. As they neared the door, Cammi turned and said, "One more thing, did you share Browning's address with Meechum?"

"No, I don't believe I did."

"But you did tell him he was expecting you that evening for a meeting at his home?"

"Yes. That's when he told me Browning was not to be trusted."

"Well, thank you, Mr. Larson. Have a good evening."

"Stay safe, detectives."

Out in the hallway, the detectives agreed that it was highly unlikely that Hank Larson was connected to the disappearance of Browning. But Cammi had reservations.

"You think he was involved?" Moss said.

"Maybe no. But having his brother murdered and the whole JFK thing and Browning being on that committee."

"What committee?"

"Senate Select Committee on Assassinations."

"Wait, I thought you said that was your brother who was into all that?"

"Yeah, and he kind of tortures me with every new detail he finds, he always starts off the same way, 'As a cop, Sis, what do you think about this...'"

"He couldn't just ask you to fix a parking ticket... Jeez."

30 | BARBEQUE

During the first two days in Phoenix, Hank ate dinner in the hotel's restaurant. This morning Hank risked opening his hotel room door in his underwear and putting the Room Service dinner plates out in the hall. He snapped up the newspaper left in front of his door. He was headed for the shower when he heard Senator Browning's name on the morning news on his hotel room's TV which was tuned to CNN.

"...for more on this story and what American officials are now saying we now go live to our own Chuck Wills in Martha's Vineyard, What's the latest on this bizarre story, Chuck."

Hank sat on the bed, glued to the screen as the scene switched to the reporter outside what looked like a local courthouse or police station.

"Laurie, French immigration authorities last night confirmed that Ex-Senator, Harold Browning had never entered France, and his apartment off the Champs-Élysées was unoccupied for several months, fueling speculation that the senator may have met an untimely death in this country. Upon the report from France, Chief Harmon Wainwright of Martha's Vineyard police made this statement, during an 8 a.m. press conference which just concluded." The reporter stayed looking at the camera as the boys in the truck rolled the chief's press conference from 15 minutes before.

The chief was standing at a podium in front of the same police substation. "In light of recent information from the French government, we are declaring a swimming accident as the likely cause of Senator's Browning death. The Senator was known to take night swims. Therefore, we concluded that based on clothing found on the beach near his home last week, Mr. Browning has suffered a swimming accident. At this time his body has not been recovered."

They switched back to the reporter. "The Browning family has made no official announcement of a funeral date, but now it seems more likely it will be a memorial service. Reporting from Martha's Vineyard, for CNN, I'm Chuck Wills."

Hank's jaw dropped. "Son of a bitch." He wondered if Meechum had invited the senator out for a swim. He looked in the free copy of USA Today to see if there was anything else on the senator's demise, but this must have just happened because there was nothing in the paper. He decided to let sleeping dogs lie. His plate was full enough. Besides he couldn't take another failure. He was heading home defeated as he checked out of the Phoenix hotel. It was possible that Arizona was just a quick layover for Dalton.

Hank dropped off his rental car and used his airline ID to enter the Phoenix Airport crewmember area. The phones were free there and you could get a cup of coffee or a shower. He grabbed a cup and headed to the phones. Hank called Dixon.

"How'd did you do, Hank?" Dix said.

"A complete fucking dead end. Three days in beautiful downtown Phoenix and I can't find anyone who saw this guy or remembers him."

"Can't help ya here either buddy. We ran a search all night. This Dalton guy hasn't used an airline anywhere in the U.S. or the free world since that day."

"I'm jumping a company seat tonight and going back to work tomorrow. Drinks are still on me."

"Sorry, this guy disappeared on you, Hank."

"Yeah, me too." He hung up and headed for the crew bus to take him to the Flying Tigers 74 that was headed to France, by way of JFK. He'd ride the jump seat. As he walked through the terminal he passed a newspaper machine with the local headline, Fire Kills Couple. He made a left and headed out of the terminal and grabbed a cab. "Police Headquarters, please."

Hank approached the sergeant's desk. "Excuse me where can I find the blotter?"

"Current or backlog?"

"Almost three weeks ago."

"The bulletin board on the right."

Hank walked over to a bulletin board with 10 overstuffed clipboards hanging from it. The Sergeant followed. "Looking for something in particular?

"I'm looking for a death sometime after June eighth. Possibly by fire."

"You a claims adjuster?"

"Does it show?"

The officer reached for the first board. He flipped through it, reading out loud. "There were two deaths reported on June ninth. The first was a highway worker, his tractor overturned while he was mowing grass. The blades got him."

Hank winced. The cop continued reading and editorializing. "The other a "person: unknown" who was burned beyond recognition in a "freak accident" involving a leaky gasoline reserve tank and a carelessly thrown match, presumably thrown by the same 'person: unknown.'"

"Fire!"

"There's a notation - Body held for coroner's inquest."

"Do you think it would still be there?"

"That, you would have to check with the coroner's office."

"May I see that report?"

"Knock yourself out. Just put it back when you're done. Okay?"

"Sure thing." Hank read the entire report. There was the address of the coroner on the receipt for mortal remains that he guessed was for purposes of preserving the chain of evidence if the cause of any death was considered suspicious or as a result of criminality.

He had to wait almost an hour to meet with the coroner. During that time his mood kept swinging between hopeful and hopeless. He saw a man in an apron come through the glass doors.

"Mr. Larson?"

"Yes,"

"Doctor Jefferies, Nice to meet you."

"Thank you for seeing me on such short notice."

"You're lucky. It was a quiet night in the 'west's most western town.' He made air quotes as he repeated the phrase from the Scottsdale Visitor's Bureau. "My assistant tells me you are inquiring about the death by fire from more than three weeks ago?"

"Yes, The SPD file said you were holding for inquest. Have you completed that yet?" So far Hank was getting by with just his official-sounding tone. It amazed him to some degree.

"Although last night was a rare low death night, the last few weeks we've been quite busy. So no, with no next of kin demanding answers and no police interest other than a dead body in their jurisdiction it kind of went to the back of the line as more pressing cases came in. What's your interest?"

Hank decided a grain of truth would better serve his needs. "This one is more personal in nature. My sister's husband, Harvey disappeared on a business trip here sometime after June 8th which was the last time she spoke with him. I was circling back to the police when I came across your mortal remains ticket." Hank hoped his instant jargon creation would sell his deception as someone 'freelancing' for a good reason. "The police here don't connect missing persons with unidentified cadavers." Hank's stomach tightened; cadaver was a medical school term he plucked out of the air. He hoped he hadn't just blown it.

"Who are you really? Why are you here?"

"I guess I blew it, huh?"

"You almost sold it, but the insurance investigators around here don't speak like that."

That made Hank laugh. "What gave me away?"

"I was willing to roll with 'ticket,' but cadaver? Nope."

"I knew it when I said it."

"So why the ruse, Mr. Larson? That is your name, right?"

"Yeah, it is. You see my brother died in a fire in New York City. Three weeks ago. He is being wrongly accused of killing two men in Texas, who also died in a fire."

"So, who do you think I have in there?" He hitched his head in the direction of the morgue.

"Well, because of the two different states involved, no one was looking at the big picture. I couldn't live with myself having my brother's name smeared with a murder accusation. So, I picked up the baton. I'm an airline pilot and used my connections to follow an individual who was in both places where and when the deaths by fire happened. His trail ended here in Phoenix. Whoever you are holding here may have also been his victim."

"Wow. I followed most of that, airline pilot you say? Did you fly in the military?"

"Yeah, two tours on Buffs during Desert Storm."

"Buffs?"

"It's what we called the B-52, big ugly fat fuckers."

"Hmmph, cute. I'm a colonel in the Arizona National Guard. Army medical corps during Bosnia."

"Can you see your way to helping me out, Colonel?"

"That's a sticky situation."

"Is there some way we can unstick it?"

A minute later Doctor Jeffries said, "Actually, you might be able to help me clear this case if you can get me closer to the facts surrounding the John Doe's death."

"You genuinely do use that name?"

In the morgue, the coroner pulled out drawer E6. He unzipped the plastic zip-lock-style body bag. The body looked like a charcoal-burnt steak in the rough shape of a man. The arms were gone up to the biceps, as were the feet. Hank gagged.

In a matter-of-fact tone of voice, the coroner sympathized with Hank's reaction. "The effects of fire on flesh turn most people's stomachs. I always think it smells like barbecue."

"You should eat out more," Hank said holding his handkerchief over his face. "Why haven't you been able to identify him?"

"Although patches of charred clothing are still stuck to the corpse, the wallet and any paper or ID are gone. And of course, no hands - no fingerprints.

"Is there a barbeque, er... men's room?"

"Sure, out the door and on the left."

31 | CHECKING OUT

Hank was at the front desk of his hotel checking out. As the concierge worked the computer keyboard she asked the usual question. "Well, Mr...." She read from the computer screen, "Larson, how did you enjoy your stay in the Phoenix area?"

"Unfortunately, I didn't find what I was looking for."

She spoke while continuing to enter keystrokes. "Did you check with guest services? They have shopping guides and directories."

"No. It wasn't that sort of thing. I just ran into a dead, really dead, end."

She was still not looking up from the keys, "Fine. Okay, now how will you be paying your bill?" She looked up, then mechanically smiled.

"Credit card. American Express." He caught himself, "American Express!"

He looked at his Breitling Aviator's watch. "It's past the first of the month, isn't it? Excuse me."

Hank headed to the phone booth. He sat and dialed the toll-free number to make a calling card call while reaching into his wallet. He pulled out the slip of paper with the widow Dalton's phone number that he called a week ago. After a few rings, she picked up.

"Mrs. Dalton, this is Mr. Larson again, I realize this is still a bad time for you, but I need to ask you something very important. Have you received your husband's last American Express bill?"

"Yes. I know I saw it somewhere..." She found the unopened envelope under other mail on the desk. "I haven't gotten to going through all Harvey's..." There's a catch in her throat, I don't even know how I'm going to pay these bills now that Harvey's gone."

Sensing her pain he reassures her, "Mrs. Dalton, you may not have to pay this bill, I believe charges were made erroneously. If you'll only just, please look at the bill and tell me when and where the last charge was made."

She opened the envelope and unfolded the bill. She put on bifocals and took a moment to get her bearings then read into the phone.

"The last charge on the list is Hertz Rent-a-Car, Phoenix on June the eighth... why there must be some mistake! Harvey died on May 27th. Something's wrong here."

"No need to worry about a thing, Mrs. Dalton. Please accept my deepest apology for disturbing you, but I think I'll be able to clear this up in a few days."

"That's quite all right Mr. Larson, thank you for being so nice."

"You take care, I'll call you in a few days." As he hung up, he realized he just gave a grieving widow hope that he could ease her financial worries somewhat. He decided that even if he is wrong, he'd pay at least that month's bill for her.

Hank called a local number next.

Hank left the booth and went back to the front desk, "I er... won't be checking out after all..."

She ripped up his bill.

"What can I help you with today?" The Hertz rental agent said.

"May I talk with your manager?"

"Sure. Just a minute, please."

A minute later the manager came up to the counter, "I'm Dave, what can I do for you, sir?"

"Can we go to your office, it's somewhat a private matter."

A little confused the manager nodded, "Certainly."

Once in the office, Hank explained himself, "My brother-in-law, Harvey. Harvey Dalton rented a mid-sized sedan from you on June 8th."

"Hold on." He punched some computer keys. "From the airport or the downtown location?"

"I'm not sure."

"No problem. Dalton spelled as usual?"

"Yes."

"Here we go. Airport...Malibu... 2-day rental. Wait there's an extra charge. What? Oh, I see now. We had to retrieve the vehicle from the Los Arcos Mall parking level 2. He didn't return it. The police called it in 4 days later."

"So, you're telling me that my brother-in-law rented a car and left it abandoned in a mall garage on the ninth of June?

"Had to send a lot man down to pick it up."

"Can you tell me if there was anything left in the car, a suitcase, clothes, a matchbook? My brother...in-law, had a silver Haliburton attaché case. Was that found in it?

The manager hits the space bar a few times. "No, the code here says the car came back clean. If any personal belongings were left behind there would have been a PB code here and a lost and found index number. However, we did check the fuel pump."

"Why?"

"The guy that picked it up said there was a strong smell of gasoline, but no maintenance is listed here, so I guess the pump checked out. Sorry, that's about all we know."

Back at his hotel, Hank passed the same woman at the front desk. He stopped,

Good afternoon, I'm in room 1028..."

"Yes, I remember. Mr. Larson."

"And I'll be checking out early tomorrow morning. I'd like to settle up right now if I could."

"Certainly." She, once again hit the keys. She noticed something. "Mr. Larson, you have a message. Would you like me to print it out?"

"Could you just read it to me?"

"Certainly." She read from the screen. "A Mister Wells called to say, and he asks this be quoted exactly, "Direct doesn't mean non-stop."

"God, he's right! Why didn't I think of that?"

"There's more. The message went on to say, "American Flight 436 made a one-hour layover in Dallas. Good hunting. Wells."

Hank heads back to the phone booths.

She called out, "How about I don't check you out of your room this time till after you make this call?"

Hank turned and nodded in agreement.

"Mrs. Dalton..."

By now Mrs. Dalton knows his voice and she answered in an exasperated sigh, "Yes, Mr. Larson."

He was surprised she recognized him. "You know it's me?"

"Mr. Larson, this is getting to be just too much for me."

"Mrs. Dalton, I know I have no right to keep pestering you like this, but please, I need to know one more thing.

"Well, all right Mr. Larson but this just has to be the last time."

"Yes ma'am. Last time. I need to know if there were any other charges made to your husband's account in either Dallas or Phoenix. I'll hold while you look it up."

"I don't have to look it up, Mr. Larson. It's the same thing I told that other fellow who just called from your office there was a charge made at the Dallas Airport Bookshop. A book for 19.95.

"Did you get the name of the gentleman who called from my office?"

"A Mr. Kendall. He said he was from American Express, and I naturally assumed he was calling from your office... You are from American Express aren't you Mr. Larson? Mr. Larson?"

Hank freezes for a second, "Yes. I'm sorry, Mr. Kendall must have followed up and didn't tell me. So sorry to have bothered you twice. Good night, Mrs. Dalton."

He hung up and went back to the front desk. She awaits his decision. "I'm out of here."

She pushed the button and the laser printer spat out his bill.

32 | EXECUTIVE ACTION

"...for this generation and generations to come. Goodnight and God Bless America." With that, the president left the platform as the Navy band struck up, 'Hail to the Chief.'

As the President of the United States walked through the hotel kitchen with the Secret Service in tow, they made a left at the elevator. The door was held open. The president turned to his secret service detail. "Just Warren."

A little confused, the others held back. Warren hit the button, and the door closed.

The president took the opportunity to check his Blackberry and asked without looking up. "How long has he been waiting?"

"Ten minutes, sir."

"What did you tell the detail?"

"Unscheduled personal, sir."

"Great, now they'll think I'm Kennedy meeting a honey."

Warren just looked straight ahead.

The door opened, Warren held his hand back, and the president waited. He quickly checked the floor, then waved the president on. They walked to a suite at the end of the hall. Warren knocked. A man opened. Warren held out his open hand, and the man surrendered his weapon. Warren then checked out the suite. He drew the drapes closed. He paid no attention to the man in the high back chair. When he was satisfied there was no danger in the suite, he nodded to the president. Then he and the man who answered the door left closing the door behind them.

The president of the United States sat across from the man in the chair. The president's favorite bourbon was in the glass, the bottle beside it. He took a sip. "Brent, now I know what you are going to say..."

"No, you don't. You have no idea what I am going to say, just like you have no idea how your flirting with the idea of peace talks is bad for business."

"Brent, it's an election year, I need to put some points on the board for my base. It's just talk."

"First off, fuck your base. We got you elected, and we will get you re-elected if you are worthy."

"And who decides that?"

"I do."

"Brent, be reasonable." The President said.

"No, dammit. You listen to me your junkie brother-in-law was a gnat's ass away from getting caught with that underaged girl, we fixed that. Your wife's little drinking problem? We made the press look the other way. We have been more than reasonable."

"Yes, and I am..."

"And you will scuttle these peace talks. Both sides are arming up. We are selling to both sides. Don't fuck this up?"

"Yes, Brent."

"Tomorrow the deputy for the premiere will wind up dead in a hotel room with a dead male hooker. We will have kompromat on his person that will give you the pretext to call off the talks."

"That's a little extreme isn't it."

Brent smacked the armrest on his chair. "Because you forced us into this. You and your liberal bullshit. We don't want these countries talking. We want them blowing the fuck out of one another with our very expensive platforms and systems. And just to remind you, don't ever question our tactics. We are doing this to clean up the mess you and your 'kumbaya crap' has created."

The president sat there, looking at the art on the far wall. "Anything else?"

"Yes. When Senator Grimes comes to you and wants to talk about releasing the government files on the executive action, you stonewall the bastard. If you don't, we'll do it."

He turned to the Admiral "The public is starting to question the Warren Commission."

"And it's our job to not supply the answers. Look, before that pussy Browning quit the senate over his wife's cancer, I had a hook into that committee. A good one. Plausibly deniable. Now you have to shut it down. Do I make myself clear?"

The president tried one more time to avoid having this senator, Grimes, have something over him. "It's been over thirty years, Brent."

"Thirty years of containment. Thirty years of operations to minimize exposure. Thirty years of unimagined profits, world prominence, dominance, and superiority! Do you sincerely want to threaten all that just to appease conspiracy nuts and romantics?"

"No, of course not, Brent, but I..."

"Good, then we are finished here."

The president nodded. He got up and walked out the door. He stopped and turned "Browning was a friend. Did you have a hand in his disappearance?"

"That is need to know, only."

The president turned and headed out of the room.

Brent's security man appeared at the door, and Brent gave him a wave off. The man closed it.

Admiral Brent R. Howser sat and drummed his fingers. He could not believe the insolence of the man. Everything the current president had achieved politically, financially, and historically was all made possible by his committee. That was the problem with politicians. They have short-term memory. They start to believe their own press releases: that it was them who surmounted the odds, defied the critics, and ascended to rule. How soon they forget what he and the committee did for them.

He reached into his breast pocket and pulled out his cigar case. It held three petit Upmanns. The Cuban cigar was the only thing good that ever came out of his time working in that Irish Mick's administration.

As he rolled the petit corona in his fingers, he remembered when he was in the oval office on February 7, 1962. He knew the date because it became historic right before his eyes. At that point, he served as military attaché to the president of the United States. He was on the couch with the briefing papers on the situation in Belgium Congo spread out on the coffee table before him. Kennedy sat on this stiff back rocking chair. He preferred it over the one behind the Resolute Desk because of his bad back. He had injured it in World War II. Mrs. Johnson, one of his secretaries, announced, "Pierre is here."

"Send him in." then he said to Brent, "This will only take a minute."

"Certainly, sir," Brent, the young military aide to POTUS, said.

As his Press Secretary, Pierre Salinger, was walking in, the president said, "How did you do?"

"Well, yesterday was short notice sir, but by last night at midnight, I managed to wrangle 12 hundred." He placed a box of H. Cuban Petit Upmanns Coronas on his desk.

"Excellent.," he said as he reached into his desk and pulled out a legal-sized paper. He picked up a pen and signed it. "Pierre, call a press conference to announce this." He handed it over.

Pierre scanned it and read out loud the first provision, "One. I Hereby proclaim an embargo upon trade between the United States and Cuba in accordance with paragraphs 2 and 3 of this proclamation."

Brent remembered thinking, *"What balls!"* He waited until he had his stash before he banned every product from Cuba as illegal. Brent had stood on the bridge as the massive 16-inch guns of the battleship Iowa belched out shells as heavy as a Volkswagen. Until this point that was his definition of power. As Kennedy blew out that first inhale of the Upmann, like the smoke rising from the barrel of the massive cannon, he had a new perspective on real power.

Immediately, Brent separated the power of the office from the man occupying that office. The power resided in the desk, the drapes, the carpet, and the oval room itself. Kennedy was just the temporary inhabitant who used it, no, borrowed that power for his own ends.

It was a week later that he was first approached by the committee. He was called to the Office of Naval Intelligence in New Orleans. In the room, he was the only man in uniform. He did recognize some out-of-uniform flag officers and a military contractor he had met at a Washington meet and greet. No names or pleasantries were offered.

The man, whom he would later replace, was the only one who spoke. "Brent. We've been watching you."

He tensed even though he had no reason to. He had never strayed, was a patriot all the way, and always erred on the side of national security and American sovereignty. But the ONI was the Navy's spook house they might have something on him something innocent, or something someone with a grudge proffered against him. He set his chin and was ready to take any hit on it.

"Who do you work for?"

"Sir, I serve at the pleasure of the Secretary of Defense."

"No, I mean above that?"

Brent was thrown for a second, then he caught on. "The people of the United States of America and the constitution of this nation under God."

"We all took that oath, Brent. That's who, in the end, we fight and die for, not for a commander, or commander and chief." He leaned in, "They only rent the office. We patriots, we warriors, we who hold the blessings of liberty in our hearts, we are the continuum, the never broken thread that connects and holds together this country while the politicians do their best to tear it apart from within."

To Brent, this was a confirmation of the very thoughts he had the other day in the oval. He involuntarily nodded.

"That uniform you are wearing is reflective of a chain of command. We are not in uniform, but we are part of a higher chain of command. A force to ensure America is now, and will always be, the preeminent power on the face of the earth."

"Permission to speak, sir?"

He waved his hand dismissively. "No uniforms here, Brent."

"Yes. I take it I am here because of my proximity to the president?"

The man looked around the room with a proud smile.

That told Brent that he must have been the one who convinced the rest to bring him in.

"That, and let's just say, certain opinions of yours, overheard over time."

Brent immediately knew that the only way for them to overhear anything was to spy on him. These guys were surveilling him. For how long, he wondered.

The man read his facial expression. "Don't take umbrage. Consider it scouting for the major leagues...are you ready, Brent? Ready to step up to the plate?"

"What do you expect of me?"

"Right now, just what you are doing. Keep your head above water and maintain your position with the president at all costs. At some point, we may call on you for assistance."

Brent left that meeting with a sense of a new responsibility added to the single stars riding atop his epaulets. A more direct and effective way to fight for his country alongside a cadre of men--men who knew the cost of freedom and were willing to bear the price. He did not know what they would call on him to do, or what the assignment would be, but he knew that he was ready, willing, and extremely able.

That call came in late August of '63. The committee had found out that Kennedy's staff was going to have a meeting on the security issues surrounding a planned trip to Miami. The committee knew that Brent was on the attendee list. Ostensibly to give, from a military perspective, the threat assessment of the disgruntled Cuban exiles over the disastrous Bay of Pigs. It was a flat-out loss and embarrassment for the CIA. Through their press allies, that agency let it be known that it was Kennedy who sabotaged their mission to retake Cuba by denying U.S. Air support, leaving the CIA's exile army as target practice for the overwhelming Cuban Army. Brent was there to offer his conclusion that there was no imminent threat assessed and that he saw no reason to scrub the Miami trip on that basis.

Brent learned that later on that trip, the committee had informed the mob of the motorcade route. The plan was to shoot the president as he traveled in his open-top car from a high building in downtown Miami. It was the first time Brent was aware of the committee gunning for Kennedy.

Brent didn't make Admiral in record time or catch the attention of the committee by being timid. Aggressive and decisive action was his winning formula. In that vein, he requested and received permission to meet with the committee at their compound in the suburbs of Phoenix.

Three men sat across from him. One he knew from the newspapers; he was the CIA man that was fired by Kennedy. Rumor had it that he was the architect of the Bay of Pigs invasion. The man in a brown suit and tortoiseshell glasses that he had seen around the old executive office building across from the White House. The third man, who sat silently in civilian clothes, was the definition of a grunt with stars on his epaulets. A general who was probably a product of meritorious field promotions.

Brent was immediately direct and didn't mix words. "Why are we trying to terminate Kennedy?"

"Do you have an issue with that?"

"In principle, no. But I was just requested to affect the southern swing he's making in late November. I could be more effective if I knew what the mission parameters were, including the cause."

"What was the subject of the September 30th meeting in the PEOC?"

Brent was impressed. The Presidential Emergency Operations Center under the east wing of the white house was the SCIF of all Sensitive Compartmented Information Facilities, and the men around the table knew the sensitive details. The fact that they were even aware of the meeting meant he was not the only government insider to have a position with the committee. *They must have ears throughout the entire federal system.*

Based on the topic of the meeting, Brent put two and two together and quickly verbalized, "I get it now, POTUS is vehemently against ratcheting up the police action in Indochina. He feels it's a losing game. He knows the CIA and military are pushing for a proxy showdown with the Commie Reds. But he is convinced it a fool's errand, a waste of blood and treasure,' as he called it."

"Do you agree with his assessment, Brent?"

"No, I think it's short-sighted. If Kennedy pulls out, the Reds are free to topple every country in the region like dominoes. But he seems more interested in Civil Rights and the Moon."

Knowing looks were exchanged between the three men. The CIA guy spoke up, "What we are about to discuss never leaves this room."

"Yes, sir."

He turned to the man next to Brent and nodded, "Okay, Howard."

Howard threw down a picture of a goofy-looking marine, a skinny kid in a helmet that was too big for him. He's our blind, he has a history and we have fabricated an identity for him that will allow us to utilize him."

"How was he recruited?"

"He was an Air Cadet in the Civilian Air Patrol in Louisiana. One of our contract pilots identified him as malleable, and a psychological analysis confirmed that field diagnosis. Since then, we've groomed him as a prime asset. He was a bright kid, despite his anti-social demeanor, which, again, was perfect for his specialty. He aced radio and radar, and we got him into the DEW line and stationed at an early warning post in the Aleutian Islands. We had him defect to the Soviets in 59. His mission was to compromise the U2 flights that were stopping us from ramping up for war. When the Russians shot down the U2, international tensions rose, and the orders came rolling in for offensive and defensive armaments."

Brent considered the effect of manipulating the levers of power with just one well-placed operative. "So how does our Marine play out in this, if he's in Russia?"

"We brought him back. Perfect cover. He married a Russian girl, had a rug rat, and the Count, our operative in Texas, who works with Russian emigres, placed him in a rooming house and got him a job."

"What do you need from me?" Brent jumped to the bottom line.

"Get a message to the acting mayor of Dallas."

"Which is?"

"His cops will lead the motorcade," Howard said.

One of the other fellows chimed in. "Secret Service always lets the local law enforcement direct them through the streets and plan the route. It's their turf they know it best."

"And..."

Howard answered, "And you will tell him to divert the motorcade by making a right off main onto North Hudson, then a left onto Elm."

"Why?"

"That sets up the crossfire."

The word, crossfire, triggered Brent. They were talking about a single marine as the sole operator in this mission. One shooter does not make a crossfire. "Wait. One marine. How can you have a cross..." Then it hit Brent. "Of course. Sacrifice a pawn to get a king."

"Exactly. Any questions?"

"Just one. What makes me the best way to approach this mayor?"

"You know General Chuck Cabell?" The ex-CIA man asked.

"Yeah, met him. He was sacked by Kennedy along with your boss, Dulles."

Howard let that attempt by Brent to nail his association with the Central Intelligence Agency, by implication, go.

"Well, you served with his brother."

"Earle? Earle Cabell? What's he doing these days?"

"He is the mayor of Dallas."

"And I take it he doesn't know of the little reception you are planning?"

"No need to know until there is a need. That's when you'll reach out to your old buddy and deliver the rerouting plan with the code word, "Mongoose.""

"If I may ask, why not his brother? Isn't he one of us?"

"More compartmented this way. And your value to the committee will appreciate immensely by this assignment."

Brent took it all in. These were men of immutable action. No other 'ism' than patriotism was practiced and right then and there. The youngest Admiral ever to earn his flag decided that he'd like to run the place someday.

Over the intervening years, Brent decided that there was a better way to control national power, assassinations were messy affairs, and despite all the pinpoint planning, the beautifully executed placement of a patsy, and the successful quashing of all evidence to the contrary, the Kennedy affair raised more questions than the committee anticipated. A virtual cottage industry was formed working against the committee's installed facts and narrative. Even Congress got into the act in '79, reopening the investigation. The fools! However, some well-placed threats and one or two disappearances convinced that body to weaken their final report. The one he regretted most, but it had to be done, was the Count. Of all the executive actions he had quarterbacked, giving the order to take that man out of play was the toughest. George was a good asset. He proved himself in war and peace. His proximity to the Dallas Russian émigré's and his hatred of the communists, which he claimed any true Russian would, made his elimination a true, but necessary, tragedy. Brent had personally interceded in asking him to reconsider his agreement to testify before the House Select Committee on Assassinations. That congressional committee was getting uncomfortably close to the sources, methods, and tactics employed. Count George could inadvertently put the nail in the coffin by miscalculation or clever entrapment by the committee. The Count thought he was too smart to be trapped, but Brent just couldn't take that chance. So, he ordered his death: the death of Uncle Georgie as Kennedy's wife called him. The death of the man who skillfully placed Oswald in the building that day. Although not of American stock, a true American patriot, whose sacrifice was in the name of preserving our nation. It still bothered Brent to this day.

And now, thirty-plus years of containment that survived rogue journalists, conspiracy theories, and Congress, not to mention scores of witnesses silenced, made to disappear, or publicly disgraced as fruitcakes, were all in jeopardy because of one lousy snapshot.

His security officer knocked on the hotel suite door breaking his remembrance. "Sir, are you ready to leave?" He took one more pull on the Corona and finished off the Chivas. "Right!"

33 | CREDIT WHERE CREDIT IS DUE

The agent behind the desk gathered the ticket with the boarding pass. "Here you are, Captain Larson. One professional courtesy pass. That'll be $22.50."

Hank handed over the cash to pay for the tax on the free ticket.

"Thank you and enjoy your trip to Dallas."

Hank headed right to the phones.

"American Express."

"Yes. I'm trying to return a call I got from a Mr. Kendall. I'll hold."

"I'm sorry, I show no listing for a Mr. Kendall. I have a Ms. Eunice Kendall."

"Thank you, I must have got the message wrong. Can you transfer me to the fraud division? My mother-in-law has been getting bogus charges on her dead husband's card. I'll hold..." A minute later he was talking to the fraud division and informing them of the widow Dalton's situation. They promised immediate action.

The afternoon committee meeting was wrapping up. The Admiral had one last question. "Do we have anything further about the Browning affair?"

"The cover story we planted with the Vineyard cops is holding. The tip that he was at his place in Paris bought us almost a month," Nelson said.

"Was the disposal handled in the usual manner?"

"All three, deep trench, sealed in steel," Nelson said referring to making bodies disappear by placing them in a perforated oil drum, weighted with boulders, and dropping them over the side of the commercial fishing boat that the committee owned. That deep sea fishing boat was always traversing the Caribbean waters above the seven-mile deep Puerto Rico Trench.

The Admiral nodded. They had long wanted to silence Meechum, but as long as he was dormant, he was not worth chasing down. Aside from losing one of his good operatives to Meechum, it was a good trade. Browning had his uses, but after he left the Senate, less and less so that was not the capital loss it could have been. But there was one glaring issue. "Are the local New York authorities still digging?"

"Our source in the NYPD says that detectives were sniffing around, but once the Vineyard story hit the press, they closed the investigation into Browning. Nothing was ever opened in the case of Meechum."

"What about Browning's security man?"

"Lonzano. He did the right thing by calling us first. Halfback has been assigned to Marvin Duluth, our guy on Wall Street. His security man was convinced to retire, so Halfback is now his new guy."

The Admiral was pleased. "So, this matter has been erased?"

"Yes, sir. Tight as a drum." Nelson said.

The Admiral didn't appreciate his attempt at humor. "Tell our man in the New York PD to see what is in the detectives' files on the case. We need to know if there are any loose ends."

"But sir..."

"That is an order, Nelson. I want to know that there's no loose thread dangling in a case file in New York, or the Vineyard for that matter. Get it done!"

34 | THE TEN DOLLAR GUY

"Past the revolving car and then down the accessway on your right. Across from the lockers. There's a big sign, 'Airport Books.'"

"Thank you," Hank said to the Dallas Airport Security Guard.

As he walked through the terminal, he was starting to doubt this whole endeavor. That this whole episode came down to chasing a book purchase was pitiful. He doubted the book was the Idiot's Guide to Arson. And whoever was masquerading as Harvey didn't just buy a novel to read on the plane, but every other lead had dried up. He promised himself this would be the last of it. He had to get back to work. He didn't want to abuse Brian's generosity in giving him paid leave for much longer.

The saleswoman behind the counter was trying in earnest to help Hank.

"A silver metal case? Now that you mention it...Yes, I do remember. I think it was around three weeks ago..." She snapped her fingers, "The ten-dollar guy!"

"Ten-dollar guy?"

"It was late. I just closed and was locking up. He just bought a book but came back."

"Why did he come back?"

"He needed change for a ten. Four quarters actually. I had just locked the safe. I had four quarters, but not change for a ten, so he gave me the whole ten and told me, 'It's okay, keep it.' I guess he really needed those quarters."

"Did he say for what?... A phone call?... Cigarettes?"

"It must have been for the lockers over there, 'cause I saw him there as I was leaving."

She pointed. As Hank turned, he saw Long Term Lockers. Still looking at them, he asked her one last question. "Do you remember which locker?"

"One of those ones right in front of the store."

"Thank you. You've been very helpful."

Hank walked across the way to the rows of lockers. He dropped four quarters in the slot and turned the key. The door locked and the key was released into his hand.

As the Coroner approached the wall phone, he wiped his bloodied hand on a towel and took the call. "Yes... Hello Mr. Larson."

"I know you said that all the stuff that the John Doe had in his pockets was incinerated, but I remember those patches of cloth I saw."

"What specifically are you looking for?"

"A locker key."

"That could be what we couldn't identify in his right front pocket. Let me look at it again. Give me your number and I'll get back to you."

F-14 fighters were in a dogfight against Russian MiGs. Hank was on the fighter's control stick, pounding relentlessly the fire button on the panel.

A group of kids stood watching in awe. The video game paused as the bonus points add up, again.

"Gee mister, that's the sixth time you've reached the next level."

"Yeah, you're pretty good for an old guy. But can't you lose now? We want to play."

Just then the airport public address system crackled. "Captain Henry Larson, please go to the nearest courtesy phone, Captain Henry Larson, nearest courtesy phone."

"Well, that's for me kids. Say, do me a favor will ya." He handed them a stack of quarters. Their eyes lit up. "Keep those bad guys away from our carrier while I'm gone."

After Hank left, one kid asked, "A pilot?"

The other two reacted in unison, "No Fair!"

Hank picked up the yellow wall phone.

"I was paged?... Yes, I am. I'll hold."

"I checked and found what could be an impression in the skin in the rough shape of a locker key.

"That's great news. Can you send it to me?"

"What?... the body? - all I found was an impression. The key melted."

"Thanks... any shot at the color of the plastic?

Hank looked down at the red locker key in his hand.

"Red."

"Thanks, this could be a big help."

"Well, if it was a red key that means the long-term, 21-day lockers," the head of the airport guard said to Hank, who was seated across from his desk.

"Why doesn't your brother send you the key?"

"My brother had flown to Dallas from New York. He died here in a fire that melted the locker key."

His eyes went wide. "No shit... I mean, sorry for your loss. But if your brother was in Dallas on the ninth of last month..." turning to the calendar behind him, "the expired lockers for that date can't be opened till tomorrow, the 22nd day.

"Do you do that?"

"Every morning at eight. Anything that's been sitting in them for a month is unclaimed property. You wouldn't believe the stuff I've found. A transmission...

"Fine. Well, I guess I'll be spending the night in Dallas."

35 | REUNION

It looked like an airline convention. Ninety percent of this hotel's guests were airline employees on layover. Hank was checking in when Chris DeMarco rolled by with her luggage wheelie. She noticed Hank and came up from behind him. "Still hot on the heels of your prey?"

Hank was pleasantly surprised. "Chris, Chris DeMarco. What are you doing here?"

"I'm on a 14-hour layover, and this is a crew hotel. So what are you doing here?"

At that moment, the deskman came over with Hank's key. "Here we are, Captain Larson. Room 1144. Checking out tomorrow. Have a pleasant stay, sir."

Chris did a slow burn. "Captain! What happened to 'secret ticket agent?'"

"Okay, you got me. I'm a four-striper with Flying Tigers." Hank lays down four fingers over his right sleeve. "Look, I'm sorry for the charade, it's just... Can we discuss this over drinks or dinner? It's a long story."

"I've got 14 hours," she said guardedly.

By the time they got around to dessert, Hank had filled her in on the whole story. "So, I'm trying to find the guy to clear my brother's name and his assets." He pointed with his fork to the slice of chocolate layer cake that he was working on. "It's quite good would you like to try it?"

Chris waved him off. "Nah, I'm a recovering chocoholic. I will have another glass of wine, though."

Hank poured from the bucket at the side of the table. They caught one another's eyes. The moment lingered.

Hank became self-conscious. "What?"

"You got it too... that "military look."

"Wow, you're good. Yeah, I flew Buffs in GW-1."

"Buffs?"

"Yes, 'Big Ugly Fat Fellow.' It's what we called a B-52 bomber. My best friend and co-pilot, Brian, got out first and landed a job with the Tigers. Then when I got out, he got me my job."

"So, you went from flying bombers in Gulf War 1 to flying trucks?"

"Bombs, cargo, same thing; somebody's still paying you to deliver a payload." And besides, boxes don't bitch."

She laughed, "Amen to that. So how..."

Hank unintentionally interrupted her, "The only... I'm sorry you were going to say something."

"Oh, no, go ahead. I interrupted you."

"Well, it was… I was just going to say, how I never realized how deprived we cargo jockeys are by not having cabin service."

She held up her hand making a halting gesture. "Cool your jets, Captain."

"Right now, things are a little topsy turvy for me. Hopefully, all this will be over soon. Then maybe..."

She was considering his overture. "Maybe." But then she thinks again. "No. Look, you started off by lying to me."

"Well, I, I mean you said you didn't like..."

She held up her hand in a 'Halt' gesture. "Don't."

"Look, I never thought I'd ever see you again. And yes, it was manipulative of me, but I needed to find out what you knew."

She took it in. She didn't speak for a few seconds. "Well, thank you for that moment of honesty. It's all too rare these days."

"Besides, you got the nicest pair of..."

Chris' hand shoots up in a stop gesture, again.

"...Ruby red slippers this side of the yellow brick road."

That disarmed her.

The waiter arrived and placed the check in the middle of the table. "I'll take that whenever you're ready."

Hank reached for the check, but Chris put her hand on it.

"C'mon Chris, at least let me buy you dinner."

"No." Then she softened. "We'll split it."

They got on the elevator. Hank hit 11, "What floor?"

"Same."

"Imagine that!"

"Yeah, imagine." The smile on her face flashed the slightest glimmer of flirtation.

On 11 Hank and Chris sort of stumbled out of the elevator. "I'm not supposed to drink on layover," she said.

They got to Hank's door first.

"Just tell them you were only following the orders of a superior officer."

She smiled. They stood there for a long moment. She broke the silence. "This is awkward."

"Yeah, I know."

"We could just shake hands."

"True. We could..."

"But...?"

"I hate cold showers right before bed."

"That can be a problem, so what do you suggest?"

"This is totally random and off the top of my head, and you may or may not agree with my recommendation, but why don't I kiss you and see if it takes away some of the awkwardness?"

"You may have something there."

He leaned in and kissed her. They looked into one another's eyes. They kissed again harder. Hank dropped his key. With his back to the wall, still kissing, he started sliding down the wall. Chris caught on and lowered herself keeping the kiss going. He picked up the key, put his arms around her, and slid straight back up the wall, pulling her up with him without breaking the kiss. She let out a little laugh and then rested her head on his chest.

Hank was gently running his hands across her back. "You're just interested in me because I'm a pilot."

She moved her shoulders enjoying the touch.

"Gave him a peck on the cheek. "No, because you're an exciting pilot."

He buried his head in her neck. "Right now, I'm an excited pilot."

Chris reached down to his crotch. "I thought you didn't carry a gun?"

"Careful, that thing's loaded."

"Mmmmm. I'll remember that."

They kissed again and separated. She grabbed the key from his hand, unlocked the door, and pushed it open. "You're cleared for a solo landing, Captain."

"Now, remember, I'm right here, alone, all night... if you need anything."

Chris took a deep breath and walked down two doors to her room. She turned to him and said, "Like room service?"

"I am really glad I met you, Chris."

She slipped the key in her door and took one last look at Hank. "See ya at 0600 for breakfast?"

The shower's cold-water faucet in Hank's room was turned on with extreme prejudice.

Chris was sitting up in bed, jamming the chocolate mints into her mouth as fast as she could unwrap them.

At the D/FW long-term lockers, a yellow dot appeared through a hole in the lock mechanism that had been red for a month.

36 | SURPRISES

A pair of serving tongs grabbed three strips of bacon. Hank put them next to the omelet and hash browns on the plate that Chris was holding. They checked out the rest of the breakfast offerings.

"I wish I didn't have pre-flight in an hour. I am so curious about what you are going to find."

"I just hope this isn't another dead end."

"I was just going to have yogurt, but I deprived myself of enough last night."

"I told you; you should have tried the chocolate cake!"

She ripped into a strip of bacon, her eyes locked on Hank.

Hank smiled. "Carnivore!"

"Hank, will you call me tonight and tell me what you find in the locker?"

"What time do you get in?"

"8:45. La Guardia."

"Dinner at 10?"

She looked down at the omelet, bacon, home fries, pancakes, and a yogurt cup on her tray. "Do you think I'm ever going to be hungry again after this breakfast?"

Hank was standing outside the security office at five to eight, waiting for the head of the guard to do his sweep of the expired lockers. When he came out, Hank asked, "Would you mind if we started with the lockers in front of the bookstore?"

The guard shrugged his shoulders. "Sure."

The guard scanned the lockers and found a yellow dot showing on one locker. "Sir, would you stand over there."

Hank stepped away. The guard inserted his passkey and opened it just enough to see inside. "What is it you think is in here?"

"A silver Haliburton case and possibly a book."

The guard pulled out an Airport Book Shop Bag. Suddenly Connors and Ritter appeared, flashing their Ranger stars to the security guard. "We need to see that." He turned to Hank. "I knew you'd lead us right to it," Connors said. Ritter grabbed the bag and pulled out...a book? He flipped through it. Turned it over and shook it.

"Well, you guys have done it. You have single-handedly solved the case of the overdue library book," Hank said, as he grabbed the book from him and flipped through it himself.

The guard went on to scan for other expired lockers in the bank.

"What were you looking for, Mr. Larson?" Ritter said.

"I honestly don't know. I thought this would have been it. That whatever it was that got my brother killed would have been in there."

"Why here?"

"Cause this is where the lockers are."

"Don't get cute! Why are you here in Dallas?"

"The guy that might have killed my brother, his name was Dalton. At least that's the name he used until I figured out that it was a stolen name from a dead salesman in Silver Springs, Maryland. Anyway, he bought a book from that store over there."

"And how did you know that?"

"The widow who was slammed by big charges to her dead husband's Amex card shared his credit card statement with me."

Connors was impressed. "You ever work in law enforcement?"

"No, but I do exceedingly well on mystery weekends."

"You also a comedian?" Ritter asked.

"No, but I'm in the airline business and you'd be amazed at what the airlines have on anyone who flies."

"So, okay, now why the lockers?" Ritter asked.

"The bookshop girl remembered him and saw him putting something in the locker as she was closing up."

Ritter turned and looked at the Airport Books store then back to the Airport Books plastic bag in Hank's hand.

Hank said, "He must have come back between now and last month. It takes 21 days to clear a locked locker."

"We'll take the book."

"Why?"

"Because there might be latent prints on it, Dick Tracy."

"Tell you what. He had to touch the bag too." Hank slid the book out gingerly and handed the bag to Connors.

"You want this, get a warrant," he said holding up the book.

Just then the security guard returned and grabbed the book from Hank. "You got to fill out an L&F retrieval form in the office. When I finish my rounds."

Hank turned to make another wisecrack he just thought up to stick it to the Rangers, but they were already over at the bookstore.

"Shame, it was a good one." He said to himself as he walked back to the office to wait to sign the papers.

37 | X MARKS THE SPOT

Because somehow his brother may have come down to Texas to get his hands on something from the Kennedy Assassination, an 'artifact,' as it was called in the paper, Hank decided to visit the scene of the original crime.

He hailed a cab. "Dealey Plaza, please."

The driver started the meter, and as he drove, looked at Hank in the rearview mirror. At one point, Hank caught his eyes in the mirror, and the driver said, "Tourist or Investigator."

"Tourist. What's there to investigate?"

"Ah, so you're a normal person!"

"Okay, yeah. Just never been there and I had a few hours to kill." He looked out the window for a bit and then asked the driver, "Investigators still come here?"

"Well, the Visitor's Bureau doesn't like us to refer to them as "conspiracy nuts." Bad for business. There's always a whole slew of them coming from everywhere convinced they got it all figured out."

"I guess it's like a nut magnet, huh?"

"Bubba, you better believe it."

"What's your take?"

"Me? Oswald. Three shots. End of story."

"That must bum them out."

"Had a guy back there just a few minutes ago, just like you, wanted to go to the Plaza. He said he had proof it was Jackie."

"Wait, the President's wife? Jackie Kennedy? She shot him?"

"Not directly. But he had a whole bunch of maybes and head-scratchers. I tell you, boy, you listen to some of these fellas long enough and it starts to make sense."

"That's just stupid."

"Amen to that. Here we are. Start here. This is Main and Elm where his car turned down the street. That's the building over there."

Hank handed over a ten. "The school building?"

"Texas School Book Depository. Now, as you can see above the doorway, it's the Dallas County Records Building. They was gonna tear it down..."

"But the investigators' trade was too good?"

"Something like that. Have a good day," he said handing the change back over the seat to Hank, who peeled off a five. "Thanks. This is for you."

It was a beautiful day, hot, so he removed his sports jacket and slung it over his shoulder. There are two places, maybe three in the world where a first-time tourist will look up. The Empire State Building, and up to the 6th floor of the orange brick building in front of him. The 6th-floor window to be exact, where Oswald fired from. Then, like everybody else, a slow pan to the street where the limo was.

He walked toward that spot a little further down the street. There were many people in this one area. Some were taking pictures, some were pointing and explaining things – 30 years later!

There were many street vendors on the sidewalk, their tables and umbrellas dotting the sidewalk down the plaza. He quickly surmised that they were all selling Kennedy assassination souvenirs. Or so he thought. The one nearest him had an easel with pictures taped to a large cardboard. Atop the cardboard, in big letters, it said, "MAGIC

BULLetSHIT." It made him laugh. He had heard the term, magic bullet, before but never connected it to Kennedy.

The gentleman at the booth was older and had one gold tooth. His black wrinkled skin, grey mustache, round clear glasses, and bent-over physicality were even more interesting than his expletive-infused sign. He was just the kind of man whose warm smile and welcoming eyes just poked at you to say, "Hi."

"How you doing, young fella?" He said to Hank in response.

"Fine, sir. That's quite a sign!"

"It's the truth."

"How so?"

"I was there. I was an x-ray technician at Parkland 'fore I retired."

"Parkland?"

"Parkland Memorial Hospital. Where they brought JFK after he was shot right there." The man jutted his chin towards the street behind Hank.

Hank turned and saw it for the first time. An eerie chill snapped through his body. It was suddenly a surreal moment. In front of him, in the middle lane of the street, somebody had painted an X. He lingered on the simple mark for a few seconds as cars passed over it. A chill that went through his body at the realization of how history was changed right there - on that spot.

"We got all four victims." The man continued.

That snapped Hank out of it and turned back to the man. "Four?"

"Kennedy, Connelly, Oswald, and Ruby. They got a plaque there till this day."

"Wow, what are the odds...but how does that relate to a bullet?"

He threw his thumb over his shoulder, toward his sign. "They say that bullet was found in my trauma room."

"And you say it wasn't?"

"I was just getting back from lunch when the limo screeched to a stop right in front of me in the ER entrance. Sirens and lots of yelling. So anyway, now I am right by the convertible, it pulled up right next to me. And I see Mrs. Kennedy, and she got the president in her lap.

Two men in suits, I found out later they were Secret Service men, well, they were trying to get her to let go of him. But she wouldn't. She said something like, 'I don't want them to see him like this.' So, one of the fellas. He takes off his suit coat and covers the president's head, and she lets go. The orderlies lift him up onto the gurney and rush him into Trauma 1. That was my room. Then this other Agent guy, he looks down at the back seat, he picks up the lady's hat, her bag, and a cigarette lighter. It was covered in blood, I remember. Anyway, as he turns something catches his eye. Then I seen it, too. Two pieces of metal. Little things laying right there, all shiny, like this..." The old guy lifted his lip and tapped his gold tooth which glinted in the Dallas mid-day sun. He continued, "Then he sees it..." The man then paused... deliberately.

"Saw what?" Hank obliged.

"There, on the rear deck of the limo, you know where the top would meet the trunk, if there were a top on it that day, was a whole bullet. The whole thing - right there, laying there. Like the day it was made. Not deformed or smashed like the two fragments on the seat, but almost brand spanking new looking, only without the shell casing."

Then the old fella pointed at his handmade sign. On it was an official picture of the bullet that he just described. His finger jabbed at it. "Warren Commission Exhibit Number 399. That's the bullet I saw, only it wasn't in the governor's leg like they said it was. It was right there in the back of the car."

"So, didn't they know that?"

"Ahhh, see, that's why this whole thing is bullshit. That agent, he pockets the bullet. I didn't think much of it at the time. Figured he was like a cop and he knew what he was doing. I followed him into T1. It was already packed with agents and cops and doctors. Ronnie, the lead doc, he was ordering a tracheotomy. Mrs. Kennedy, she was just standing there all covered in blood on her pretty pink suit. She handed him a piece of the president's head, I think she said something like, "Would this help?" That just floored me. I had to turn away, so I helped with the trauma team. My buddy, Wes, was already popping exposures, so I just helped reload the plates. Not more than a minute later, I see the bullet laying there on the stretcher. The agent left it there."

Hank was having a little difficulty following where this was going. "So that was the magical bullet?"

"So they say."

"Who says?"

"The Warren Commission. They say that bullet that I saw in the back of the limo...seen with my own eyes, that that bullet was responsible for first entering Kennedy in his back," he reached around tap his back then reversed and poked his chest, "Then came out his chest and went into the Governor's back." He reached behind him again. "...and out of the Governor's chest and then into and through his wrist and wound up lodging itself in his thigh."

Hank smiled as he watched the man going through the machinations of the bullet's magical trajectory. It turned the septuagenarian into the image of a man swatting away a swarm of bees, ending with his hand on his thigh.

"So, you are saying all that didn't happen?" Hank asked.

"No, I looked into Trauma 2. The Governor was shot and in a bad way. No, he got shot alright, just not the way the Warrens say. Not with the bullet that never got into the car, that stayed in the back, and never went through anybody."

"So, who shot the Governor?"

The former radiologist turned conspiracy advocate just shrugged his shoulders. "Who knows, but Oswald's three shots are all present and accounted for."

"How so?"

The man tapped the top of the pile of his wares on the table. "It's all in my book." The ex-x-ray tech said. "It blows the lid off of Arlen Specter's Magic Bullet theory."

"How does it do that?"

"You gonna buy the book?"

"Convince me. What was so magic about it?"

The man sighed and Hank saw him check his surroundings. Hank assumed since there weren't any customers around his table at the moment, the old guy decided to humor him a little longer.

"Cause if you believe the Warren Commission. One bullet made those 7 wounds and a right turn."

"That sounds more like the bullshit part," Hank said.

"Exactly, my friend. You see if you hold to the three-shot theory, you run into a problem real fast." He held up three fingers. "Three shots, right? He peeled back each one as he made his points.

"First shot, misses, goes right over the limo altogether, hits the curb down by the overpass, and wounds a bystander, James Tague, a car salesman. He was standing down there by the triple underpass, he was." He pointed down the street at a railroad bridge that spanned three lanes of traffic. A train was rumbling across it.

He bent his ring finger down and was now holding up two fingers. "That leaves two. We know the last one was the headshot... from the Zapruder film. You've seen that right?"

He bent down his index finger for that third bullet, leaving his middle finger. "That leaves just one more that, like I said, supposed to have gone through the president's neck, then the Governor's back then out the front through his wrist and lodged in his thigh. One bullet!" He emphasized the one in the manner of flipping the bird. "The magic bullet."

"I see what you are saying. So, what do you think that means?"

"It's all in the book." The man held up his book. It was a copy shop kind of deal. The cover said, "The Magic Bullet," and right under it were the words, "An X-ray technician sees right through it."

"Five dollars!"

Hank smiled. The show he just witnessed was worth that much, and he liked this old guy. He had spunk. He found himself doing the reach and peeling off five singles. "Here ya go."

"Thanks," the man said as he tapped the book now in Hank's hand. "You'll see, it's all in there. Including that he was dead before he was brought in. But we tried anyway. Had lots of government types telling us what to do and how to do it. You'll see."

"Will do," Hank said as he shook the man's hand and turned to walk away. He folded the 20-page booklet, slid it into his back pocket, and turned only to be right in front of the X again.

Being surrounded by all this Kennedy mania, he couldn't help dwelling on what he had learned in school. Kennedy was a great man. He was the future of America. He was elected at like 43 years old. That was young, as presidents go. He started the whole moon-shot thing. The Peace Corps. They even did a movie about him when he was in the Navy and almost got killed in World War II. Then they killed his brother, too. Hank had to stop himself, they?

He understood how unimaginable things like this seem too big, too important, to be the actions of one single person. Maybe it was in our nature to believe the world, or people in it, conspired to do unthinkable things, rather than admit it could be any one of us or happen to every one of us. He guessed that some people found comfort in that. Explaining the unthinkable away as a grand plot, rather than a random uncontrollable event. Random was scary. Even the most despicable, dastardly evil event, if done by forethought and some motive, was easier to get your arms around, rather than admitting it was some random confluence of events or a lone nut.

As Hank stared at the X on the pavement, he thought of one of his philosophies about life, whenever someone hears about the death of someone they know, eventually they will ask, "How?" He always felt that question was part actual concern and part a check against one's own mortality. If the answer to "how?" was, "smoked three packs a day," they immediately had a way to gauge their own mortality. They excluded themselves with the rationale, "Great, I don't smoke," or at least, "phew. I only smoke one pack a day." But if they also smoke three-pack-a-day, they will dig deeper for a distinction: "For how long?" Especially if they feel they went to three packs fairly recently. Finally, after they have exhausted all the self-exclusionary excuses, they land on genetics, "Did cancer run in the family?".

He found it was the same, whether it was a heart attack, a car accident, or even a murder. Dig down deep enough and you could rationalize an exclusion of yourself. However, one cause of death that no one could exclude themselves from was random. A safe falling on your head, a truck crashing into your bedroom, or a crazed person with a gun just out to kill anyone. You can't separate, compartmentalize or live comfortably in a cocoon of 'that was them, not me,' because we are all, first and foremost, "random beings." To his way of thinking, burying these fears was how most humans dealt with the specter of death.

A World War II veteran in the barbershop where many of young Hank's philosophies of life were spawned, called it "whistling past the graveyard."

Standing at the curb on Elm Street, Hank had no idea he was standing exactly where Cyrus Shaw stood all those years before.

He continued on down the "flea market of the absurd," as he started to think of it. There was a loud discussion going on at the next booth. The man behind that table was arguing with a guy in a black shirt.

"No, he was a Count first, then the OSS," the seller said.

"Well, in any event, he's the one that got Oswald the job," black shirt said.

"Look, I can't spend all this time with you. Are you going to buy my book or not?"

That's when Hank noticed he had handmade booklets piled on a chair next to him.

He walked over to the table and asked, "What's the book about?"

"About 10 dollars." The black shirt scoffed and walked off.

"Cheap ass." The old man said under his breath.

Hank laughed. The guy in the black shirt came back over. "I am not cheap. That's half the story."

"So, the whole story is 20 bucks?" Hank said.

"No. I mean, we know all about Oswald and there's just as much evidence to support his claim that he was a patsy than there is proving he was the lone shooter."

Hank was starting to get into this so he bit. "So, who was the other shooter?"

"Or shooters." The Black shirt injected.

"And you know?"

"The three tramps!"

Hank laughed because he thought this guy was invoking a fairy tale, like the three bears, or the three little pigs, to belittle the huckster's theory. It made him think, what a bunch of whack jobs were drawn to this place. But then the smile was wiped from his face when the black shirt took umbrage.

"No. That's not a joke. That's what Warrens called them; but in reality, they were three hitmen from the Corsican Mafia. They were brought over on one of Onassis' ships."

Hank had heard enough, especially when this guy started invoking a different fairytale. "That's interesting, but I got to go."

"Okay. But the truth has been buried for too long. Have a nice day." And the black shirt was off, probably to find a more sympathetic ear.

He took one more look around and then decided to get out of there and walk around town a little.

It was after 5 when he got back to his hotel. His feet were complaining, and he looked forward to soaking them in a warm tub.

"Ouch." The water was a bit too hot. He turned on the cold for a few seconds. "Ahhh." While he sat on the chair that he placed by the edge of the tub, he grabbed the booklet. He read how the supposed magic bullet was found in near-perfect condition lying on a stretcher in Parkland Hospital, where both the president and the governor were taken after the shooting. Yet, no one could verify that the stretcher was ever used to transport either man, as there was no blood on the sheets. The book further stated that a CIA agent placed the bullet on the stretcher, ostensibly to confirm it was a 6.5 x 52mm bullet that matched the rifle that they claimed Oswald used. This was done to discredit earlier reports that had the police on the scene identifying the rifle in the assassin's nest as a Mauser, which used 8mm ammunition.

Hank had had enough. He put the book down. How could anyone know what was true or made up? Only a handful of people were actually there, and probably no two of them would tell you the same story afterward. You could fabricate many kinds of stories, causes, or effects over the simplest event. This was the narcotic of conspiracy theories.

This was what his brother was hooked on. All this conspiracy stuff. He ate the shit up. He would spend money he didn't have to travel to some godforsaken place to see a metal bar someone said was from a flying saucer, or once to Peru to go to some plain where supposedly ancient aliens drew huge figures with lines in the dirt, presumably by drawing with a big stick attached to their saucers and doing it free hand or something ridiculous like that.

He was about to feel guilty; he knew it. He was going down a road he traveled many times since his brother's death. He still really wasn't sure if his addiction to whacko theories was what got him killed.

Hank realized that his brother had lived in his shadow all his life. Growing up, Ben was always a tag along on Hank's ticket. He never had a chance to be "the guy." Maybe that's what sent him into alternate realities. The fact that his actual reality was that of second fiddle to a smug and self-confident older brother. Hank wished he could hug him, tell him he mattered, that he, in many ways was Hank's hero. Smart, sensitive, and caring about others. Many of the girls that Hank knew from the neighborhood would tell him that Ben had something about him that was endearing. "Sweet," was the word that they often came up with. How he would have loved to be here in Dallas today. All the nuts, crazies, and pseudo experts for him to commune with and find nirvana.

38 | 20A & 20B

Hank was able to nab a courtesy seat back to LaGuardia on an early flight. He threw his bag in the overhead, sat down, clicked the seat belt, and looked in the seat pocket. It held the same mag he read on the way down. He sat back and looked to his right. Ugh. It was the guy in the black shirt from yesterday, still in the black shirt!

He tried to get small. He scored the seat because it was the last one, so there was nowhere else for him to sit.

"Hey there," came from his row mate.

Aw, nuts. He turned to the guy, "Hi."

"Heading to New York?"

"That's what the sign said."

"I'm going to a convention."

Hank could only imagine the kind of looney toons confab this wingding was attending.

"I hope there are no delays, registration is at 2 p.m. The Waldorf is very busy, probably take an hour on line," black shirt said.

Hank couldn't believe what black shirt said: "The Waldorf? As in the Waldorf Astoria?"

"Yes. It's our 20th annual convention."

Twenty years of insanity. "Really? Twenty years?"

"Goes fast. But it's good to reconnect with the men."

"Men?"

"USACE. Out of Guam."

Hank's face read like a computer trying to figure out a problem.

Black shirt filled in the blanks. "Sorry, US Army Core of Engineers. Kyle Mann." He extended his hand.

"Hank Larson." He shook it. "You know, I had you confused with somebody else."

"Really? You live in Dallas?" Kyle asked.

"No, New York, but there was this guy yesterday, same shirt, same build. Only he was..."

"Wait, that was me. Dealey Plaza. I knew you looked familiar."

The words, 'a nut' remained on deck in Hank's brain, glad he never called them to the plate.

"What do you do, Hank?"

"I'm a pilot for Flying Tigers."

"My unit supervised the building of the airfields your name sakes flew out of China from back in 38 and 39."

"They were some real cowboys in that command," Hank said.

"All volunteers, if I remember correctly."

"In the beginning. Hey, can I ask you something?"

"Sure."

Hank turned to look him in the eye, "Do you sincerely buy into all that Kennedy stuff?"

"Good question. I don't know if it's a passion or a hobby, but there's just so much there. I mean, every time you turn over one rock, there's a hundred more. Tell me, do you believe the official account?"

"Do I believe it? Why wouldn't I? It's the official finding. It seems plausible, I guess."

"Ya see, and to me, it's anything but plausible," Kyle said.

"How so?" Hank didn't know if he just poked a hornet's nest, but he seemed like a good guy, and there were almost three hours to fill.

"Take for example what I was trying to tell that guy yesterday..."

"About some count, right?"

"Count George de Mohrenschildt. He was a double agent in World War II. Played both the Germans and the Allies. And they both knew it, but he was such a charmer they let him go back and forth, each believing they'd get more valuable intelligence and transmit more false information than the enemy. After the war, he went with the winners and became part of the OSS, which became the CIA. His cover was as a geologist in the oil business. He was also the toast of the town in New York. All the parties all the events. He was on what they call the 'a-list.'" He affected an erudite accent and became one of "those you must simply have at your soiree."

"I believe they called them, 'bon vivants,'" Hank said.

"Exactly! Then you know the type. Anyway, so he meets this high society dame. I mean, he falls head over heels for her, but she won't give him the time of day. But old Georgie, he ain't giving up. He woos her at every turn. He even travels out to the ass end of Long Island to see her, but she gives him the cold shoulder. But he keeps coming back, literally standing in her front yard. Meantime, her little girl befriends this guy. He plays with her and her toys and dollies. Right there in the yard. She's a little doll. Soon, he's shlepping all the way out there as much to see the kid, as the mom. The kid starts calling him, 'Uncle Georgie,' and that becomes a lifelong relationship. Her and her 'Uncle Georgie'--an 'Uncle' who would do anything for her."

"And this has to do with the Kennedy assassination, how?"

"Hank, this is why there was an assassination."

Hank recoiled a bit. "This oughta be good."

"So, like I said, George's CIA cover was as a geologist for oil companies. You know who got him that cover job?"

"Haven't a clue."

"George Bush. He was one of the architects of the Bay of Pigs. They even named one of the three boats in the invasion, 'Barbara.' Anyway, Bush is Texas oil, and he gets Uncle Georgie, formerly of the OSS, now CIA, the gig. He gets assigned to a Texas firm. But remember he's also a member of the Russian, aristocracy. So, he takes an interest in the Russian Émigré community and dedicates himself to finding homes and jobs for recent émigrés from the Soviet Union. Georgie hated the communists, but even this was a CIA op. He was secretly keeping his eyes out for spies and KGB'ers looking to infiltrate with their families and hardship cases.

"Anyway, he is ordered to help this one special family get a foothold in America. He gets his friend, Ruth Paine, to give them a room in her boarding house in Irving Texas, a bedroom community of Dallas. He also gets the husband a job so they can pay for the room."

Kyle stopped and asked, "You follow me so far?"

"Yeah, pretty much."

"Well, the little girl playing with her toys with Uncle Georgie? She was Blackjack Bouvier's little girl, 'Jaqueline,' named after him. And her Uncle Georgie, he gets Lee Harvey Oswald, recently returned from Russia, the job in the Texas School Book Depository.

"Kyle, is this real?"

"Welcome to the passion, my friend."

"I can see how you could get all caught up in this, shi...stuff."

"Yeah, but to answer your question, everything about the assassination is subject to mis and dis-information, cover-ups as well as ignored evidence and dead witnesses. Hell Johnson created the whole Warren Commission just to whitewash the whole coup d'état. Put a CIA man on it."

"You truly think it was a coup?"

"Follow the money, follow the players, follow the deaths."

The flight attendant came by. "What will you gentlemen be having tonight?"

"Can you make a screwdriver?" Kyle asked.

"I sure can."

"Make that two," Hank said. "So, this is what you were saying yesterday to that guy, that it was Jackie."

"No, because of Jackie. Can you handle a little more? I know it sounds crazy."

"Just a little... but go on."

"Okay so 1958, Mediterranean Ocean. Aristotle Onassis' yacht, the Christina, after his daughter. He is entertaining the young congressman from Massachusetts and his gorgeous wife. The congressman is looking for a donation to his war chest. When Ari gets her alone, he tells her, 'You know he's fucking everything in a skirt, don't you. You deserve better.' And she says, "My being First Lady is better. Ari, I know all about Jack, but he's going to be president and I am going to be right by his side."

"She knew?"

"The Kennedys were the most powerful American family in certain circles."

"So, this is Onassis, the same guy she winds up marrying?"

"Bingo. He loved her forever. He hated that Jack was tomcatting around on her. So did Uncle Georgie, from the CIA."

"You know this is really out there, don't you?"

"Yes, that's why I am going to go real fast over this part: you probably know some of it. Bay of Pigs, the CIA war, Kennedy doesn't play ball, denies air support, and a thousand Cuban expatriates that they trained to go back and fight Castro, get annihilated on the beach instead," he holds up his pointer finger. "That's one."

"His father makes a deal with the teamsters to get his son elected president, but two, his brother Robert crucifies them and the mob on TV hearings. The mob was funding, off the books, the CIA's Bay of Pigs because Kennedy stopped the flow of dough, and they were losing millions when Castro kicked their casinos out."

"And three, Kennedy was for killing the oil depletion allowance. But the number one, granddaddy of all reasons for killing him was that he was going to pull the troops out of Vietnam. So, taking him out became a kind of take-a-number and stand-in-line deal."

"Never realized he was so despised," Hank remarked.

"Throw in that he had a hired negro secretary in the 'All White' House and you can add the southern democrats and their Ku Klux Klan boys into the mix."

Hank scratched his head. "So, now I am a little lost."

"Happy Birthday, Mr. President. Do you remember when Marylyn Monroe sang that to him at Madison Square Garden?"

"I remember the dress."

"Yeah, she was something else. Anyway, that was the last straw for Uncle Georgie and Ari. Georgie puts Oswald in the building as a patsy. Meanwhile, hitmen from the Corsican Mafia come over on one of Onassis's ships, and a creep named David Ferrie flies them into Dallas from Mexico. The Warrens called them the three tramps. They set up a kill zone, a triangulated field of fire."

"Okay, so now you just made a left and are heading off a cliff."

"I know, but Oswald is documented as being in the 2nd-floor lunchroom at exactly 12:15 p.m."

"Okay, but in what I read last night, Kennedy was shot at 12:30."

"True, but that's only because Kennedy stopped the motorcade to chat with some party apparatchiks. He was scheduled by the Secret Service and the DPD to pass by the building no later than 12:15."

"Yeah..."

"So, if Oswald was out to kill the president, he had to be ready to shoot him at 12:15."

"...and at that time, he's in the lunchroom," Hank concludes.

"Exactly! How would he know they were running late? And before you ask, there was no radio in the room, and nowhere did they find a transistor."

"Two minutes after the shooting, a cop found him in the same lunchroom."

"Wow. Kyle this is a lot to digest. But what are you saying? Was it the CIA, Uncle Georgie, or the mob?"

"Perfect storm, Hank. Georgie supplied the CIA's cover story with Oswald. Onassis supplied the muscle. The mob supplied Jack Ruby to tie up the loose end. In the end, Ari gets the girl; the military-industrial establishment gets their war; Johnson and the Texas oil guys get the presidency..."

"And America gets screwed," Hank said.

Kyle tapped his glass. "Ready for another?"

"Sure."

"You know what Ruby said was the reason he killed Oswald?"

"No."

"He said he did it for Jackie, to save her from reliving it in a trial!"

"Wow."

Having OD'd on conspiracy theories, Hank got up and hit the head. It was good to stretch. As he walked down the aisle, he considered asking Kyle about what his brother might be after. He decided to do it, even at the risk of going another 10 rounds in the ring with Kyle. He thought he'd keep it to a low roar by just nibbling around the edges.

When he returned to his seat, there was another drink sitting on the tray. "What are you doing to me pal, I've had two already and I got to find my way home," Hank said.

"You're a pilot, navigate!"

"Hey, let me ask you something: what would you consider an artifact of the assassination? What could something like that be?"

"Ahhh, it could be anything. Well, there's all the stuff in the national archives: the gun, the bullets, not his brain though, that got lost, believe it or not. Hell, they even cut out a piece of the curb where the first bullet took out a chunk of concrete."

"James Teague."

"Whoa. Look at you."

"Nah, I read it last night. But okay, that's the stuff the government has. What might they not have that could be an artifact?"

"Gee, by now, almost everything has turned up. I mean, maybe stuff like a shell casing, or the foil or wrapper of the fried chicken or sandwich that they say Oswald ate in the sniper's perch. I know a guy who paid $20,000 for the Fender Flags from the Lincoln Continental that Kennedy was shot in. For a while, there was a rumor that the first draft of the speech he was on his way to deliver at the Trademart was found. Supposedly it was him announcing the pullout of all troops from Southeast Asia by 1964 and a new diplomatic relationship with the USSR after the Cuban Missile Crisis."

"What happened with that?"

"Never surfaced. Now, the question is, was it bullshit from jump street, or did some nefarious group come out of the shadows and gobble the speech up and replace it with the benign document that's now in the archives. You just don't know. Why are you asking about artifacts?"

"My brother, he's into all this stuff. He was supposed to buy something referred to as an artifact from the assassination."

"Really? So, did he?"

"I don't know. He died a few weeks ago."

"Sorry, man. How did he die?"

"Fire in his apartment."

"Eeesh, not a nice way to go!"

"So…, the speech. You think that's the kind of thing they may be talking about?"

"That, or unless you got another Zapruder film?"

They didn't speak for the rest of the flight, as Kyle took out some papers for his convention. It looked like he was prepping for a speech.

As the plane was landing, Kyle leaned over. "I don't mean to be indelicate, and please don't take offense, but did your brother die before or after he bought the artifact?"

Hank got a cold chill. "After, I think."

"And since you don't know what it was, it's possible someone took it?"

"And killed my brother for it? Is that what you are asking?"

"Look, I don't know, but there was a reason we wound up in the same row. Here's my card. Let me know if you need anything or any way that I can help you."

"Thanks, Kyle. I'll be in touch."

"Hopefully my luggage is here to meet me. They lost it when I flew to Dallas. See ya."

Hank smiled; it explained the black shirt.

39 | PREACHING TO THE CHOIR

Peter Salvo's presentation was a multimedia event. He used slides, audio tape, and a 16 mm projector. The film that he would show at the end was the convincer. Tonight, Peter was getting five-hundred dollars for a one-hour speech to share what he found out about Jack Ruby, the man who shot, some say silenced, Lee Harvey Oswald.

Everyone in the audience at the Uptown Y, was to a person, a devotee of the alternate theories of what happened, why it happened, and who made it happen in Dallas that day. The place was packed. Outside crazies were hocking everything from little jars of dirt from Area 51 to 'documented proof' that the moon landing was faked. Of course, this rankled Peter. It cheapened his true academic and serious investigative achievements. It was the reason the media always relegated him to the fringe, but $500 bucks was $500 bucks!

He had given this talk before. It was a smooth, comprehensive dissertation on the fact that Jack Ruby was a mobster with ties to the Dallas Police Department and was working for the CIA's partners in the assassination, the mob. He knew all the "Oooo and Ahhh" points, as he thought of them. Those moments when his proof made the audience gasp or at least murmur. He learned to allow time for that to sink in, so to speak, which made his pacing as he delivered the truth a model of showmanship.

The big finish was a 16 mm film copy of a Kinescope film recording of the live broadcast on the night of the assassination. Filming a TV set was a popular way of preserving what, later, the video tape would be exclusively used for. He paid $200 to the TVC Film Lab on west 43rd Street in Manhattan to make the copy. A true believer who worked at CBS liberated their copy for a day so he could have it duplicated. It was worth the money because this was the first time the Dallas District Attorney, Dade, confirmed they had 'one, Lee Harvey Oswald' in custody. That film clip would be his "big finish."

The talk was going well. Peter's 'moments' happened right on cue. In order to leave ten minutes for Q&A, he cut the second to last item and jumped right into the big close. "Finally, today, I like to leave you with, what for me is the primer facia evidence that Jack Ruby was not a random chit in the assassination game. That he wasn't just some unknown guy who somehow got into police headquarters to shoot Oswald. And with this final piece of evidence, we know the truth about who Ruby was and how he planned the assassination of the assassin." He rolled the projector that was on a stand pointing up at a screen set higher. It made the images trapezoid, like a keystone atop an arch, but it got the point across.

In the clip, filmed late the evening of the assassination, after the D.A. identified Oswald, a reporter asked if he had any known ties to any radical organizations. The D.A. fumbled for the answer. "Yes, he is a member of the Cuban Fair or Fairness for Cuba, committee." Somebody's voice was heard correcting him, "Fair Play for Cuba Committee!"

The D.A. looked up as the camera panned right to the man who spoke. It was Jack Ruby. The D.A. then said, "Thanks, Jack. Yes, the Fair Play for Cuba Committee."

Peter stopped the projector, "Thanks, Jack?" He paused for effect. "Remember what we covered in my opening, that the Warren Commission stated Ruby had no connection with the Dallas P.D.?

Remember how the official word was Jack Ruby snuck in somehow to the basement the day he killed Oswald? Poppycock! Jack was a regular at the old Police headquarters, and everybody knew him. So, I ask you, did Ruby shoot Oswald to silence him, or was he just an emotionally disturbed person, bereft of the fact that Kennedy was killed, and took matters into his own hands? He switched on the projector again. He had spliced in this next piece. "Oswald, you son-of-a-bitch, Bang!" Followed by a grunt, then pandemonium as they subdued Ruby.

A round of applause followed. The stage lights, which were dimmed during the presentation, came up, and the moderator and Peter sat in two chairs to the left of the screen, each picking up a microphone.

The moderator started the Q&A session.

Outside the Y, Peter was hailing a cab. A man approached. "Mr. Salvo?"

Peter turned to him.

"I was in Dealey Plaza."

Peter attempted to blow him off, "Well then, you were there for history." He turned his attention back to the street with his arm raised.

The man persisted. "I use to work for the CIA."

Peter lowered his arm and turned back to the stranger. "Nobody used to work for the CIA." Peter started to step backward.

A van pulled up behind him, the side door slid open, and the man pushed Peter backward into the van and climbed in. The door slammed shut.

A few people on the street witnessed the grab. One ran into the Y to call the cops.

40 | DISCRETION

Hank came through the apartment door and headed straight for the couch. He laid down and closed his eyes. It had been a long day. The phone rang ten seconds later.

"Yell-ow."

"Mr. Larson?

"Yes, I'm Hank Larson. Is that you, Doctor Jefferies?"

"It seems the dental records finally came up with a match. The corpse was I.D.'d as Burt Dreesan, a former special forces operative and security expert."

Hank hears a dog bark and the sound of kids loudly coming through the room the coroner was in.

"Are you calling me from home?"

"I'm calling from my home because as soon as the ID was made, official traffic started getting intense."

"Sure, special forces, tough customers!"

"Tomorrow, my boss and some bigwigs are launching a discrete investigation. Since many people have seen you come and go, I might have to tell them about you."

"Would you also mention the money I gave you for the information?"

"I was hoping..."

"Doctor, if my name never comes up, then nobody will call me..."

"A mutual protection of sorts."

"Exactly. Then we have an agreement? Fine. Good night."

"Hank hung up the phone. He took the locker book out of his flight bag. He thumbed through it. He shook his head in disbelief and tossed the book on the nightstand. The clock radio next to it read 9:40 P.M. Noticing the time, he got up, removed his shirt, and headed for the shower.

With the shower running, he didn't hear the doorbell on the first ring. He shut off the water and was smoothing back his hair when he heard the second ring. He opened the shower door and reached unsuccessfully for a towel. There was none on the hook. He stepped out, dripping. The doorbell rang again. He looked on the shelf, no more towels. Doorbell.

"Shit." He calls out. "Just a minute."

Still dripping wet, he walked into the room. He yanked the tablecloth off the dining room table, wrapped it around himself, and opened the door. Chris stood there her smile growing. They spoke on top of one another.

"I'm running late."

"I'm running early."

They laughed.

"Well, you didn't have to get all dressed up just for little ol' me," she said.

He looked down, "This old thing?"

She made a gesture that said, 'Well, are you going to let me in?'

He swept his arm in a grand entrance manner, and she entered.

"So? All day long, I couldn't stop thinking about what was in that locker... Tell me."

Now it was Hank's turn to hold up his hand in a halting gesture. He walked into his bedroom. Chris used the moment to check out his apartment. A few model planes on pedestals: B-2, B-52, 747, and 727. A picture of him and Benny at a ball game.

She called out, "No pictures of women?"

"I put them all in the drawer because you were coming."

"Is this... was this your brother?"

Hank entered wearing a robe.

"When you look up Yankee fan in the encyclopedia, it says see Larson, Benjamin. I took him to his first game."

She looked around, "Well this is a nice place you got here."

"Thanks. Here's what was behind door number 1."

He handed her the book. She was confused.

"I don't get it!"

He flopped into a chair in front of her. She handed him back the book.

"It's easy. I failed."

He flung the book all the way back into his bedroom. "I went through all this on a hunch, just so I could play detective. What a jerk!"

She began to rub his shoulders.

"Failing while trying to do something noble is a very attractive personality trait."

"I just couldn't accept the fact that Ben could've... I mean maybe there was so much that I didn't know about him... What happens to people?"

"Hey, you were just trying to do the right thing."

His hand found hers.

He sighs, "I'd better get dressed for dinner."

"I had a big breakfast today, I'm not very hungry."

He slowly put it together, "So... I... shouldn't... get dressed?

She slid her hand down his robe and across his chest winding up inside the robe. She followed her hand with her body and snaked around him coming to rest in his lap without breaking the kiss. He gathered her up in his arms and took her into the bedroom.

There was a shaft of light from a streetlight cutting through the curtains and it spanned across the bedroom ceiling. Chris' head was in the middle of the bed circa Hank's crotch, her right arm wrapped around him. "Oh brother, did I need this!"

"You really are incredible."

"It takes two, my dear." Two kiss sounds fill the room. "

She pops up her head. "You know what I was thinking about?"

"What?"

"Ice cream."

"Macadamia Crunch or Rocky Road?"

"Surprise me..., again."

Hank rolled out and was off to the kitchen. Chris wiggled up to sit with her back against the headboard. She shifted uncomfortably. She reached under herself and pulled out the book which was under her. She thumbed through it again. Hank returned and she put it on the nightstand. He had a tray with two pints of ice cream and two glasses of champagne.

"Here, take the glasses and put them over there."

Chris took the two glasses as Hank sat on the bed. As Chris put the glasses on the nightstand, she did a double take at the book. There was a slight separation between the pages. A line.

Hank served the ice cream. "It's okay to have this because we just burnt up a million and a half calories."

She didn't respond. She was reaching for the book. He watched as she opened it again, but this time, she felt one page between her fingers. She then tore the very edge of the page and revealed that it was actually two pages scotch taped together. She opened them. Hank reached in and pulled out the Polaroid. A sharp black and white photo of a badly composed shot of President Kennedy - in that he was out of focus in the lower left-hand side of the picture. At first, they just see Kennedy in the car. Upon a second look however, in the center of the image, clearly focused, was a man in a policeman's uniform, standing behind a fence, pointing a rifle right at the camera. A muzzle flash was clearly visible.

"No wonder they kill everyone who's touched this."

"This is creepy." Then she noticed the rifleman. "Oh! Dear God!"

"So, that's why the coroner was freaking out."

"The who?"

"Doctor Jefferies, the Phoenix coroner. That G.I. Joe with the silver Haliburton you helped me trace, turned out to be a flambéed ex-special forces alumnus. "

"Can I pick 'em out or what?... You think your brother was involved in this?"

"No, my brother wrote articles like, "Elvis Was an Alien Spy," and stuff like that." He looked at the Polaroid again, this was going to be his biggest story - maybe even a book - but this, it's bigger than that, this changes history."

"What are you going to do now?"

"In the morning, I'll call Peter Salvo and find out who killed my brother."

As early morning light was cascading through the curtains, Chris was snuggled under Hank's arm fast asleep. He was wide awake. He bolted up from bed in a cold sweat and turned on the light. Chris was startled.

"What?"

"I signed for the stuff in the locker!"

He grabbed for his pants and found the property retrieval slip. He dialed the number. It rang and rang. He looked at the clock radio. It would be 6 a.m. there.

"C'mon, c'mon... I don't believe I signed this thing. I left a direct trail right to me…, to us."

He hung up and dialed the number again. Chris stirred and propped up on her elbow, waiting by his side as she stroked his arm.

"Dallas airport security, please hold..."

Hank waited for what seemed like an eternity. The Guard picked up.

"Thanks for holding, can I help you."

"Yes, my name is Hank Larson."

The office the Guard was standing in was in shambles. "Yes Mr. Larson, can I call you back?-- things are a little crazy here this morning."

"Look, I just need to know if anyone came by to ask about my brother's locker yesterday.

"I have no idea, and right now there's no way for me to look that up because someone broke into our offices last night and made a mess of our files."

Hank hung up fast. "C'mon Chris, we've got to get out of here."

Hank grabbed his go bag and started putting his clothes on. Chris threw everything on and grabbed her flight bag. He reached into his wallet and took a slip of paper and dialed the number.

"Peter. It's Hank Larson. I got it. The thing Ben was after. When you get this message, call me back...no, on second thought, meet me at the coffee shop across from my house in two hours. The lasers are starting to point this way."

Hank took Chris into the basement, and they came out of the building from the service entrance and carefully slid out the side gate.

They went to the payphone on the corner. Hank pumped in a quarter and dialed.

"Miller..."

"Brian, it's me, Hank."

"Hey, we miss ya' here, Hank. Need my old squadron commander back."

"Big favor time, Brian."

"Whatever you need, buddy."

"If anyone calls or comes looking for me, I need you to stonewall. I mean completely."

"I'll just tell whoever the hell asks that you went hunting."

"Only now, I've become the hunted. Thanks, Bri."

He hung up the phone and turned to Chris. "How long before you're due in pre-flight?"

"Got a check-in at 6:30, then I'm out of town for 4 days."

"Good, it would be best if you stayed out of New York and away from me until this thing is over." He looked into her eyes and was about to say something, but changed his attitude back to business. After he explained his plan, he asked. "So... we'll meet back here at 11:30? Will that be enough time?"

"I think so. It's not complicated."

They kissed. Chris touched his cheek, looking at him for a long moment, then walked off.

"And the Bosco...Got it!"

"Police are speculating that last night's abduction could be a publicity stunt because neither Mr. Salvo's agent, publisher, or his manager have received any ransom demands," the reporter said into the camera as he stood on the street outside the Y. In his ear was an earpiece that had IFB and mix-minus, which allowed him to hear the control room tell him when he was on and when to wrap it up, as well as what the anchor in the studio was saying. The producer called it "jib-jab" when the reporter and the anchor talked casually, either before or after the report. The reporter doubted "jib jab" was the correct word, but the man was from the south, so...

"So, Stu, let me get this straight," the voice of the anchor came back over earphones during the jib-jab outro. "We now have a possible conspiracy about the alleged abduction of a conspiracy theorist?"

"Sometimes, Dan, you just can't make this stuff up." Stu said with a smile, "From 92nd street on the east side, this is Stu Simons. Back to you in the studio." He waited for his cameraman to give him the clear sign. Over his headphone, he heard the producer say, "Great job, Stu." The anchor intro'd the next story, "The mayor has been battling the head of the city council..."

He removed the earpiece and handed the mic to the cameraman. "Get some B-roll for the 11 o'clock package." His live report would be edited to be self-contained. The Jib Jab at the end would be cut off, but his signoff would remain. Shots of the outside of the Y and the poster in the lobby touting the talk would be used to cover cuts in his report to shorten it.

Chris was hard at work in the closet darkroom. Being based in Dallas, she would stay at her brother's whenever she was on a New York layover. Her brother had turned one of his two walk-in closets in this prewar building into a darkroom. Mikey was the person who taught her photography growing up. He was now a stringer for various wire services and was out on assignment more than in town. Sometimes, they'd even both be in the apartment at the same time. As long as she replaced any chemicals and papers she used, Mikey had no problem with his baby sister using his stuff.

She had her Nikon F2AS 35mm camera loaded with Kodak Pan-X film on a tripod, aimed at the Polaroid on a black card against the wall. Two photo lights on either side illuminated the picture.

Using the close-up lens, she was able to fill the frame, which insured the most detail that could be derived from her copy of the "camera original print" polaroid. She got a chill looking through the viewfinder. It was almost as if she were in Dealey Plaza at the moment the president was shot. She bracketed her exposure, taking 5 shots in all. She rewound the film, then shut off all the lights and turned on the safety light. Only then did she remove the film canister from the camera. She loaded the film into the developer tank. Once it was safely in the sealed tank with the developer, she turned on the room light, took down the photo lights, stowed the tripod, and gingerly placed the original back into a dark sleeve that she bought at Peerless Photo, along with a new quart of developer and a bottle of Stop.

A punch rocked Peter's bloody face. He spit blood. Croft adjusted the brass knuckles over his fist. The burly ex-special forces grunt righted Peter's head and wailed off on him again. "Do you have it?"

"I don't know what you are talking about," he screamed through guttural moans, his eye swelling.

Fallow was going through Peter's bag. He found something and held it up to Croft.

"What's your phone number?"

"Wha..."

Croft pulled Peter's head back. "Your phone number, you puke!"

The encrypted satellite telephone suitcase was in the other room with Belson. The 30-pound military unit had a whip antenna and ran off batteries. There was no phone service in the abandoned building in which they had sequestered. Once they dialed the number, they held Peter's remote message beeper to the mouthpiece and pressed the button. The warbly tone cut off the outgoing message. "You reached Peter Salvo. I can't..." There was a beep, then rewinding. The first message played, "This is Madison Cleaners, Mr. Salvo, your dry cleaning is ready for pickup." Then another beep. "Peter. It's Hank Larson. I got it." Croft looked at Belson, as the message continued. "The thing Ben was after. When you get this message call my office... no, on second thought, meet me at the coffee shop across from my house in two hours. The lasers are starting to bounce off the glass surfaces." That was the last message.

"Well, it seems the brother has made our work easier. Go to the coffee shop, kill the son of a bitch, and bring back the photo."

Belson then walked to the room across the hall, there bleeding from his lips and nose with his hands tied behind his back, was Peter Salvo.

Belson screwed the silencer into his gun. "Good news, we won't be needing you to talk anymore. The man you were working with has the Polaroid."

Peter's mind raced like a computer. "The Polaroid? Mary Moorman's! The seventh picture? It exists!" Peter started laughing.

Belson was confused. "Why are you laughing? Do you have any idea what's going to happen next?"

Peter wasn't paying attention as he was enraptured by an almost religious revelation. "Sure, don't you?" He spit more blood. "This means it's true. I knew it. You. The picture. It's true! There is a conspiracy. Always was. I knew it! I was right!"

"I'm happy for you... Take it to the grave." With that, Belson pumped a shot into Peter's temple, freezing the smile on Peter's face.

41 | DON'T KILL THE MESSENGER

Waiting for the Admiral to attend, Nelson separated the pages of his report into three piles on the conference table in front of him. It was how he controlled his nervous reaction that came to him whenever he had to deliver bad news to the Admiral. In his mind, he went over how he would make his report. The Admiral had ordered him to ensure there were no loose ends in the Browning death that might blow back at the committee. Under the Admiral's command, the committee had stayed below the radar by insuring 100% containment of every operation and air-tight isolation of any complicity in any course of hard or soft action.

The door to the conference room opened, but only Sorrells came in. "Admiral wants to do this in the den. He's in one of his moods."

Nelson gathered the papers and took a deep breath. "Into the lion's den...," he said as they exited.

The brandy snifter was alongside the Admiral's plush chair with the heat and massage that was his oasis when his back acted up. The low level of booze in the always full decanter told Nelson that the old man may not be too aggressive this afternoon.

Nelson sat across from the Admiral and Sorrells on the couch flanking them. Three other members sat around the den that was decorated as an homage to the hunting lodges back in the good old 1950s, complete with roaring fire, which kept the AC running on high, here in the desert-like climate of Arizona.

Nelson waited for everyone to settle, then started, "Sir, ..."

The Admiral held up his hand while he scanned the room. "Where is Belson?"

A little uncomfortably, Nelson informed him, "Sir, He's finishing up an interrogation up in New York."

The Admiral nodded. "That's right, Yonkers..."

"Yes, sir." He waited for the Admiral to possibly continue, but the Admiral was finished, so he started again. "Upon further digging, some disturbing facts have come to light in the Browning matter. A review of the detective bureau's form five," Nelson held up the facsimile of the NYPD DB-5 form that all detectives use to record the progress of their cases, "...shows they interviewed Henry Larson."

"Him? How does he figure into this?"

"Somehow, and it's not made clear here to a certainty, Larson learned of Thomas Vallee."

The real name of the Chicago Oswald had the Admiral punch down hard on his armrest. "That pain in the ass, Meechum!"

Nelson was impressed with the old man's encyclopedic instant recall. "Apparently, he was living as Dennis Meeks. And..."

The Admiral held up his hand. "And Larson reached out to Browning, Meechum interdicts him, and Meechum takes it from there."

"That's essentially what happened, sir." It wasn't, but Nelson wasn't going to correct the Admiral's errors. The man got the result, and that was all that mattered.

The Admiral leaned in. "All the more reason to rid me of this boil on my ass, Larson. Is there anything in the police report about Browning alerting us to Larson's inquiry?" Secrecy was the key to the committee's longevity. Being mentioned in an official NYPD document would have been a major breach in that wall of security. He'd hate to have to order a raid on the NYPD to contain it.

"That's where we missed an opportunity." Nelson had decided on that language rather than the more descriptive, *'That's where we fucked up.'* "Admiral, Browning's call came into the operations center through the safe number. The duty officer transcribed the name Larson to Lawson. So, we missed it. Or Browning himself may have mistaken the name. We don't record the safe line."

"Who was on the desk?"

"Pratt. A good man, years of a spotless record."

The Admiral waved his hand. "Okay, it was probably Browning's error."

Nelson thought, *"Pratt you just dodged a bullet...literally."*

The Admiral adjusted the way he was sitting with a painful grimace, "So Browning is not connected to us...good. What else did you find?"

"As I mentioned, the DB-5 also referred to one Dennis Meeks of Patchogue. Our state police contact went into their files. Larson admitted to the detectives that Meeks was actually Meechum. They noted that Meechum had abandoned his single-family residence with no forwarding address or suspicion of foul play, but referred the matter to county detectives in case of further developments. His house is up for public auction due to the arrears of real estate taxes."

"At least something went right. The New York police have no idea we disposed the bodies of Browning Meechum or... or..."

"Hosty, sir."

The Admiral blustered through his lapse of memory. "Yes, Hosty. Good man. Shame to lose him. The clean-up crew did a good job." Then the Admiral had a second thought. "Have Duluth bid on and buy the house. Rip it apart, find anything you can, and then burn it to the ground."

"Yes, sir."

42 | STAKEOUT

For the one-thousandth time, Hank chided himself for being so stupid for leaving his name and address when signing for the book in Dallas. Whoever ransacked the guard's office at DFW had to have found what they were looking for, namely, him.

Hank sat in his brother's blue Acura TL, which was parked across the street from his place. As soon as they left the building, he went to get Ben's car, figuring that whoever was after him would already know his car and plate number.

He watched the day unfold on his street. Cabs, buses, and trucks rumbled down 42nd Street to and from the West Side Highway. People walked dogs, which he assumed happened around the same time each day for them and their pets. Deliveries came and went. Nobody he would call suspicious or "military type" entered his lobby. He looked up at his window from time to time to see if anyone was in his apartment. He also kept an eye on the side gate that lead to the alley beside the building and the rear entrance.

It took a while, but a Sears Service Truck pulled up to Hank's Apartment building. A man got out of the passenger side and walked across the street to the coffee shop. Hank watched as he went in. Through the window, he saw the man looking around.

"Son of a bitch," Hank muttered under his breath. Somehow, they knew he told Peter Salvo to meet him there. For an hour, he watched the man observing for anyone looking for someone else. Then the serviceman exited empty-handed and returned to his van. Rather than pulling away, the van sat.

The man got out of the van timing his exit just as Mrs. Weinstein was walking her dog again. He smiled as he held the door for her, then entered the lobby. Four minutes later, Hank saw activity in the window. The Sears serviceman's gray uniform passed by a few times. He imagined he must have been trashing his house.

The Sears guy came out of Hank's building and got into his truck. When the van pulled into traffic Hank followed.

Connors and Ritter, the two Texas Rangers, were pulling up in a Ford Crown Vic Police Interceptor, borrowed from the NYPD motor pool. Although they had no arrest powers in the city, they were given the car and a portable radio as a professional courtesy. If there was a collar to be made, they had to call in the NYPD. That was the deal. However, since the crime they were working on was a Texan jurisdiction, NYC waived any right to contest extradition. At that moment they spotted Hank pulling away in the blue TL and followed.

"This could be interesting," Connors said, as he executed a U-turn to follow the car.

"What if he's going shopping or to the airport?"

"Then we'll know we can activate the search warrant for his domicile."

Getting a warrant would mean calling in an NYPD cop to serve the warrant, hence the real reason for the portable radio.

Down the Westside Highway, close to the World Trade Center, the van stopped. Hank rolled by, not to raise suspicion. The Serviceman got into a red Chevy. Hank drove further South, took a guess that the driver was going to go North, and swung around. Bingo! The Chevy made the big U-turn around at the end of the Westside Highway and headed north. Hank stayed 3 to 4 cars back in the heavy northbound traffic.

There was a blast of an air horn.

"Watch it!" Connors called out.

The two Texas Rangers nearly got creamed by a cement truck as they were following him.

"Damn New York drivers," Ritter said.

"He couldn't have made us."

"Maybe he's just another crazy New York driver, too?

North of the city they were now on the Saw Mill River Parkway, the traffic thinned out, making it harder to hide. It was then that Ritter caught on.

"Notice something?"

"That he seems to be following that red Chevy?"

"Exactly."

Suddenly, the red Chevy took an exit. They saw Hank slow down.

"He's good. Not calling attention to himself."

"This looks like it's going to come to an end soon." Connors hit the radio, "This is 19th Squad Special Portable to central K."

"Central to 19th Squad K," was the dispatcher's response.

"We are in..." He turned to his partner.

"Yonkers was on the last sign," Ritter said.

"Yonkers. We are requesting local backup. Silent approach. Possible drug deal going down. We are undercover in an unmarked, black Ford Interceptor with NYPD New York tags. Our N.C.I.C. joint task force authorization code is, able baker 37..."

Hank approached the turn at the bottom of the exit ramp. A quick look left caught the brake lights of the red car going around the corner. Hank found the Chevy parked head-in, near the front door of what looked like an old abandoned commercial building on the Hudson River. He didn't see the two Rangers drive up in the distance. He pulled his car across the back of the "head in" parked Chevy, trapping the car between his and the wall. Hank rifled through his brother's trunk and came up with a 1/2-inch nut driver. He then patted his pockets and came up with the Lost and Found form from Dallas Airport. He placed them under the Chevy's wiper blade and got out of sight, hoping that the Serviceman came out alone.

She compared the image on a wet 8x10 photo with the original Polaroid. Although the original was yellowed, the copy was crisp Black and White. She went to her family album and found an old Polaroid. It's the one with her high school Junior Prom date, Larry. He was a jerk. She hated him and that photo that they took. Her mother put it in with her stuff when she went to college. She was always going to throw that out. Now she needed it.

The "serviceman" exited the building, wearing a sports coat and carrying an overnight bag. At first, he was taken aback by the car blocking his. He opened his door and started blowing the horn. He then noticed the folded paper under his wipers. With one arm propped up on the door of the car, he read the form.

Hank pressed the cold nut driver right into the nape of the guy's neck. The "serviceman" didn't get rattled.

Hank put on the toughest voice he could muster. "Don't be stupid or your brains become this thing's new hood ornament."

Hank breathed easier as the man instinctively put his hands up. "Stretch out with your hands on the roof of the car."

As the man complied, he made a professional critique.

"Real cowboy, huh?"

"What makes you say that?" Hank asked as he patted him down from behind, looking for a gun.

"Broad daylight, out in the open, large bore weapon... 44?"

"Etiquette my friend. I get to ask the questions. Did you kill Dreesan?

"Don't know who you're talking about."

The serviceman was cool. Hank tried a different tact.

Connors and Ritter managed to slip into the yard and were crouched behind their car as a Yonkers PD, Blue and White, unit rolled up silently.

Connors flashed his Star to the local cops who came over, staying low.

One of them, talking in a whisper asked, "What do we got?"

Connors practiced the sin of omission. "The guy holding the piece on the other guy is a suspect in a contraband case in Texas. We don't know who he is holding at gunpoint, but we followed them here from Manhattan."

"Are we taking both of them?"

"Let's just see what plays out."

Hank was starting to get into the role. "Look, I don't want to sever your spinal cord and leave you a vegetable for the rest of your life, but if I shoot here between the fourth and fifth disc..." He pressed his finger into the man's spine with his free hand. "...I'll probably miss all the vital organs, so you'll rot away for the next sixty years. Bye."

"No, wait!"

"No time left, daylight and all. Sorry, we couldn't work things out." Hank released some of the pressure of the ½-inch socket on the man's neck like he was adjusting his grip, getting ready to fire."

"Okay... Okay listen, I'm just a hired hand here. I really don't know who Dreesan was."

"Come on. Special forces? A real wizard with a match? I'm wasting my time here."

The serviceman was calmly trying to talk sense now. "Look, all I know is they called me to do some research on a guy."

Hank smiled. "Who?"

"Hank Larson."

"Why?"

"He stole something that belonged to them."

"Who's them?"

"The Committee..."

Suddenly, a bullhorn crackled. Hank was startled.

"Drop the gun and put your hands up!" Connors, ordered from behind the car.

The serviceman didn't move a muscle. Hank, the lesser experienced of the two, turned to look at the cops. The serviceman took immediate advantage of the situation. He turned as a spring-loaded holster, strapped up his sleeve, and put a 9 mm automatic in his hand. Hank was stunned. He didn't pat down his arms. He watched the whole thing in slow motion. Hank saw the momentary incredulous look on the serviceman's face as he realized Hank only had a nut driver. The serviceman hesitated, deciding on putting a bullet in Hank's head or shooting it out with the cops. In that split second, a cop's shot ricocheted off the roof of the car and nailed the guy in the temple. He crumpled. Hank put his hands up.

Chris waited by the back service entrance to Hank's building for as long as she could. Hank was supposed to meet her before 12. It was 12:10. She took a chance and went to the front door. She slipped in behind a tenant coming back with groceries.

She knocked on Hank's apartment door just to be sure he wasn't home. She wrote a message on the envelope, slid it under his door and left.

As she left the building her head was turned by a cry for help. She turned just in time to see a homeless man on the ground take a punch from a big bruiser who stole his bottle in a bag and ran off. Chris went to the poor soul. "That was terrible, are you okay?" She froze, the man on the floor pointed a gun at her and she backed away and into the arms of another man. He swung her around and threw her into the open side door of a van that pulled up at that instant. The homeless guy jumped in. On the next block, they stopped long enough for the bruiser to climb into the front seat.

43 | TOOLS OF THE TRADE

Hank was seated in the Chief of the Yonkers' Police Department's office. Connors, Ritter, and the two cops stood at the door. The veins in Chief Walsh's neck were popping as he questioned Hank to make sense out of this mess.

"A nut driver! This guy had a 9 mm, and all you had was a nut driver! And you got the drop on him?... Son of a bitch!" He flipped the tool and put the 'weapon' down on his desk.

Hank was getting pissed. "For the tenth time, he cut me off and gave me the finger. I just snapped that's all."

"Who was this guy?" Connors was impatient.

"I don't know. Maybe you should have asked him that before you killed him." He turned to the Chief, "Am I being charged with something here or can I go?"

The Chief looked up at his officers, "So tell me about the drugs."

"We didn't find any boss."

The Chief popped a few Kleenexes from the box behind his desk and handed them to Hank while he flicked his fingers over his own cheek.

Hank followed suit with the tissue. He looked at it. Blood. He nodded to the chief.

The Chief looked to the two Texans. "You called us in on a drug bust. What happened?"

"No, we never said drugs. We said, contraband," Connors said.

He put his hands on his hips. "Contraband? What was the contraband?"

Ritter hesitated a bit. "Well, ...er, Chief the nature of the contraband has yet to be identified."

The Chief got in his face. "Let me get this straight. You almost got my men shot on a fishing expedition?"

He turned to Hank, "Do you know what this is about?"

Hank just shrugged his shoulders.

The Chief aimed his rage at the Rangers. "Okay, here's what you two are going to do, you are going to sit with my detectives and tell them what the hell this is about. Then you are going to swear out affidavits in this officer-involved shooting death. Then you are going to get the hell out of my city. And never come back, unless and until you are called as material witnesses if this goes to trial." He turned to Hank, "You're free to go, but don't leave the state. You're still a material witness in this case."

Connors objected, "You can't let him walk."

"I don't know about Texas, but up here 'suspicion of some kind of contraband' doesn't qualify as a crime!"

"Chief, he's a person of interest in two murders in Texas. You've got to hold him on something!"

"For what? Assault with intent to tighten some guy's nuts!"

44 | THE ENVELOPE PLEASE

Hank came through the door to his ransacked apartment after 8 p.m. Chris was long gone and probably on her way to work. On the floor was an envelope that was slid under the door. In it was the original Polaroid, and an identical enough-looking copy. Scribbled on the envelope itself was a note. Hank read it.

"Hank, I was here at noon, waited, and went back to my place to get ready for work. It took a few tries to get it just right. I think I ruined my iron, though. Call me when you get this, 212 887-...."

He headed right to his phone to dial the number on the piece of paper. It rang as he neared it. He picked it up.

"Chris, I was just going to call. Great work."

"Hank, do whatever they say..."

He stiffened.

She was terrified and then it sounded like a gag was stuffed in her mouth, cutting her off.

A man's voice came on next. "Larson, she might still be able to bear children if you come quietly. There's a car downstairs. Be in it in two minutes. Bring what was in the locker. Don't do anything noble or this fly girl crashes and burns." He heard the beep from whoever it was hitting the wrong key before he hit the disconnect button of her PDA.

Hank slammed down the phone. He lost it. He grabbed at his face with his hands. He kicked the end table over; it now matched the rest of his ransacked decor. "I can't take this!" He stopped and grabbed the phone. "Operator, give me the number of the FB...I..."

His voice trailed off. He thought twice and threw the phone so hard that the cord came out of the wall.

"Fuck!... I've got to think!" He bit his knuckle. Then he had an idea. He went through all his stuff strewn about his apartment, turning over everything. Eventually, he found what he was looking for and dashed out.

The Yonkers detectives identified the "Sears serviceman" as an ex-army ranger through his prints. All they could gather on him pointed to him being a Mercenary. Eventually, they found his small, classified ad in "Soldier of Fortune" magazine. He was a soldier for hire. Those types typically never operated within the U.S., mostly because they'd be thrown in a federal pen for a score of federal offenses that being a Merc within U.S. territory would trigger. They reached out to the Pentagon for his service record and sought a warrant to his P.O. box where respondents to his ad would send inquiries and payments. His gun was traced to be part of a cache of weapons stolen in a robbery of an armory in Westchester County a few years back. Thus, there was no ATF registration to help with the forensic picture that was forming of Terrance "Trip" Saffrin.

The shoot-out had happened right in front of an abandoned factory building. The Yonkers Crime Scene Unit made quick work of checking out its interior. They found some homeless people camping on the main floor. Only one heard the shots. None of them admitted to seeing anything. Given the state of inebriation of four of the five, the cops didn't suspect them of lying. They instead called social services, and those individuals were taken to a homeless shelter on Nepperhand Avenue.

On the second floor, the CSU officers found two gray Sears uniforms. The one that was on the floor showed fresh sweat stains and the wrinkles of having recently been worn. The other was pressed and untouched on a hanger. Upon closer inspection, it was determined that one was a large size and the other extra-large. The slim Trip opted for the smaller size. They found no toolboxes or other items around it. Once the uniforms were dusted for prints, they were bagged and tagged. The CSU police locked and sealed the scene. It was now part of the evidentiary chain.

In the adjacent abandoned building that shared the same parking area, in a dank and dusty former conference room on the second floor, Chris was gagged. Her wrists were restrained with a piece of cloth that was tied around a standpipe.

"For your sake, let's hope your boyfriend really does care about you and does the right thing," Belson said before walking out of the room.

On the street outside Hank's building were Fallow and Croft, the two men Belson had dispatched to bring Hank to him. They stood alongside a Lincoln town car, in their dark suits and sunglasses. They put their hands on their hip holsters when they spotted Hank coming at them with something in his hand. He was holding the photo and something else in his hand. As he neared, they got a good look at what it was and took a step back. The photo was wrapped around a grenade. "I've pulled the pin and let it go to four. There's maybe a half second left, I wouldn't hit any bumps boys."

The two hesitate. Fallow, the smaller of the two, made a suggestion. "Maybe we should call this in?"

"Fuck no! Fuck him! This shitbag isn't going to blow himself up, let's go!" Croft said.

Hank was surprised they were following the route that he took following the serviceman. It was confirmed when they pulled into the same parking area but pulled up to the other building in the complex.

As Hank gingerly got out of the car, the two men kept their eyes on the grenade.

"Got bad news fella's... My hand is cramping up."

Fallow was in a near panic. "Switch hands man!"

They made him walk up the stairs well ahead of them. He waited at the landing.

As they entered the room, Belson, demanded, "Why the hell isn't he blindfolded?"

"Hank," Chris said, through the gag in her mouth, hands tied to the standpipe.

"Er... He's got a grenade there." Croft said.

"And you brought him here?!!!"

"He insisted," Fallow said.

"HE insisted!!?"

Hank interrupted. "Look, I don't know how much longer I can keep squeezing this thing. Let me have the girl and I'm out of here."

"I'm afraid I can't do that."

"Listen, I'm real tired of being shot at and threatened. You people have made my life suck and I'm at the point where I'll take you all with me just to get out of this nightmare. Now, hand her over or they'll be picking frags out of what's left of us."

Belson ignored Hank's threat. "Is that the photo?"

"Wrapped around the grenade and the first to go?"

At that, Belson relaxed a bit. Hank realized his error. He thought out loud. "Now I get it! You don't actually want the photo. You just want to make sure no one else sees it."

"The game is over shithead; we'll leave you with the fly girl. If you try to leave, we'll shoot you from a safe distance. So please, do indeed blow yourself and the photo, to hell. Just have the decency to wait for us to leave the room."

Belson nodded to the two others. Croft holstered his weapon and grabbed a briefcase and they started to leave. "Hold it!... In the event of my death, three envelopes get opened. One at my lawyer's, one at a TV station, and the other at The New York Times."

First, thanks to retouching and trick photography it's only the original photo that counts. And second, you're bluffing, Mr. Larson. And three, now I'm tired."

The men continued leaving.

Hank was thinking fast. "Was Dreesan bluffing?"

That stopped Belson in his tracks. "Now that's a surprise, Mr. Larson."

"Dreesan told me everything."

As Hank got their attention, he moved closer to Fallow, the nervous one, who looked to Belson for a second. At that moment, Hank hauled off and punched Fallow in the face. The weight of the grenade packed more punch than a brick. As the man fell, Hank threw the grenade at Belson and Croft.

As Belson and Croft ducked for cover, Hank grabbed the gun from Fallow's hand. Hank walked over to Croft, the macho one, who was behind a desk, briefcase shielding his head. Hank put the gun to Croft's head. "Bang!"

The befuddled guy looked toward the grenade in the center of the room. It had fallen in such a way as to hit the striker button, which created a spark, that ignited the butane, making a blue flame. Just right for lighting a cigar.

"Son of a..." were the last words Mr. Macho uttered before Hank cold-cocked him with the butt of the gun.

As Belson, the boss, came up from cover, he went for a drawer in his desk. Hank warned him while waggling the gun, "Uh, uh, uh! This one's real."

Hank kept it trained on Belson as he went over to Chris. With his free hand, he loosened the rag from around the pipe freeing her.

She pulled the gag from her mouth. "They got me, leaving your place."

"Are you okay?"

She nodded, rubbing her wrists.

"We got to get out of here." He turned to lead the way.

"Wait. There was someone else."

"What?"

"When they brought me in, I saw a man in a room down the hall. He didn't look well."

"Okay," Hank went over to Croft and took his gun. He handed it to Chris, "Wait here. If he moves shoot him."

Hank went down the hall. He opened a door to a closet. Then he tried the door across the way. He slumped when he saw Salvo. "Oh no," he said as he took in the grotesque sight in front of him. Peter's head was cocked sideways. His left shoulder was covered in brains and blood. His hands were tied behind the chair, holding up his dead body. Hank didn't dwell on it, but it looked like an ear or part of it was sitting in a spray of blood on the floor. It was odd but Hank could swear there was a smile on the dead man's face. Hank shuddered and left.

"Well, did you find him?" Chris said as Hank returned to her.

"Yes. He's dead."

"What?"

"No time. We got to get out of here," He took the gun back from her and slid it into his waistband, "...and we are going to take him." He pointed his gun at Belson.

When Croft came to, he rousted Fallow. "Hey, c'mon we got to bug out."

Fallow rose groggily. He was a little unsteady for a minute. "Where's Belson?" He asked rubbing the back of his head.

"I don't know. Let's get to the safe house. This place is compromised."

As they were leaving, they passed the room with Salvo's body.

"What about him?"

"We can't call for a clean-up because we don't know where Belson or that Larson guy are. Besides he doesn't tie to us, the room is clean, and we all used gloves."

As they exited the building, they made sure the door was locked behind them. The Lincoln they used was gone, so they hot-wired Belson's car.

As Chris drove the Lincoln back down the parkway to New York, Hank sat in the back with the gun trained on Belson, whose hands were bound by the same rag that held Chris.

"Chris, let me have your PDA thingy."

She rifled through her bag with one hand and held it over her shoulder to the back seat. "Press the green button after you punch in the number."

Hank first called 411 and got the number of the Yonkers Police. He informed them of the body in the abandoned factory building by the water. He finished the call and asked Belson, "Why did Peter Salvo have to die?"

"Peter who?" Chris asked from the front seat.

"He was the man you saw. A friend of my brother."

Belson remained silent.

Hank drew back the gun like he was going to smack him with it, but instead tried the easy way first. "I don't suppose you'd be willing to tell me who you're working for?"

All he got was a stare.

"Fine, you'll tell them."

"Who?"

"The FBI."

Hank couldn't see it, but Belson smiled as he turned away to look out the window.

Chris pulled the Lincoln up in front of the federal building. Hank got out with his jacket over his forearm, which hid the gun trained on Belson. With his other hand, he gave Chris her flight bag.

"Here, you nearly forgot this. I'll call you once I'm finished. You okay?"

"Sure, I can still make pre-flight."

"You're incredible."

He leaned over and gave her a peck on the cheek. Then he marched Belson into the building.

As they entered the building, Hank saw the metal detector. "All right, this is going to get a lot of attention so don't try anything cute."

As they walk through it, the machine went off. Two security guards approached.

In a voice intended to sound calm, Hank informs them, "Gentlemen, this man is dangerous and a kidnapper and killer. When you put him into custody, I'll give you my gun."

A cold steel barrel nudged Hank's cheek. Special agent Foster, in shirt sleeves, had his chrome-plated .38 snub-nosed at full extension and spoke in a very calming voice. "Sir, you'll surrender your weapon now."

"O.K. But watch this guy." He let the gun swing around his trigger finger as he raised his hands. Foster grabbed it and proceeded to frisk him.

"Second gun in the waistband," Hank said nodding to his right.

Foster retrieved it and led them both to the elevators, uniformed officers assisted.

In an FBI interrogation room, Hank watched Special Agent Foster try to figure out who's who. An agent standing by Hank remained mute. Belson, now sitting in handcuffs, whispered something to Foster and then the agent left the room. Hank and Belson were left to stare at one another for a few moments.

"Did Dreesan kill my brother, the two men in Texas?"

Belson sat silent. Foster and another agent returned, and he opened Belson's handcuffs. Foster tossed them to the agent next to Hank.

"Cuff him!"

Hank was stunned.

Foster declared, "Henry Larson, you are under arrest for the murder of Burt Dreesan."

"Beautiful, just beautiful!" Hank said shaking his head.

Hank was led from the room by Foster and the other agent. They marched him through the open office area filled with FBI agents at their desks. He saw Belson walking down the corridor with a guy in a suit with an FBI building badge hanging from his lapel pocket. It identified him as SAC Ben Holloway, Director New York Field Office. They were talking and nodding. As they approached, Belson spoke first. "Gentlemen, I am taking charge of the prisoner."

The agents looked to Director Holloway, who confirmed this.

"Sorry men. Mr. Belson has jurisdiction on this one."

"Who is this guy, and where am I going?"

Ignoring Hank, the Director told his men, almost regretfully, "Better escort them downstairs boys."

Hank tried one last ploy. "Look, I can't go anywhere, I'm a material witness in a police shooting."

That got Holloway's attention, "Local case?"

Belson was annoyed, "What difference does that make?"

"Yeah, a police shooting in Yonkers."

"We'll have to check that out."

The Director nodded to one of his men, who took that as an order and left. Belson protested. "Look, I have to get going here. He's my prisoner and..."

The Director got in his face. "Look, you may have jurisdiction over the bureau, but you don't have the juice to pull a material witness from a murder case."

"I don't believe I'm hearing this!"

"Well hear this! I am not going to take the heat in a judicial dispute with any local authority without getting someone above my paygrade to clear it, got it?" He turned to his man, "The prisoner stays here until further notice."

Belson exploded, "Look, you fucking bureaucratic asswipe, I'll have your posting for this. You're screwing with the big guys now, buddy boy, and you're going to get your administrative ass kicked!"

The Director glared back and took out his pen and offered it to Belson. "Write down my name. Call your DIA buddies. Get the Attorney General on the phone. But I go by the book until a boss from the 7th floor orders me differently!"

The Director locked his eyes on Belson's and said in a lower and more confidential voice, "And if you ever talk to me, or my men like that again, I'll arrest you for obstruction of justice and threatening a federal officer... fuck face."

The agents around the room reacted with choruses of "You tell him Chief" and "Way to go, sir!"

The Director quieted his men down. "Okay, forget this little sideshow." He turned to the agent with his hand on Hank's arm. "Get the prisoner down to holding." He turned to the room, "Get back to work, people."

45 | DEATH GRIN

"Thank you, Hal," the Chief of Yonkers Police, Walsh, said as he dipped two fingers into the green Vicks VapoRub jar the officer held out to him. He rubbed it under his nose before he entered the room with the bloody, rotting corpse strapped to the chair.

The Vicks made the gagging smell of death more tolerable, but it was still rank. The Chief had seen a death grin before. A phenomenon that happens when a corpse decomposes. The tightening facial skin creates a garish mask-like grin. Although on this victim, the eyes and cheeks were different, almost part of a frozen expression, almost as if this man died with a smile on his face. He quickly dismissed the ludicrous idea.

He noticed a standing numbered card on the floor next to what looked like a severed human ear. His homicide detectives were busy with the crime scene. One came over, "What brings you here, Chief?"

"Proximity. We had a shootout next door. This is just too much of a coincidence. Was he tortured?" The Chief said jutting his chin at the ear on the floor.

"No, he's got powder stippling on his temple. That ear was blown out with the exit wound when they put the gun point blank into the other side of this head."

"Any ID?"

"Wallet says, "Peter Salvo. Ronnie thinks he knows him." He turned and called out to the Medical ExamineWatergate r's assistant who caught this case. "Ronnie, come over here and tell us what you know about this guy."

He walked over. "Afternoon Chief, yeah, I know this guy, well, know of him. He's an author and a researcher." He made air quotes on *researcher*.

"How do you mean?" The Chief asked.

"Well, he's a JFK conspiracy type. Holds big seminars, gets on TV, and espouses all kinds of, what he calls evidenced, about the assassination of president, Kennedy."

"Is he a local?"

The detective answered, "No, the license is from Texas, address in Dallas."

"Naturally." The Chief looked around, "Find out what he was doing here?"

Ronnie spoke, "I think I remember that he recently had one of his seminars down in Manhattan."

"How do you know all this?"

"Kinda professional curiosity, Chief."

"How's that?"

"He was the one who released the JFK autopsy photos, so..."

'Got it. Thanks."

Back in his office, the chief pulled out the Texas Ranger's card. "Officer Connor's? Chief Walsh from Yonkers. We got a homicide victim here, one," he read from the license, "Peter William Salvo, age 56, who is from your jurisdiction. We found him in the building adjacent to where you had that shootout."

Connors snapped his fingers and got Ritter's attention in their squad room, "Chief Walsh, I am going to put you on speaker so my partner can join in. Hold on." He placed the call on hold and filled in Ritter, then hit the speaker on the desk phone.

"Howdy Chief," Ritter said. "Was this a robbery gone wrong?"

"An execution. Possible torture as well, my ME is looking into that now." The Chief said over the scratchy speakerphone, "This may or may not be connected to your extradition or whatever you boys were doing up this way. I'm just alerting you out of professional courtesy."

"Thank you for that, Chief. Do you have any suspects?"

"Not at this time. The body was ripe. Best guess is dead for at least two days. Clean crime scene. As if this was a clean execution."

"So as far as you know, no motive?" Ritter asked.

"Nothing has emerged, although do you remember what this Hank Larson was saying?"

"You mean about his brother?"

"Yes, well, turns out this dead guy was what you might call a JFK conspiracy nut, also."

Ritter's eyebrow went up as he looked at Connors.

"So, I was wondering if you had a fix on Larson. He's not responding to my calls."

"No sir, we were ordered off the case."

"Well, maybe this isn't anything, just wanted to match notes. Thanks for your time gentlemen. If I hear anything or you do, let's get back on the blower again."

"Sure thing, Chief."

Connors hit the button and the speakerphone went dead. "Whatcha thinking, pardner?"

"Larson maintains that his brother didn't kill Cyrus and Howard, but that someone killed his brother."

"You think it was this Salvo guy who popped the brother?" Connors said.

"Maybe, the thing that sticks in my craw though is that the newspaper said..." He flipped open his detective's notepad, "Where is it?" He flipped a few more. Here it is." He mumbled through the clipping of the small Pecox Telegraph article he had copied into his notes, "...brokered a deal between... a New York feature writer... a historical artifact from the day President Kennedy was shot." He looked up. "There it is, the Kennedy killing."

"And the editor of that paper was murdered."

"And now this conspiracy guy ends up dead where we shot it out with that serviceman."

"Well, we know Larson's brother didn't torture and kill this Salvo guy."

"Or Millie Hensley."

"So, you're thinking his brother, Hank, killed him?"

"I don't know. Wanna take this to the boss?"

"Do you?"

Connors just shook his head. "No." He didn't want to poke the bear... again.

46 | FLIGHT OR FLEE

In the FBI holding area, Hank was sitting in a small, windowless office with a bench and a pipe running along the floor. Hank's cuffs were chained to it.

Holloway, the director, entered and opened the cuffs. "Come on, let's go."

"Where?..."

"Shut up and do what I tell you or I'll have you gagged and shackled."

They walked down to the security doors. The Director flashed his badge. The doors buzzed, and he and Hank walked through. They reached the elevators.

When they got to the garage level, the Director turned to Hank and pulled a gun from his waist and pointed it at him. "Okay, you're free to go. Here's the gun back."

The Director flipped the gun in his hand around so that the butt was now pointing toward Hank. Hank grabbed the gun and Holloway turned to walk away.

Hank was shocked, "That's it? Listen, what about that Belson guy?"

"He won't bother you."

Hank thought for a second. Then handed the gun back. "Hey, look, they'll just send somebody else. Shit, I'm safer here. Take back the gun. I'll take my chances with you."

The Director looked him in the eye as he took back the gun and put it in his pant waist. He then yelled, "All clear... code 5."

Ten agents came out of nowhere. They were hiding behind cars and pillars.

"Mr. Larson, you just passed the J. Edgar Hoover "Fight or Flee" test. You could have run or tried to shoot me, without a firing pin by the way, or you could have done God knows what else. But you did exactly what someone, who claims they're in your position, would do. You're no killer."

"When did you know I was telling you the truth?"

"I didn't, till just now, but Belson was in such a hurry that it just smelled wrong. So, I thought I'd give you the benefit of the doubt."

"Thank you, for that."

"You know, like I told your other man, this guy or one of his men blew the brains out of Peter Salvo in a building in Yonkers. Where they were holding Chris after they kidnapped her."

"Who's this guy, Chris?"

"Someone trying to help me," Hank said. A sixth sense telling him to let it ride.

"Where is he now?"

"Ran. I can't blame 'em."

Meanwhile, Agent Foster was in front of Belson, whose face was red with anger and disbelief. "He did what?"

Special agent Foster tried to hide how much he was enjoying this. "Sir, the Director had to release the prisoner."

"What. He really fucked up this time. I need a phone."

Foster then said matter-of-factly, "Sir, I have been asked to escort you to the holding area."

"Bullshit. On who's authority?"

"Some bureaucratic asswipe's, sir."

As he said it, two agents locked Belson's wrists in cuffs.

They brought him into the same room where Hank was held. As they chained his cuffs to the pipe, Belson protested.

"You can't do this to me. I'm an agent with the Department of Defense."

"Sir, if you'll give us a name or contact at the D.O.D., we'll be glad to check out your story."

"I can't do that. I told you. I'm on a classified mission."

Foster bent over to address him face to face. "Till someone, from somewhere, tells me different, you're not going anywhere...sir.

"I'll have your ass in a sling." He went for Foster but was stopped by the chain.

"Here's a pen...." Foster said as he clicked the top.

In Director Holloway's office, he and Hank were talking across his desk.

"By the way, what's your name?" Hank said.

"Yeah, I guess we missed that part, I'm Special Agent in Charge, Ben Holloway, Director of the New York Field office, for now."

They shake hands.

"Who was the girl?" Holloway said.

Hank decided to level with him. "That was Chris, Chris DeMarco. I got her into this. I was trying to protect her. She doesn't have anything to do with this. She had one of them as a passenger a few weeks back and I pushed her into helping."

"Belson mentioned she drove you to my office."

"Like I said, she was helping me. She's innocent of any of this."

"And where is she now?" Holloway said.

He checked his watch. "By now, she should be at her place, then she's going to work."

Holloway handed him a pad. "Write down her address. I'll have someone keep an eye on her."

Hank did. Just then Foster walked in.

"How'd it go with Mr. Belson?"

"He's pissed, but not budging on his story." He changed his tone. "Sir, what if he indeed is on an authorized D.O.D. black op?"

"Foster, that's why I want all the paperwork on this signed only by me. I don't want any of my people being hit with shrapnel if this thing blows up."

"Sir, on second thought, I don't believe he's going to call anybody legal at DOD, because I think he's free-lancing for a sub-group..."

That caused a light bulb to go on in Hank's brain. "The Committee?"

"What Committee?" Holloway asked.

"That's who the repairman said he was working for just before he was killed. The Committee."

"Foster, run a computer sort on The Committee, both outside and internal databases. Let's see what comes up... and keep it between us. Only I sign the search request."

After Foster left, Hank was curious. "Why are you doing this, Ben?"

"Well Hank, let's just say it gets my goat when people start using the system for their own gain... That, and I got shut down big time on my investigation of Enron a few years back, and this smells like the same pile of happy horse shit."

"What if you follow it into the barn and it leads up the chain of command?"

"Hell, Hank, those guys up there get real touchy when somebody starts looking under their dress. We could both disappear."

"Thanks, that's comforting."

47 | THE NITTY GRITTY

Snuggled in the foothills of Paradise Valley, just outside Phoenix, was a ranch spread that was more of a compound. Bucolic, classic, and innocent looking, like the opulent family home of an oil tycoon from out west. That is, until and upon closer inspection, sensor units in the trees could be seen. An untrained eye would mistake the 150-foot killing zone in front of the walls as a landscaped lawn intended to separate the architect's vision from the hilltop it rests on. But the turrets atop the stone wall corners concealing the guards with MP5 machine guns ruin the notion that it's just a home for a loving family.

Inside, in a heavily paneled room with priceless fine art on the walls, the 13 men of the Committee were convened. Each held the strings on major arms manufacturers and bureaucrats who at once benefitted and were controlled by the committee. Some willingly, others by kompromat. That blackmail was either revealed or inflicted by the committee. It all added up to everyone making billions as long as they kowtowed to the committee. This was guaranteed by their need for self-preservation of their corporations and personal power, which became the shackles that held them in check and loyal to the Admiral and the committee.

"What about the status of the red team?" Admiral Howser said.

Sorrells stood and put a picture down on the palette. "As you know, Admiral, Red Team was headed by operative LB/COLT and manned with three independent contractors..."

On the screen, a photo of Belson appeared with the code name LB/COLT in the lower right corner. "No contact for 48 hours, no local news or police records so far, so I would classify them MIA, until further notice."

The Admiral chews on this for a moment. "Do you think the brother is responsible? I mean, have you grossly underestimated his operational ability?"

"Negative, sir. At best a bad sequence of mishaps... and a little luck on his part."

"Losing a prime operative to the, what was it, Yonkers police force? - makes the brother, more than a little lucky!"

Sorrells shrugs.

"I can't explain it."

Nelson scanned a folder that had just been handed to him. "Maybe I can sir. Seems the brother, Henry "Hank" Larson, was a wing commander 9th Air Force, 43rd Tactical Bomb Group. B-52 driver, 52 sorties. Awarded Congressional Medal of Honor for running into a burning bomber that crash landed, and pulling out the wounded pilot, one Colonel Brian Miller, right before it exploded."

"A hero! I knew there was more to this man. It's been a little over a month since Polaroid 7 re-appeared. We are still no closer to it. I'm very disappointed."

The old man looked away to the crackling fire. Sorrells tried to offer up some defense.

"Sir, aside from Dreesan turning on us for more money, there is a percentage of risk associated with any operation. Statistically..."

"Up your ass with statistics! This isn't some shit-hole banana republic we're overthrowing here or blackmailing some congressman with the hots for a schoolboy. This is our asses on the block."

"The details in this particular case..."

"I don't want to hear about details, percentages, or luck. I want action, goddammit! I want this contained and the threat neutralized, at all costs! Do I make myself clear?"

The room disintegrates into a mass mumbling of "Yes sir."

In Director Holloway's Office, Hank was looking through mug books. Holloway was filing notes.

Foster burst in, beaming. "Got it! Went to the surveillance files. Dead match on The Committee for a Strategic Superiority. It was first formed on January 18th, 1961. They laid heavy bucks into the campaign of hawk politicians. An analyst posted in their file; the Committee was formed in the wake of Eisenhower's military-industrial establishment speech."

"Makes sense. Kennedy was going to pull the advisors out of Viet Nam by `64. Somebody would have lost billions."

"Student of history, Hank?" Holloway said.

"It's a long story about lasers bouncing off glass and... and... Achoo!" Hank sneezed.

"Gesundheit!" Holloway then turned to Foster. "Go on Foster."

"They folded in late '63, December 1st."

"When Johnson made the war an official police action," Hank said.

"They've been dormant since then."

"So, where's the match?" Hank said.

He started entering passwords.

"Foster, how did you get access to these files?"

"This part of the main frame is password protected."

"Okay, so where did you get the passwords?"

"Birth records, sir."

"You going to have to explain that one, Foster."

"DDCI's daughter's birthday plus her initials. He used her initials first and no 19 on the year."

"Shit, I am going to have to change mine then."

"Yeah, boss. People just don't understand it's 1993 and computers are here to stay."

"Foster, remind me to have the director issue a directive on secure passwords, you write it up."

"Roger that, sir." He smiled and pulled up a file with graphics. "The head of the Committee back then was Rear Admiral Upper Half, Brent R. Howser, USN Retired. He and General Cabell founded the Special Forces training camp where Dreesan was an instructor. Let's see, sound bites, sound bites, here it is Geopolitical speeches Rutgers 61 Nov."

Hank pointed. "Try that one, 'on Kennedy – 8 seconds.'"

He dragged with the mouse and a video window popped up, and a clip of a younger Admiral Howser rolled.

"Kennedy is committing treason in high office. You know what we do to traitors don't you?"

They look at each other.

"Ben, this all fits perfectly," Hank said. "Kennedy was a threat to them. He was making nice with the Russians, banning nuclear testing, threatening to pull out of Vietnam, and was repealing the oil depletion allowance."

"Well, that gives most of the big money in this country a motive."

"And the Committee took the contract."

Hank thought for a second, "So the Deputy Director of Central Intelligence wasn't keeping these files of evidence of subversion..."

"These were proof of loyalty to the cause." Hank reasoned.

Foster returned to the screen. There was a flurry of keystrokes. "And the final piece of the puzzle. The Admiral lives in a compound outside Phoenix, Arizona."

"Foster, you're amazing," Hank said.

"Not me sir, the system."

"Well, nobody gets out of it what you do. Well done."

The beaming agent then asks... "Well, sir, what now? Do we go for a court order? Notify the Phoenix Office?"

"No, I don't think so Foster."

Holloway walked over and took the printout from Foster. He removed his lighter from his pocket and set the pages aflame and dropped them into the waste basket. He shut down the terminal, which went immediately dark.

"Foster, this report isn't worth the paper it's printed on. It's pure speculation, and the Bureau only 'Acts on Facts.' I'm going to assume, for the sake of your career, that you never gave me this report. Do you read me?"

Dejected and crushed, Foster acknowledged.

"And Foster, on your way out... book Hank and me on the next flight out to Phoenix, then lose the travel req for at least a month."

Foster pumped up again. "Yes sir. What travel req, sir?"

The recharged agent took his moment and left. Ben went to his desk and took out Hank's gun. He released the magazine and it dropped into the drawer. He press-checked the chamber. Tossed the gun to Hank then tossed another fully loaded magazine to him. "You might want to have live ammo this time."

Hank smiled. Automatically, due to his training, he also press-checked the chamber. Then he seated the mag, but he didn't rack the slide, which left the weapon uncharged.

"Hank, I assume you want in on what could be the last case of my professional career."

"Just you and me, huh?"

"I'm out on a limb here. I can't ask any of my men to be involved in this. Besides, the last thing we need is official traffic crossing some bad guy's desk. That leaves me and you, if you want in?"

"Ben... "

"Yes?"

"That was my brother's name."

"Just tell me you never called him, Benji. I hated when my brother called me that."

48 | A STROLL ALONG THE GRASSY KNOLL

With all the connections to the JFK assassination, and Connors not wanting to push his luck with the boss, Ritter felt that maybe he could learn something to either connect the brother, Hank Larson, to the murders, or get him and his partner back on the case. With three unsolved murders in their jurisdiction and the one he just heard of up in New York, all connected in some way to the crazies who can't let it go. Ritter drove into Dallas and the 'nut line,' Which was what he and some officers called the loons who lined up in Dealey Plaza with tables and kiosks claiming all manner of conspiracy theories.

Ritter hadn't been to the Plaza in 20 years or so. He didn't particularly hold any position on the assassination, nor did he really care. As far as he heard from his dad, who was a nearby Fort Worth cop, the Secret Service and the DPD botched the whole murder investigation. Ritter always took that with a grain of salt because his father was friendly with a DPD Officer, J.D. Tippit. Tippit was murdered by Oswald right after he shot the president.

Ritter's dad felt that that was the investigation they blew. The murder of Tippit. Shell casings found around Tippit's prowl car indicated an automatic weapon that ejected shells as it was fired, however, when they captured Oswald at the Texas Theater, he had a revolver on his person. The revolver holds the shells from fired bullets. But DPD was out for blood that day, and they had Oswald for shooting the president, so hanging Tippit's murder on him went unchallenged by anyone. Except for Ritter's dad, who had his doubts.

He parked on Elm and walked to the Grassy Knoll, which itself had become synonymous with crazies who doubt the Warren Commission's official findings. He came upon about twelve Grassy Knoll types hawking their wares, videotapes, books, and leaflets in the shadow of the sniper's nest.

The first fella was all about how Castro killed Kennedy. On his table were museum-like cases, obviously not from a museum, which held what was supposedly a poisoned cigar that the CIA tried to kill Castro with. There was a bandana from one of the exiled Cubans who was killed in the Bay of Pigs. A poison fountain pen by which the CIA had tried to get a sexy lady to stick into the bearded leader's neck. The supposed clincher was a yellow leaflet, which sat below a picture of Oswald handing out leaflets in New Orleans. It was from the Fair Play for Cuba Committee. Ritter guessed that from all this, one was supposed to assume Oswald, who was pro-Cuban, shot Kennedy for Fidel! Ritter didn't engage the man behind the table. Instead, he moved on.

This next guy had an umbrella on the table. And a grainy picture from that day of a man standing with an Umbrella as the motorcade passed by. The sign on the table read, "The Umbrella Man is the Key!"

He passed by that table. The next one kind of grabbed him. "Watergate!" wthe Tippetas on the sign behind the man in his Kiosk. Ritter thought, how is Watergate connected to Kennedy? Then he saw the smaller print under the big letters. The Three Tramps are the Watergate co-conspirators! E. Howard Hunt's plumbers were there to stop the leak of assassination documents.

He listened in as a tourist from Germany was asking how it was connected. The man behind the table had two pictures. He pointed to the first one and said, "These are the real shooters. And see this picture here of the Three Tramps being led away from the Plaza on the day of the assassination? Now look at these two men. Aren't they the same?"

The German tourist responded in a thick accent in the affirmative. Then in a small bit of table-top showmanship, the man lifted a slat of cardboard revealing the names of the men in the second picture. E. Howard Hunt and Frank Sturgis. Ritter seemed to remember those names.

The man filled in, "These men were caught breaking into the Watergate office complex for "Tricky Dick" Nixon 10 years after they shot President Kennedy right there." The man pointed towards the street and the tourist, and Ritter both looked at the X painted in the center lane of the street. They are CIA operatives and have a lot more blood on their hands, believe you me."

Ritter didn't think the pictures were a particularly good match, but conspiracy theories die hard, he guessed. He shook his head as he walked away, "Watergate." He scoffed.

Next was an unmanned table. It was all about the Babushka Lady. Some photos and a Yashica Super 8 camera lay on the table. Ritter figured, even conspiracy nuts had to pee from time to time.

The next one hit home. It was 3 photographs of J.D. Tippit, Oswald, and Jack Ruby. The sign said, "Thick as Thieves." The cop, and the father's son in him, wanted to rip down the poster, but this nutjob had a constitutional right to be stupid in public. He just had to ask, "So, what proof do you have that Officer Tippit knew his killer?"

The man looked him straight in the eyes and said, "He didn't know his killer... but Tippit damn well knew Oswald and Ruby!"

Ritter rolled his eyes. "But Oswald killed Tippit!"

"There's no proof of that. What there is, is nonsensical...don't make no sense. Here."

The man held up a black-and-white picture of three men around a table in a nightclub. He pointed to each one, "Ruby, Tippit, and Oswald, nice and cozy at the Carousel Club."

"That's a fake."

"No, it ain't. Taken by Joyce Gordon, a stripper and sometime cigarette girl or photo gal at Ruby's club with a Graflex Speed Graphic 4x5 with bulb flash and developed in the darkroom in the back of the club."

"That's all you got?"

He recoiled a little, "Well ain't you a tough customer." He pointed to a picture sealed in plastic. It showed shell casings around Tippit's Dallas Police squad car. Then another from the Warren Commission Report showed Oswald's .38 caliber snub-nose Smith & Wesson pistol. "Any cop will tell you a revolver doesn't eject shells."

That gave Ritter pause. "Yeah, I know. A cop told me that once."

Ritter thumbed through some of the pictures and leaflets on the table. He found an old black and white with a caption below:

David Ferrie (second from left) and a teenage Lee Harvey Oswald (far right) in a group photo of the New Orleans Civil Air Patrol in 1955

Ritter held it up to the man, "So who's David Ferrie?"

"Ah, he was a pilot. Worked for the mob. Ruby and he would make frequent flights to Havana to collect the mob's take of the casinos there. It was Ferrie that introduced Oswald to Ruby."

Ritter had enough. "I'm done." He walked off.

The next hawker on the street threw him a little ______. The banner this guy had was something you could make on a dot matrix printer and fanfold computer paper. He used all "S" letters to make big block words proclaiming, "SECRET SERVICE KILLED JFK."

Ritter debated whether to engage this citizen, but he must have gazed a few seconds longer than he should have.

"Don't believe it? Think it's crazy?" The man said.

"Your words not mine."

"Those good ole' boys on the presidential detail...they did some major league drinking that night before. Hell, half the detail was hung over."

"So?"

"When the first shots rang out, Agent G. Hickey, riding in a car behind the limo, fumbled with his weapon. Accidental discharge! Took the top of the president's head right off!"

Ritter's first instinct was to feel bad for the agent, a fellow law enforcement officer. Thirty years after what was probably the most horrible day of his life. "Amateur Researchers" are accusing, no, convicting him of firing a bullet into the head of the man he was duty bound to, instead, take a bullet for. His ire just came out. "How do you sleep at night, man?"

"I sleep under a blanket of truth."

"I'd check it for moth holes, bubba." Ritter just walked off.

He looked down the line. There were a few more crazies left. He skipped them and decided he had the stomach for one more. He went down to the last table. On it was a yellow book "Ruby, The Mob and The CIA," by Peter Salvo.

Ritter immediately realized the author was just found dead an hour or so ago in Yonkers. He picked it up and thumbed through it. There were pictures in the center. The Carousel Club. A frame from TV where Ruby, in a Fedora, was in the police station. Of course, those shots from the TV coverage of the shooting of Oswald that was done like a film strip six pictures long across the center of two pages. He turned it around and read the back cover. It told how Peter Salvo was the premiere critic of the Warren Commission and a leading alternate theorist. Ritter chuckled at the term, "alternate theorist," like it was a science or some such academic balderdash.

"It's a good book!"

Ritter looked up. It was the woman on the other side of the table. She was young, pretty, and in a sweater that Lana Turner would envy.

Ritter thought, what a nice change from the men he had encountered this far. *She must sell a ton of whatever horse shit she is selling,* he thought to himself as he realized he was smiling at her. "Is it now?"

"Yes, it's the definitive link to Ruby's connection with the assassination, he did have the last word you know." She made a gun with her right hand and jutted it forward like Ruby did into Oswald's side and winked. As offbeat as that was, Ritter thought it was cute. He laughed, "Yes when you put it that way," he did the same gesture, "I guess you can say he did."

They both laughed, and out of that, she asked, "What's your name sugar?"

"Beau, Beau Ritter."

"Howdy Beau. I'm Beth. Beth Salvo."

It hit Ritter like a bucket of cold water. Suddenly his mind hardened. He was no longer a goofy tourist. He was back to being a Ranger. "*Go easy*," he said to himself.

"You related to the author?"

"He's my brother. He's away, so I am watching his stand. Where you from, Beau?"

"Originally Fort Worth, now Dallas.

"Ah, Cowtown!"

"We like to think of it as Panther City."

"As you like."

Ritter was torn. He wasn't here to make a next of kin notification, and since it was clear that this was not a woman in mourning, he assumed some DPD cop was going to get around to next of kin notification at some point later today. He could casually interview her and find out what he could about the murder victim...her brother. And let her find out through official channels. But he couldn't just stand there and not tell her. He decided he was about to ruin her day and make the notification without official sanction, but it was the human thing to do. "What do you do for coffee around here?"

"There's a coffee shop in the TSBD."

"May I buy you a cup, Miss Beth?"

"That'll be nice."

She turned to the man at the table next to her. "Bill, watch my table for me. And if anyone wants the big book, they're four dollars, okay sugar? Can I bring you back anything? A cruller, or a coffee?"

"Nah Beth, the wife's coming by soon with lunch. Take your time."

"Thanks, Bill."

49 | HOUSE OF PAINE

As they walked up the slow incline, Ritter figured out TSBD stood for Texas School Book Depository. Although when they got there, that wasn't the name on the doorway. But he figured if you are a JFK alternative theorist, the new name of the building, the Dallas County Administration Building, didn't have the same ring to it.

They found a table by the 6th Floor Museum, the place his dad called the sniper nest, which was now a tourist attraction. Lots of people were moving around. It was lucky that he nabbed a table as three French tourists got up to leave. He cleaned it up while she grabbed a couple of napkins to wipe it down. The waitress came over and they ordered.

"So, what do you do Beau?'

"Well, Beth, I'm a police officer."

"Is that a fact? I'm a High School English teacher. I edited all my brother's books."

"Look, Beth, this is totally by accident, but I need to inform you of some bad news."

"Is this a joke?"

"No, Beth, I wish it were." The weight of the heavy situation that he so suddenly found himself in, turned his demeanor to all business.

It was the only way he could get through it. He took out his star. "I'm a Texas Ranger, I came here to find out a little about this whole JFK thing because a case I am involved with touches on it, but I am afraid I have to notify you that your brother has passed."

At first, it didn't register, "What?"

"Your brother is dead, Beth. He died up in New York, maybe two days ago. I'm so sorry for your loss."

'Peter is dead?" She started to breathe in short breaths. Her eyes filled with tears. "How?"

"I don't know any details yet, except to say, the police department of Yonkers just notified my office. I didn't expect to find his next of kin, you, here. I was just looking to understand the whole JFK thing better. And I am sorry to deliver this awful news to you. Is there someone you can call to get you?"

The tears were starting to flow, and she shook her head.

"Would you like me to escort you home?"

"Just give me a minute," She dabbed her eyes and cleared her nose a few times. Ritter sat respectfully. He felt awful.

"How did Peter die?"

"Again, I don't have the official report yet, but it is most likely foul play."

"Dear God..." she started crying again.

When she caught her breath, he said, "Someone will notify you officially about arrangements and that sort of thing. Is there anyone who you need to notify? Relatives, mom or dad? Was he married?"

"No, we buried our parents. It's just him and me." She looked off. "Now just me."

Ritter didn't believe it as he did it, but he reached out and took her hand. "If there is anything I can do for you."

She looked up with red eyes. "That's sweet. If we could just sit here a while longer?"

"Of course, take all the time you need."

Later, he helped her pack up the table. When she told Bill what happened, all the street vendors came around to offer their condolences. It was like they lost a member of their family as well.

When one of them intimated that maybe it was the CIA, Ritter took it as his cue to escort the woman to her car.

Ritter followed her home, maybe she would feel up to talking about her brother and that might help him get a jump on who killed him or why?

She rolled through a red light, and a DPD cop pulled up behind her and pulled her over. Ritter pulled up behind his RMP. The cop turned and said, "Stay in your car, sir."

Ritter took out his shield, "Ritter, Texas Rangers. I am escorting her home."

The cop came to him.

"I just notified her of the death of her brother. I guess she is distracted."

"Okay, if you got her, then I'll let her go."

"Thanks, officer. I appreciate it."

"Just tell her to be careful, okay?"

He nodded to him and walked over to her car. "How much further?"

'About three minutes. I'm sorry, I didn't..."

"No problem, we're good. Just pay a little attention, and let's get you home safe."

Beth watched him walk back to his car in her sideview mirror. He was a nice man.

She lived at 2515 West 5th Street in Irving, Texas. He pulled into the driveway behind her. He went to help her in with the table and the boxes.

"Just leave those. I'll deal with them tomorrow."

"As you say."

"Thank you for doing this."

"Are you going to be okay?"

She nodded, looking down.

He had to ask, "Do you feel up to answering some questions? It could help our investigation."

She took a deep breath. "Maybe in a little while. Would you like to come in?"

"I can wait out here."

"Don't be silly. Besides, I need to remove this make up my mascara's running down my face."

"As you wish."

They went inside. It was immediately apparent that she lived with her brother. His name and hers were on the mailbox. She excused herself and he sat on the couch in the living room while she got herself together. Every once and a while, he heard her sobbing.

He looked around, there were pictures and posters, mostly all JFK-related. His cop sense triggered, as for the third time, a car stopped on the street and then pulled away. It happened three more times in the ten minutes she was in her bedroom. The next time one stopped, he went out onto the little covered portico and saw that the people in the car were taking pictures.

He went back inside, and she came out in different clothes, no makeup, and her hair tied back. She was still pretty, even with red eyes.

"Would you like something?" She asked.

"No, I don't wanna take up any more of your time than I have to."

"That's all right, you're helping me get through this. I can't believe he's gone." She plopped down in a big easy chair and the sniffles began.

"We can do this another time if you are not up for it."

She wiped her nose with a tissue, "No, no, if this will help..."

"Beth, I assume your brother and you shared this residence?"

"Yes, he bought this place after our mom died with her insurance money and some of the proceeds from his books. I was in a dinky little apartment, and he said he would be on the road most of the time and why should I pay rent. So, yeah, I been living here the last 6 years or so."

"Do you know why your brother was up in New York?"

She rummaged through the items on the coffee table and handed him a flyer. It was a poster for his appearance at the Uptown Y in Manhattan to speak on Ruby, the Mob, and the CIA. It also mentioned that copies of his best-selling book would be on sale in the lobby and that all convention attendees were welcome.

"What convention?"

"Any convention. My brother would get these posted in the lobbies of the biggest hotels in whatever town he was appearing in. Those hotels always had conventions going on."

Ritter looked up and saw somebody peering through the living room window. He put his hand on his holster and bolted for the door.

Beth turned and called out, "Beau, it's okay!" Too late. He was out the door.

"State your business," he said to the man and the woman peering through the picture window, while his hand was on his weapon's handle.

"Hey, mister, we don't want no trouble. We was just wondering if she was home?"

"You a friend of hers?"

"No, sir. Just wanted to see if she was still alive."

Ritter gave them a funny look. Beth squeezed by him and patted his shoulder. "It's okay, Beau." She spoke to the couple. "She moved a while back. Now you're welcome to take your pictures and be on your way."

Ritter was thoroughly confused. "Who's she?"

Beth smiled, "You don't know where you are do you?"

"No."

"This was Ruth Paine's house."

"And who was Ruth Paine?" The cop asked.

"She rented the spare room to Lee Harvey Oswald's wife Marina and her baby."

"His wife?"

"Yes, and this is where he kept the rifle that he supposedly used to kill Kennedy. When my brother heard it was up for sale, he just had to own it."

"Of course," Ritter said rolling his eyes.

"Get a lot a folks come round wanting to see if she's here or take pictures. They don't mean no harm."

"Sorry, It's just..."

"Yeah, I know. If you're not used to it."

They went back inside.

"The National Registry of Historic Places wants to list the house."

"That sounds like a big deal."

"Except then once it's a national landmark, it will take an act of Congress just to change the carpet or the drapes. No, thank you. But now with Peter gone, maybe someday I'll let them do it.

They sat back down.

"Beth, did your brother have any enemies?"

She got up and went to the secretary's desk. She came back with a pile of letters in an oaktag folder. "These are just from the last two months, there are boxes in the garage."

Ritter went through them. They were mostly insults and calling Peter crazy. "Are any of these direct threats?"

"You mean like I'm going to kill you? Not really. Just general threats."

"May I have these and those in the garage?"

"If you think it will help."

"It might. Have you ever heard of a Hank or Henry Larson?"

"No, but there's a Benjamin Larson...and he's up in New York."

"You just happened upon the murder victim's sister?" Captain Colson asked.

Ritter and Connors sat across from his desk. The only good thing about it was they called the meeting, instead of being called on the carpet by the boss. Colson was a by-the-book Texas Ranger. He saw Ritter and Connors as adventurers and major budgetary sinkholes.

Connors gladly let Ritter do all the talking. "I was getting some background, seeing if any of those Grassy Knoll people knew Salvo or could tell me about him. I didn't know his sister was filling in for him in the nut line."

"Is she nuts?" Colson asked.

"She helped her brother. She doesn't seem to be a Kool-Aid drinker, but again, I hit her with a dump truck of bad news. So, I couldn't tell for sure." Then he thought about it. "But you know, Boss, she didn't immediately jump to the government or the CIA or the Army killed her brother. So, she probably isn't that deep into this crap, personally."

"What are you geniuses using as a new working theory?" The cynicism in the captain's voice was born out of a few expensed trips and a lot of man-hours chasing down Hank Larson.

"Ben Larson and Peter Salvo were connected to the "artifact out of Pecox, and by extension, the Shaw and Lance murders up there and the Hensley murder back here." Ritter said.

"You two are not going back up to New York."

"We think we can work it from this end, boss," Ritter said.

"No overtime!" Colson pointed his finger at them.

"Not a minute, Cap."

"So, what do you got?"

"The prints on the bag from the locker at DFW came back as a Burt Dreesan. Ex-military type. Mercenary. Foggy background. Nothing current and no certificate of death"

"Kinda like government agency fog," Connors said.

"Okay..." Colson said.

"Well, the guy we took out up in Yonkers also came back ex-military and the same fog."

"So, you think these guys are connected? That's pretty thin."

"Except both are connected in some way to whatever JFK horseshit came out of Pecox," Ritter said.

"Why not just kick this up to the FBI. We are talking interstate here." Colson said.

"Agency fog could be coming from the FBI."

"Wow. Just don't turn into one of those conspiracy nuts. Keep the man hours low on this, and don't short-change your current cases."

"Will do, Thanks, Cap."

50 | SOUTH BY SOUTHWEST

On their way to the gate to board the plane bound for Phoenix Hank sneezed.

"You coming down with something?"

"Hope not. Ben, look I just thought of something. I'd better call my boss and tell him I'm going to be out for a few more days. You go ahead. I'll meet you at the gate."

Hank stopped at the pay phone as Holloway continued ahead. He hit 0. "Collect call operator from Hank Larson to Flying Tigers, Brian Miller."

Holloway walked away and looked back once.

"Brian? Hank. You are going to shit when I ask you this one..."

It was an empty flight that night. Sitting in the back, with no one within three rows of them, Hank and Holloway talked at a level just under the drone of the engines. Ben Holloway whistled as he inspected the yellowed and delicate photo.

"No wonder everyone who touched this is dead."

He then did what Cyrus, Ben, and Hank did. He ran his thumb over the stain in the upper corner of the photo's back.

"This is his blood, huh? Spooky."

"Yeah, but after a while this little fellow begins to grow on you."

"How so?"

"I haven't worked a day since this thing started. My house has been wrecked, and every dime I've squirreled has been eaten up by playing coast-to-coast detective."

"So, this becomes your meal ticket?"

"Shit, I was told by the guy Belson killed that I could get a 100 grand advance in a publishing deal."

Holloway was impressed.

"I'm gonna need some money to put my life back together after all this is over."

"A publisher saw this?" Holloway handed it back.

"No, nobody's seen this, yet. And now, with Peter dead, I'm going to have to find a publisher." He slid it back into the protective sleeve.

Holloway nodded in agreement and then looked out the window, with something on his mind.

51 | PAIN IN THE HOUSE

Croft was dispatched by the Admiral to search the home of Peter Salvo. Since Salvo was working with Larson and the brother, it was a good probability he was in possession of Polaroid 7.

As he sat across the street, he saw a car in the driveway. Someone was home. Then he saw a woman in the window. He assumed that the wife was home. She might be able to tell him more than just searching the property. He was curious about the activity outside the house. Three or four cars momentarily stopped in front of the place.

He walked up to the door and knocked. A young woman answered.

"Mrs. Salvo?"

"Miss."

"May I come in?"

"This is really not a good time. I have..." She stopped when she saw the gun.

"What was your husband's business with Benjamin Larson?"

"He is, was, my brother, and I have no idea."

"Who is Beth Salvo?"

"That's me. We lived here together."

"No wife?"

"No, Peter never married."

"I'll need to see everything you have on Benjamin Larson.'

"I wouldn't begin to know where to look."

"Let me put it another way." He took out his gun and removed a silencer from his pocket. He methodically screwed the silencer into the end of the barrel. "You either find what I am looking for, or you will soon see your brother again."

Ritter turned onto 5th. He was running a little late. He had promised to be there with Beth when her brother's remains arrived at DFW from New York at 3 pm. He parked on the street so as not to block her car in case she opted to drive herself. He walked up to the door and knocked.

Croft turned in the direction of the door. "Are you expecting someone?"

Beth smartly decided to not offer up who was at the door. "No. But since Peter died, a lot of folks come by to express their condolences."

He picked her up by her arm and manhandled her to the door. He stood alongside the doorway and pointed his gun at her. "Get rid of them or I'll kill you both."

Beth started shaking.

"Stop it!" He shook her. It didn't help. She just shook more. "Aw hell," He cold-cocked her with the gun. She went down. He dragged her into the hall to the bedroom. He answered the door. "Can I help you?"

Ritter wasn't expecting a man. "I'm here to pick up Beth. Who are you?"

"A friend of the family. She's not feeling well. Maybe come back some other time." He attempted to shut the door, but Ritter stopped it. "We haven't met. I'm Beth's cousin, in from Kansas. We were going to pick out a coffin." He looked at his watch. "We have a three o'clock appointment."

"I see. Well, come in." Croft said.

As Ritter passed him, he spun around and pulled his gun from his shoulder holster. Croft pulled his gun, too. Ritter fired a split second before Croft. Both men went down.

52 | BY THE TIME WE GOT TO PHOENIX

Holloway retrieved his and Hank's guns from the captain in the cockpit as they left the plane. The last time Holloway was in Phoenix, he was issued a government vehicle. This time, not being on an official case, he had to rent one. They had the MapQuest that Foster printed out, and they were ready to go find out about the Committee.

"You think we can just walk up and knock on the door?" Holloway said.

"Okay, yeah, maybe that isn't the smartest idea. I agree."

"We'll park out of sight, wait for dark, and hoof it in. This way we can assess what we are dealing with." He turned his eyes from the road to Hank adding, "I hate surprises."

At five miles out, they pulled down a dirt road off the main and shut the engine. The sun was setting, making the southwest sky streaked with red. Holloway was tapping his finger on the steering wheel. "Did you know this Peter Salvo?"

"Met him once. He was working with my brother. That's pretty much all I know."

"We called it into the Yonkers P.D. They must have processed the body and the crime scene by now."

"It just doesn't make sense to kill him," Hank said. "He had no idea what this was about."

"How can that be? You have the photo."

"Now I do. But when he came to me, I had no idea, and neither did he. I hopped jump seats and dead-headed, crisscrossing the country following the trail to get this thing."

"So why do all that if you had no idea what you were chasing?"

"The Texas Rangers were hanging a double murder charge on my brother. That's what started this. Eventually, I came to realize, maybe if I found this, it could lead me to who killed the two guys in Texas and my brother."

"Long way to go..."

"I owed it to him; it wasn't easy being my kid brother going through school."

Holloway smiled.

"I got to take a piss." Hank got out and headed for a tree.

Holloway lit a cigarette. Checked his watch.

When Hank came into the smoke-filled car, he sneezed.

Holloway rolled down the window. "It's time."

They drove back up to the main road, turning on the headlights only when they reached the concrete.

Watching the odometer, Holloway pulled over. "This is as far as we should go." He reached up and switched the dome light off, so it wouldn't go on when the door was opened.

They trekked through about a quarter mile of woods. Holloway actually brought along a compass.

"You must have been a boy scout," Hank whispered.

"Yeah, Troop F, BI."

They came over the crest of a hill. The compound lay before them. It was like a fortress. Radio-equipped guards with night vision goggles were everywhere. From their point up high, Holloway and Hank planned how to get in. Hank had to sneeze but stopped it.

"It's not going to be easy," Holloway said.

"Is that your professional, Troop FBI, opinion or just a guess when you saw the A-team down there...?"

The command center in the compound was always on full alert whenever the Admiral was in the house. His personal security when he traveled was handled by a small cadre of men. More men were added during the "Home Games," as they called it.

The captain of the guard was called to the room after a guard watching an infrared display saw two life forms breathing and making their way toward the perimeter.

As their boss watched, a third life form was skulking towards them.

Holloway pulled his gun and pointed it right at a startled Hank. Before Hank could react...

"Duck!" Holloway said in a loud whisper as he assumed a combat stance."

A voice, in a louder whisper, came from the bushes behind them. "It's me, chief!"

Holloway safetied his weapon. "Foster! What the hell are you doing here?"

As Foster came to them, he crouched low and spoke only when he got close enough to whisper. "I did some further checking. The whole file on these guys is blacked out. That's scary shit chief, and I thought you should know before you tangled with them.

"What's that mean?" Hank asked.

"It means that someone at the bureau has knowledge of this group and has removed all info from our files under a national security code."

"The scary part is that, usually, you get a reference name. This file's reference is also classified."

"It's the bureau's little way of saying don't even remember you saw the blacked-out report!"

"Also, Belson was sprung the moment you left. What are we going to do now chief?"

"We?"

"I figured you guys might need a hand."

Just then flood lights went on, and a voice came out from speakers placed in trees. "Stay where you are! You are on private property. Do not attempt to run."

A four-wheel drive vehicle broke through the clearing and two guards, toting MAC-10's got out.

Commands continued to blare over the speakers. "Remain calm. Stay where you are." The message was then repeated.

Holloway put his hands up and Hank followed his lead. While one Guard kept his MAC-10 trained on Holloway and Hank, the other stripped them of their pistols and frisked them. He found the photo in Hank's sock. The other Guard motioned them into the back of the vehicle, and they headed down from the hill as another vehicle passed them going up. Hank and Holloway looked at each other. After a moment, they heard machine gun fire.

Holloway looked away. "Damn it, Foster, why couldn't you stay put!"

53 | COMING TOO

Beth started to stir. She rolled over on the floor in an uncertain daze. Her head hurt. She felt a large bump on the back of her skull. Her vision was blurry. She lay there for a few seconds as her thoughts cleared. She remembered... She went to rise, and her head pounded. She forced herself and when she looked towards the front door she screamed.

Beau and that man were sprawled out on the floor. There was blood. She rose on shaky legs and picked up the phone. "Operator, I need the police. There's been a shooting at the Paine house. Please help, 2515..."

"Put the phone down." She turned and saw the man who hit her holding a gun on her from the floor."

She dropped the receiver. The scratchy voice of the operator continued.

"Mister, you are going to need help."

"You are going to help me. Bring me a towel and alcohol. You are coming with me." He inspected his bloody side.

"Drop it." Beau managed to grab his gun and was holding it on him.

"Croft couldn't roll over or turn to Ritter, so he just arced his arm over and started firing behind him.

Ritter shot him five times and he was dead. Then Ritter collapsed.

54 | COZY NOT HOMEY

Hank paced in an empty room, alone. There were no windows, doors, or furniture in the room. Hank checked his wrist out of habit, but his watch was gone. He stopped, placed his ear to the wall, and listened.

He heard footsteps, low at first, and then growing louder. He waited a moment, listening to them come closer, closer...until there was the mechanical sound of locks and gears whirring.

A small piece of the wall swung outward into the hallway. Two guards with M16s stepped into the room. "They're ready for you."

"Who?"

"Come on, move."

Hank stepped between them. One moved into the hallway, and the other took up the rear.

Hank watched the guards from the corner of his eyes. Suddenly, Hank stopped and was about to sneeze. The Guard next to him prodded him on and he moved. Hank hesitated again, his nose scrunching up, - nothing - and then continued with the guards.

Hank said apologetically, "Thought I had to sneeze."

They took another two steps and Hank sneezed hard, his arms flailing with the force of it.

"You all right?"

"Yeah, I must be allergic to something."

"There's nothing in here. The atmosphere is controlled."

As they take another step, Hank hesitated like he's going to sneeze again. The Guard next to him stopped for a moment, and Hank relaxed his face and signaled that everything was O.K. As the Guard turned forward to keep moving, Hank threw his weight behind a right cross to the Guards temple, knocking him into the wall. As the front Guard turned around, Hank grabbed his M16 and twirled him to the floor next to the other guard.

Training the gun on them, Hank said, "Well now, things seem to be looking up a bit."

Hank's smile died on his lips as he felt the barrel of a .45 automatic pressed into the back of his skull. The voice behind the gun chilled him with familiarity.

"Gesundheit!"

The guards grabbed their guns back and trained them on Hank once again. Hank turned as Ben Holloway re-holstered his weapon.

"You didn't think we'd let you get away with a stunt like that, did you?" Holloway nodded his head to the door at the end of the hall.

Hank scoffed, "Beautiful, just beautiful..."

They reached the conference room. Hank stopped just inside the door.

"Come in Mr. Larson, sit down. You've been quite an impressive pain in the ass," the Admiral said.

Also seated around the black marble conference table were the Committee members and Belson. Holloway sat in the empty seat next to Belson.

Everyone stared at Hank. He stared back and moved to the empty chair next to Holloway.

Hank shook his head. "Anyone ever tell you that you guys take yourself way too seriously."

The Admiral allowed a smile to touch his lips. "I think the time for levity has passed, Mr. Larson."

"Maybe for you, but this has to be some kind of comedy routine. Otherwise, why didn't Holloway take the picture from me before?

Why put on the act with Belson? They had me in jail. I had the photo on me..."

"We needed to be certain it was the original. Ben has been with us for thirty-five years. He has an honest face, and in your case, a person is more likely to tell something to someone they trust than to someone like Belson torturing them."

Hank turned to Holloway, nodding his head. "It was all an act. The fight with Belson at headquarters. Your Hoover test... it was good Benji."

"Don't call me that."

Something came to Hank. He started nodding, "That's why you wanted everything signed by you alone."

"Too bad you put yourself into the middle of this," Holloway said.

"Don't write me off yet."

Holloway's smile fell away as Hank turned to the Admiral.

"What do you want?" Hank asked.

"We have what we want."

"Did I miss something? The photo doesn't point to you or your group. There's no solid proof there, just speculation. Was it worth murder?"

"Presidents come and go, but since World War II, this Committee and its predecessor have protected the foreign policy of the United States. We crafted and perpetuated the single gunman, 3 shot, no conspiracy finding for 30 years. We can't have speculation or publicity about our involvement in the Kennedy affair."

"Be bad for the bomb and missile business..."

"For America. The business of America is arms! That's the power. That's the real global currency!"

"You murdered my brother and framed him as the killer of those men down in Texas."

"The man who murdered your brother and those other two men, is dead, Mr. Larson. There was no reason for you to pursue this."

Even at a moment like this, Hank was still relieved that the Admiral just confirmed that his baby brother was not a killer, and that he was indeed murdered by these creeps.

Hank stared directly at the Admiral and let a small smile crease his lips. "A friend made copies of that picture, and if I don't make a call within four hours, they get sent to every News station in New York."

Once again, the Admiral allowed a small smile to crease his lips. "We are not fools, Mr. Larson. Copies of this particular photo can easily be maligned as another conspiracy fanatic's hoax."

Hank turned defiant. He continued to stare right into the Admiral's eyes. "Yes, of course. I see it now. You know, I didn't realize this till just this second, but it's you. You're in that photo. You were the shooter."

The men around the table reacted in a hushed shock as every head was now turned in the direction of the man at the helm, seeing him for the first time in a new light. The Admiral faced them defiantly. "How do you think I got this job? He was a traitor; he was undermining America's status amongst our friends and enemies. He was a foreign policy disaster. Yes, my initiation into the committee was to take an active role in this purging of the cancer foisted on the America we love." He found some strength and resolve and straightened up. "He was about to announce our pull out from Viet Nam at that goddamn market speech." It was the first time the Admiral displayed any sense of self, albeit with the sudden affectations of an older man, just barely holding it together. When he stopped talking, he defiantly looked at each committee member around the table. The silence seemed to last for minutes, but it was only seconds before one of the men started clapping then he was quickly followed by the others. Some added, "Here, here!"

The Admiral was visibly affected, like a returning conquering hero. He held his chin up and panned the smiling faces of his men.

Hank could swear he saw his eyes moisten, but with old guys, that's sometimes a constant condition. Hank felt defeated. That was his 'big play' that had just come to him. Almost with an air of resignation, he looked at the Admiral and dismissively said, "Now what?"

At just that moment, the intercom next to the Admiral buzzed. The Admiral raised his eyebrows and clicked the button. "This is what we are waiting for."

The Admiral watched a monitor by his side. He pushed another button, and the door at the other end of the room opened. A man entered with the photo in his hand. The Admiral beckoned him to stand next to him. "Dr. Stevens will certify its originality." He turned to the Doctor. "What about it, Stevens?"

Doctor Stevens handed the yellowed picture to the Admiral. "This is a decent attempt to disguise the fact that it is not the original."

There was a murmur around the room, and Holloway glared at Hank. Hank sneezed.

"Bless you." The Doctor said, "You did a very nice job on this Mr. Larson. I especially like the blood stain in the corner here. Very convincing to the naked eye.

"Thanks."

Holloway protested. "It looks authentic. It's old."

"Are you telling us he faked this picture?" The Admiral said.

"An old science lab trick. High school?"

"Elementary... Dr. Stevens." Hank said.

The doctor explained to the Admiral. "You sprinkle lemon juice on a sepia-toned copy. Then heat it with an iron. It turns yellow and brittle giving the appearance of age."

"What about the blood stain?

"It's not blood..." the Doctor said.

The Admiral turned to Hank.

Hank opened his palms, like it was so obvious. "Bosco."

"Brilliant!" The doctor said.

"Thank you. I'll tell her that."

"Enough!" The Admiral slammed his open hand down on the cold marble. "All right Mr. Larson, cards on the table. Where is Polaroid 7?"

"As I said, it's on its way to a news station by now."

The Admiral stared at Hank, measuring him a bit more carefully now. He pressed his intercom and a voice answered.

"Yes, Admiral?"

"Bring her in."

The Admiral buzzed the door opened again, and two guards brought in Chris DeMarco.

She was in uniform, carrying her flight bag. "Hank!"

She tried to go to him, but was restrained. Hank knew there was nothing he could do, so he stayed put. "Are you O.K.?"

"I've had to handle tougher guys in first class." She yanked her arm from one of the guards.

Hank smiled and realized why he was so attracted to her in the first place.

The Admiral was insistent. "Mr. Larson? Where's the Polaroid? I don't think we have to dwell on what will happen next if you refuse to tell us."

Hank held up his hand in a halting gesture. Chris smiled. He stood up and walked around the table toward the Admiral. Two guards were about to intercept him, but the Admiral waved them off.

Hank put his face in the Admiral's. "V2. Point of no return Admiral. If I do tell you, me and the lady are good as dead anyway, right?"

"There's no doubt, you are both going to die. The only question is in what manner."

Hank was thrown. He wasn't expecting that kind of detail. "Right. Well, I vote for old age. And my insurance is that photo."

"I'm certain you understand that Belson here could make you tell us things you didn't know you forgot."

"Admiral, you can take your best shot, but I'll bet you I can hang in for at least 4 hours - that's all I need to shorten all your life expectancies. Ya see, Brent, the real question is who gets the photo first."

"Why don't I just kill her first then see how macho you are then."

"Then I'll hate you for the rest of my life."

"Well, that won't be too long," Belson said.

The admiral glared at Belson and then focused back on Hank.

"I propose a trade. Me and Chris for the picture, straight away schoolyard swap. Agreed?"

The Admiral swirled this thought around his mouth for a moment, then conceded. "Agreed. Tell us where it is, and we'll have it delivered here..."

"Brent, if I were that stupid, I'd be dead already. We swap in a public place where we can each go our own way."

"And where do you propose this Mr. Larson? The library perhaps?"

"That wouldn't be too safe. You kill librarians, or don't you remember Howard Lance."

The Admiral genuinely looked innocent. Hank dismissed the notion with a disgusted wave of his hand.

"The Phoenix Airport, on the tarmac. I'll get the photo and meet you there..."

"Now who's playing who for a sucker? We're not letting you go, Mr. Larson."

"Fine, then we'll all go together. The photo and our way home will be there anyway. And believe me, this could easily be the eleven o'clock news."

"If you're trying to dick us around Larson, you will be the eleven o'clock news," Belson said.

55 | GRATITUDE

The first face Ritter saw when he awoke was Connors. "Hey pardner, you gave us quite a scare there for a while."

He looked around and saw he was in a hospital room. He went to speak but his mouth was cotton dry.

"Here." Beth held a Styrofoam cup to his lips. He sipped, then smiled. "You're okay?"

"Thanks to you," she patted his hand.

Ritter had the wherewithal to grasp her hand in his.

Connor saw this. He had figured his partner of 10 years was sweet on this gal. "Beau, this lady is in a room down the hall, but she's been here like a nurse."

"Much obliged," Ritter said as he looked at her noticing the head bandage. "Are you okay?"

"Mild concussion, and I am here for observation."

Ritter smiled and turned to Connors. "Who was the shooter?"

"Miss Beth, would you excuse us for a minute?"

"Sure thing, I'll be back, Beau." She patted his hand as she let go of it.

As she left, Connors nodded at Ritter. I like her, Beau."

"Me too."

"The guy you tapped, Edward 'Ned' Croft, same M.O. as the others; ex-military, foggy files, and false ID."

"Why was he there?"

"Beth says he was looking for information on Benjamin Larson."

"More JFK...," he said and turned his head away.

"What is it, Beau?"

"My dad had doubts. And I think of all these people who are looking for an answer. Thousands, maybe millions, and yet, nobody kills anybody. What makes these guys go tactical? Why are the bodies piling up? Who is doing this?"

"We have a partial lead. We think Croft flew in from Arizona. We have alerted Arizona DPS. They are tracking him down from their end. And we asked about any possible connection to a committee or commission."

"What the serviceman said up in Yonkers. Good."

Just then the doctor appeared. "I heard you were up. How are you feeling?"

"Okay." He looked up at the I.V. on the hook over the bed. "Whatever moonshine you are pumping into me, I am feeling no pain."

"There's only so much of that you can take, after that you'll feel something."

"How bad is it, doc."

"The bullet perforated your spleen. You almost died on the scene from internal bleeding. I don't know how you were able to fend off that attacker after you got shot."

"When can he get back to the job?" Connors asked.

"Twelve weeks, at least two here, where I can watch and make sure it's healing. Then regular visits and some meds. But notwithstanding any complications, you should return to a normal life. That is if what you Rangers do can be considered normal."

56 | LET'S DO IT AGAIN

Hank was held in a room with an antique spinning wheel in it. The room was decorated like something out of the colonial days. It made him think this was maybe the old bastard's house as well. It made him laugh as he imagined a typical day in the Howser household.

"Mommy, where's Daddy?"

"Don't bother your father dear, he's busy assassinating the leader of some third-world country. He'll look at your homework when he's done."

The Admiral's words came back to him. *Since World War II this Committee and its predecessor have protected the foreign policy of the United States.*

That meant that these could be the guys who wanted Kennedy dead. And that's why they were going to such great lengths to get the picture. He thought about how all he was out to do was clear his brother's name, now he was the target of the most powerful group of men in history.

He had always been able to control fear. As a pilot, he got into some hairy situations where he would have bought the farm if he panicked. When he and Brian crashed landed, it was one hell of a fix. But he somehow remained calm and got them both to safety. Some people believed that he never got the fear gene. He knew he was plenty scared many times. Yet, it was all he could do to remain calm standing in that room with those merchants of death. It got intense when they brought Chris in. *God, what did I get her into?* He looked down at his hand, it was shaking. He was fine until he thought about her. He was responsible for her life. She was innocent. He brought her into this. And now there was a slim chance they'd get out of this alive. He grabbed his shaking hand with the other and reprimanded himself. *Focus. I need to focus to get us out of this.*

He wondered where they were keeping her. He dreaded to even think that they may have killed her already. That started another round of the shakes.

I got to stop my brain. I got to get in control. I got to get in control.

The Admiral chose to hold this sensitive meeting out on the Spanish-tiled veranda. The entire Paradise Valley spread out before him. Sparse desert-like vegetation and a terrain that would challenge a Patton tank. The man across from him was advocating an executive action that would be transformative and decisive in correcting the course the current U.S. government was on. A wayward vector that would endanger America's standing and erode the strategic superiority the committee achieved over the last three decades.

"Timing?" The Admiral asked.

"Next 45 days." The advocate for regime change in Washington responded.

"Tight timeline."

"It's before the G8 and the disastrous alliance he's looking to make."

The Admiral pondered this. He had no moral compunction about the plan, if he were a younger man, he'd pull the trigger again. But two of the operatives could trust to execute this mission were lost to this stupid Polaroid affair. That, in itself, told him how important total containment would be this time. *Maybe Croft is ready*, he thought and made a mental note to speak to him when he returned from Dallas.

Just then there was a knock on the door frame that led to the Veranda. The Admiral turned as Nelson approached. "Sorry to interrupt sir, but there's an officer from the Arizona Department of Public Safety here and demands to speak with you."

"Demands?"

"Insists, strongly."

"I don't have time for some state trooper. Call our man there, Lieutenant Colonel Harding, and tell him I said to make this cop go away."

"Sir, the officer that's here is Harding."

The Admiral found this disturbing. "He's here personally?"

"Shall I have him come out here?"

"Yes." The Admiral looked at the man he was engaged with. "Could you give me a minute?"

"Of course, Admiral," he said, and he got up and walked back into the main house, passing Harding on the way out.

The Admiral turned to the limits that his bad back would allow in order to speak with Harding before he was in front of him. "Goddamit man, are you crazy coming here yourself?"

"Admiral, believe me. This is ears only."

"Very well." He waved at the now empty seat across from him. "What's so important you needed to interrupt a very crucial meeting?

"Sir, the Texas Rangers have requested information on Edward Croft and his connection to something called, the committee."

"Damn." He got lost in thought for a few seconds then said, "Has Croft been compromised?"

"Croft is dead, sir."

"Dead? It was a simple assignment."

"Somehow, the Rangers interdicted him. There was a shooting. One of theirs survived, as well as the woman Croft was interrogating before he was shot to death."

Croft dead? Shit. The Admiral had a sinking feeling. He was about to assign Croft to the next mission. His building rage and frustration came out. "Hell Harding, you're number two in the state police squash this. Better yet create some misdirection. Get these tin star sheriffs off my ass, man."

"Already done, sir. This is more of an after-action report, if you will."

"Good. Good man. Continue monitoring the situation and report back to me as the situation warrants."

"Of course, Admiral."

"We're done here."

The man nodded, and without any further eye contact with the Admiral, left.

The Admiral felt that God was fucking with him. This stupid, penny ante issue with this photograph had devastated his upper command structure leaving him in a less-than-desirable strategic predicament when the next big Executive Action, bigger than Dallas, was spinning up to keep America preeminent on the world stage.

57 | THE BLACK-TIE SWAP MEET

It seemed longer to Hank but an hour after he left, the guard returned. "Come on. Time to go."

He walked Hank to the outside of the building. The guard was smart this time. He stood 5 feet back and to the right of Hank, hands on his machine gun. Four black Chevy Suburban's drove around to the front of the compound.

"First one," the guard said.

As he walked to the vehicle, he saw Chris being walked out to the second car to his left by another guard. He was relieved she was alive. He called out, "Are you okay?"

"No talking," the guard said.

She nodded and got into the vehicle.

Hank couldn't believe what he saw next. The Admiral and the rest of the 13 members emerged in black tie. They loaded into the 2nd 3rd and 4th cars. Belson and two more rifle-toting guards came last. The Admiral and Holloway entered the car Hank was in. They took off through the electrically opening gates as the sentry waved them past.

The ride wasn't very long. Hank's hand hurt from his stupid attempt to take on the guard. He was glad Chris was okay and seemed spirited. How horrible this must be for her. Some strange guy chatted her up, and soon there are dead bodies, kidnapping, and confinement, just because Hank couldn't let go of the notion that his brother wasn't a murderer.

The man who killed your brother and those other two men, is dead. There was no need for you... The Admiral's words reverberated in Hanks's head. He had his closure, albeit possibly at the cost of his and Chris' lives. That led to a dark thought; if he and Chris didn't get out of this, they too might someday be the basis of a conspiracy theory.

This whole committee was the proof that there was a conspiracy. It seemed every whacko theory that he had heard in the past weeks, had some connection to the men in these cars. *Maybe that's why Peter had a smile on his face.* Kyle and all those other folks would orgasm over what he was in the middle of right now.

"Where in the airport are we going?" Holloway asked.

"Over by the cargo load, on the tarmac. I don't know how many people you've positioned inside the terminal."

"It's just us, Hank."

"Just us?" Hank threw his thumb over his shoulder. "What about the entire intramural Committee football squad following behind, all dressed for the prom?"

"We have a charity function to attend this evening." The Admiral said.

Hank laughed. "Yeah, real pillars of the community! Achooo!"

Holloway hands him his handkerchief.

The driver in the lead car flashed some kind of identification at the runway's gatehouse guard, who waved the three SUVs through. The cars rode over to the cargo area of the airport.

"Right there by that plane." Hank pointed.

Hank directed them to a Flying Tigers 747 standing silently on the tarmac. The cars stopped, and everyone got out. The guards looked at Holloway, who motioned to them to stay by their cars. Hank and Holloway stood before the plane.

"Is the original picture on the plane?" Holloway asked.

"First, hand over Chris, and then I'll give you the photo."

Holloway whispered into the walkie talkie and Chris was brought forward by one of the guards. She ran the last couple of feet to Hank. They hugged; she looked up at the plane with a questioning look.

Hank just winked.

From back by the cars, the Admiral called out, "Now the photo, Mr. Larson." He nodded and two guards racked the bolts on their guns to punctuate the Admiral's request.

Hank grabbed Chris' flight bag and began to slowly remove her items. A guard drew a bead on Hank. Holloway raised his hand motioning to the Guard to hold his fire.

"What are you doing?" Chris asked.

"Just giving 'em what they asked for." He dumped the remaining contents on the tarmac. He picked up one of the ruby slippers. He reached in and took out the curled original Polaroid.

"When did you do that?" She asked.

"Yesterday, in the car."

"Very clever, Mr. Larson." The Admiral nodded, approvingly.

Hank put the photo back in the bag and flung it to Holloway, who handed it to a Guard. The Guard brought it to Doctor Stevens, who was waiting at the back of one of the SUVs. Stevens reached into the back of the vehicle and opened a metal briefcase. Inside was a mini-test kit, complete with Alkaline trace solutions and litmus papers.

Chris leaned over as they watched the man test the photo, and said in a low voice, "I know I wanted a little excitement in my life Hank, but this is a tad more than I bargained for."

"Don't worry, they got the photo. We'll get out of this okay?"

Doctor Stevens checked the photo, and confident of his findings, brought it to the Admiral. Holloway walked back to Hank and Chris.

The Admiral was anxious. "Well, Phillip?"

"It tests positive. This is, without a doubt, the long lost, original, Polaroid 7."

"Very good. Very, very good." He turned to go back to his car. He waved his hand, "Ben, clean this up."

Holloway held up a fist, and the guards trained their guns on Hank and Chris.

"Hank, I don't like this. Do something." Chris nudged his arm.

"Be calm. We're waiting for a sign from above."

Chris squinched her nose at Hank's sudden show of heavenly faith.

The Admiral held his hands up to Hank in apology. "Sorry, Mr. Larson, no loose ends."

Suddenly someone shouted, "Don't!" The loud command voice came from the forward cargo door of the Flying Tigers plane. Everyone looked up. "Brian had his M16 trained on the committee members. There were 9 more armed men at every door on the 3 story-high cargo airliner, their guns aimed at them. Two from the forward lower deck door, three men aiming from prone positions in the main deck cargo door, two from the alternate lower deck door, and two more on each side of the bulk cargo door in the rear.

The guards appropriately froze.

"Who the hell is that?" Holloway said.

"Who the hell is that?" Chris said to Hank.

"Brian's Brigade."

On cue, Brian Miller poked his head out of the door, an M16 in each hand. "Who the hell is she?"

Hank smiled and ushered Chris up the service steps of the plane. He stopped by Brian.

"Major, good to see you." He handed him one of the rifles from his "Me Wall."

"Flying Tigers—you call, we deliver, Colonel." He nodded at Chris. "Welcome aboard ma'am." Back to Hank. "Who is she?"

Hank called to Holloway from the door. "Sorry Ben, but if you hadn't turned on me this would have been both our tickets out of here."

"I knew I shouldn't have let you make that call at the airport."

"We'll each go our separate way now, O.K.?"

Holloway turned to the Admiral.

"A capable man, our Mr. Larson, eh Ben?" the Admiral said.

"What do you want to do?" He asked the Admiral.

"Hell Ben, we've got the picture, our primary objective. Why start a firefight when the other guy has the high ground? We'll get all of them later."

Holloway nodded his head and grabbed the walkie-talkie. He clicked the button, his eyes on Hank. "Into the cars everyone. You've got a concert to attend. I'll cover your back. Then catch up with you later."

The Committee members, the Admiral, the guards, the doctor, and the drivers got back into their cars. Belson and a guard remained outside. Holloway stood watching Hank.

Hank watched Holloway from the open forward cargo door as he and Brian had their guns trained on the scene below. Chris was standing on the side of the door, hazarding a peek now and then.

"What is this, a waiter's convention?" Brian said.

"Only these guys serve up missiles, bombers, and the occasional assassination."

Miller understood and turned to Chris. "Hank saved my life, so I know why I'm here. How did you get mixed up in all this?"

"At the risk of sounding stupid, I honestly don't know."

On the tarmac, Holloway checked his watch and trotted over to the lead car.

Belson watched. He was seething.

Chris was still grappling with Miller's question. "The buns."

"Excuse me?" He asked momentarily taking his eyes off the gun sights.

Suddenly, Belson grabbed a rifle from one of the guards. "You can't let that son-of-a-bitch live!" He took cover behind the fender and started firing.

"Belson! You fool." The Admiral yelled.

Bullets ripped into the skin of the 747 near Chris. She instinctively ducked. Hank, Brian and the rest of Brian's Brigade opened up, returning fire.

Holloway hit the deck and rolled clear of the car, but didn't return the fire. The cars were sprayed with automatic fire as Hank and Brian's Brigade fired their air-cooled, fully automatic recoilless rifles from the sides of the forward cargo door.

The three cars exploded in a fiery blast. The fire from the plane ceased.

Holloway shielded his head then, turned and coldly watched.

Hank came down from the service steps of the 747 and, keeping the gun trained on Holloway, walked over to where he stood. He was puzzled. "We couldn't have hit all three tanks simultaneously."

Holloway nodded his head as he held up a small radio-controlled detonator. "Magic bullet."

"Very fitting," Hank said.

"The end of an era, Hank. They were dinosaurs. The world changed, but they didn't. They started to buck policy. They were planning to rearrange the Washington furniture again. So they could finance a rebellion and start another war."

"So, you were going to take them out all along?"

"This whole affair was sloppy. They left too many loose ends. It was the perfect cover for me to get inside. I had to go along with their plans for you to get them all together."

"You would've let them kill us?"

"To avoid assassination and another war? Yeah. I would've shot you myself if I had to."

Hank let this sink in. "And now?"

"Now the only one you're a threat to is me, and I probably won't live long enough to indict anyway. So, go. It's the least I owe you."

Hank hitched his head towards the inferno. "What about this?"

"As far as the world will be concerned, I just dusted some major drug dealers off the planet. We'll set it up to look like they were dirty all along." The flames reflected off Holloway's face as he turned to Hank. "Want to live a long life?"

Hank looked at him, cautiously.

"Forget all about this and me, or others will come. They'll make that firebug, Dreesan, look like a girl scout. Follow?"

"Thanks, I think. So, who do you work for, or did you just blow up your paycheck?"

"I can't tell you that."

"No, I guess you couldn't."

They both watched as the cars burned.

Without turning, Holloway said, "But odds are you probably voted for him."

Hank nodded his head and laughed, then had another thought, "Shame the Polaroid got destroyed."

"What?"

"It's a shame the Polaroid got blown up, too."

"What Polaroid?"

"The picture. The one showing the Admiral on the grassy knoll, that proves Kennedy was killed by the Committee."

"What Committee? What are you one of those conspiracy theory nuts?" Holloway turned back to the burning cars.

"Beautiful. Just beautiful." Hank said.

As emergency equipment and firemen started to arrive, Chris trotted down the service stairs to Hank and they hugged. Together with Holloway, they watched the burning cars.

100 yards down the airfield, the wind blew something against one of the short, stubby blue taxiway lights. The Polaroid, its edges singed, waggled in the breeze. The next gust of wind blew it tumbling away.

LETTER
FROM THE AUTHOR

The Story That Keeps on Giving.

This book is an homage to one of the longest-lasting, self-perpetuating cottage industries in America. JFK Assassination Conspiracies, Inc. A national obsession that has pervaded our culture since that awful day in Dallas on November 22nd !963.

Why?

Why has this shocking murder, this mass disillusionment with the world as it truly was, not as we wished it would be, why is this still running on full power 60 years later?

Trust in our institutions has steadily been eroded since that day. People now question their government, more specifically what the government tells us. Right now, UFOs are the subject of congressional inquiry. Transparency issues with the vaunted FBI and other here-to-fore "trustworthy" agencies are nipping away at that paradigm and raising a question that we would all, collectively, rather not consider. "Are we being lied to?"

Above the politics of any given moment in time, is the notion that some things are immutable, reliable, can be counted on, and can be taken to the bank. Therefore, the recurring speculation of the Who What Why Where, When, and How of the Kennedy Assassination still percolates throughout our society.

Who What Why Where, When, and How is a founding tenant of Journalism. It is the basis of all reporting. And as this book will show; the conspiracies within, and the dangers they present to the characters in my story, exist in the absence of a thorough reporting of the Who What Why Where, When, and How of the Kennedy Assassination.

As a case in point, I attended a Times Talk on the 50th anniversary of the Assassination. It was a blue-ribbon panel of reporters and journalists who were there in Dealey Plaza on that day and the days that followed the national nightmare.

It was an almost romantic, nostalgic, and at times poetic remembrance of the events of that day. On the stage, the venerated practitioners and icons of the Journalistic profession brought us in the audience back to that day. The color, the air, the emotion, and the reality.

One instance struck me as emblematic of why we are still dealing with non-stop conspiracy theories of that day. Thomas Wicker, a wonderful newsman, with a long and distinguished history of reporting for the Times and speaking on TV and other events, recounted in lovingly descriptive detail his remembrance of a moment outside Parkland Memorial Hospital, where Kennedy was rushed to after he was shot.

Wicker, like the other reporters, was forced to wait for news outside the emergency room entrance. He told us how the Lincoln Continental in which Kennedy was riding in when he was shot was right next to him. He then proceeded to wax eloquently about what he witnessed.

I'll summarize his recollection: Members of the Secret Service were wiping away the blood from the back seat. And as they rinsed the sponge in a bucket, I remember the crimson color of the water mixed with the President's blood. I never forgot that water in that bucket."

With apologies for the lack of actual transcription, that was the gist of his memory of this moment.

Hauntingly beautiful right? Eerie and so counterpunctual to the aftermath of what caused the blood to be sprayed on the backseat in the first place.

What immediately hit me was, 'Has anyone on that stage ever covered the crime beat?'

Since the 1930s newspaper men and women have covered the gory details of murders and reported from blood-soaked crime scenes, and for almost that long they have known the rules; 'You touch nothing, you alter nothing, and you leave a crime scene intact until the investigators, (today called Crime Scene Units or Crime Scene Investigators,) have fully documented the scene. Otherwise, evidence is lost or compromised.'

And yet, here in the aftermath of the greatest murder of the century, newspaper folk just watched longingly and lovingly as the Secret Service erased the evidence of the shooting, Namely the blood spray pattern, and any incidental bone and flesh fragments that could be instrumental in determining the direction of the kill shot based on the blood and brain matter splatter pattern. That branch of forensics is expert testimony that is accepted in all courts and is instrumental in leading to a conviction of murderers then and now.

Right then and there I saw the root cause of Conspiracy theories. It became clear that the first contributor to the ongoing love affair with conspiracy theories is the mishandling of the crime scene. We are all free now to make up or decide or just flip a coin and which way the blood splatter would indicate the direction the shot came from...because hard, incontrovertible evidence wound up as a simile of descriptive writing... instead of evidence in court. But maybe the murder never getting to court was the point. After all, Secret Service is law enforcement and surely somebody in their ranks knew they were tapering with crime scene evidence...so that no court could touch the murder...and thus the conspiracy theories begin.

Two days later, there was no doubt that Jack Ruby killed Oswald, everyone alive with a TV set witnessed it. That televised murder immediately ticked off the Who, the What, the Where, the When, and some of the How. Half the 'How' we all witnessed: Ruby put a gun in his ribs and pulled the trigger. The other half of the 'how' was, How Ruby got that close in the basement of the Police Station? Half of the How and all of the Why were not immediately apparent to the viewers of the grainy black and white. And in just those one-and-a-half questions a whole sub-cottage industry emerged on Ruby, the Mob, the Dallas PD, Dorothy Killgallen, dead strippers, live strippers, money transfers, and Oswald. I touched on some of these within these pages.

Conspiracy thrives in the fertilizer of bad journalism and bad policing. Americans and many around the world today can be divided into two categories. Those who believe, three shots, lone gunman, no conspiracy. And those who have some lingering doubt. Like the House Select Committee on Assassinations in 1973 who admitted in their final report, "President Kennedy's assassination was probably the result of a conspiracy." They released that assessment with no indication of who what why where when or how of the conspiracy, so have at it, instead of open and shut it's a free and open field.

ACKNOWLEGEMENTS

Writing a novel is a solitary endeavor. Just you, your thoughts, and an unblinking, unforgiving screen. When you get to the end of a second draft, the question is; will anyone else make it to the end? Is it readable? Does it hold a reader? Are there distractions, disinformation, or needless moments? At that point, you are glad they invented Beta-readers. Brave, intrepid individuals who, without concern for personal sanity, dive into your uncorrected manuscript and apply the human filter. Their comments and impressions form the nascent draft of my book and catch issues that elevate my narrative. I am ever so grateful for their time and attention. For Ask Not! I thank Billy Blake, Joe Badal, George Camron Grant, John J. Kelly, Michael Berenbaum, John and Angel Pasquarosa, and Al Contrera who opened my field of view and encouraged me to forge ahead. I started this project back in 1993 and I would be remiss not to acknowledge the input and confidence bestowed upon me then by Robert J. Groden, who released the Zapruder Film on National Television in 1975, served on the House Select Committee on Assassinations as a photographic expert and also advised Oliver Stone in a similar manner in the movie, "JFK." His book, The Search for Lee Harvey Oswald, and a very delightful and instructive dinner way back when, were fundamental to my early research. By the way, it was Robert who painted the X on the pavement of Dealey Plaza.

All this however means nothing if it doesn't get published and that's where longtime friend, David Ivester and Suncoast Publishing drummed up the most courage and took the big risk of meeting an impossible deadline. You are reading this because they put the pedal to the metal.

ABOUT THE AUTHOR

Tom Avitabile's experiences in government, the arts, engineering, journalism, and advertising, serve as a catalyst for his plots and characters. But his work as a film and stage director affords him the human insights and discerning eyes, ears, and heart to engage the reader and deliver an immersive and satisfying read that has made him a #1 bestselling author.

A native New Yorker, he'll proudly tell you he has the 'X' factor. That unique trait that hailing from the Bronx, the only borough with an 'x', imbues. He'd love to hear from you, drop him a line: AskNot@Author.nyc